THE
FOLLOWER

NICHOLAS BOWLING

TITAN BOOKS

The Follower
Print edition ISBN: 9781789094220
E-book edition ISBN: 9781789096798

Published by Titan Books
A division of Titan Publishing Group Ltd.
144 Southwark Street, London SE1 0UP
www.titanbooks.com

First Titan edition: July 2021
10 9 8 7 6 5 4 3 2 1

A CIP catalogue record for this title is available from the British Library.

Printed and bound by CPI Group (UK) Ltd, Croydon CR0 4YY

For the JAB and the CPB

1

VIVIAN OWENS stepped from the bus at Mount Hookey with two black eyes and five hundred pictures of her twin brother bundled under her arm. The journey had been almost eleven hours, including the hour-long interchange at Lewiston, which she'd spent in the post office getting her brother's poster photocopied. The pictures hadn't even come out right. The toner was faded and smudged and made him look more like an escaped convict than a missing person, but she hadn't had the time or the energy to ask the little man behind the counter to do them all over again. She'd just thanked him and gone back to the bus station, where she'd picked up the black eyes.

The bus pulled away and left Vivian squinting in its exhaust. It was nearly midday and the street was baking. Apart from the backdrop of the mountain, the town of Mount Hookey was like all the others she'd passed through on that interminable bus ride, not much more than a stretch of highway huddled with tall billboards and squat, nondescript buildings: two bars, a thrift store, a supermarket, a gas station, a Chinese restaurant called Wing's, closed and shuttered. There was a single traffic light dangling above the interchange at the far end of town, and beyond it the motel where she was staying, Cedar Lodge, whose sign was held aloft by a carved wooden bear. After that the town stopped. Five hundred posters was too many, she thought. That was twenty-five dollars she'd never get back.

Vivian had an address for her brother in town but decided to check into the motel first. Jesse had already been missing for a month and a half, and she figured another couple of hours wouldn't make much

1

difference. She needed a shower and a nap. Her head was throbbing and she hadn't eaten a thing since Lewiston. She wasn't holding out much hope for the address, anyway. It might not even have existed. In six weeks they hadn't once picked up the phone or answered an email. Hence her coming all this way. Hence the posters.

The town unfurled as she made her way down to the motel. A few quiet streets led off the main highway to residential neighbourhoods, a barbershop, a school, and then petered out into pines and cedars and yellow Californian scrub. There were hints as to Jesse's purpose here, too, in the back alleys. Palmists, shamans, a gallery displaying "transdimensional artistic interventions". An improbable number of shops selling crystal skulls. She was in the right place, then.

Vivian reached Cedar Lodge and crossed the parking lot. The motel looked dusty and worn-out. No cars out front. The wooden bear held its sign like it was enduring some sort of divine punishment, its face grim and stoic. Behind the L-shape of the motel building was dark pine forest, and beyond that the foothills of Mount Hookey itself, rising to a white cone against the huge blue sky.

It was dark inside the lobby and smelled of perfume and old cigarettes. She'd been hoping for a roaring wood fire, but it was too warm for that, even in October. It wasn't that kind of place, anyway – everything inside looked synthetic and flammable. There was a man of indeterminate age sitting on the couch who Vivian suspected wasn't a guest. He was surrounded by shopping bags and was wearing his woolly hat so high on his head it had an almost ceremonial look, like a bishop's mitre. He saw her and nodded and the hat wobbled.

Vivian put the five hundred copies of her brother's face on the reception desk and rang the bell. A woman appeared from a little office out back who seemed far too glamorous to be working in a place like Cedar Lodge. She wore a fuchsia jacket and a lot of gold jewellery and her hair was permed into an almost perfect sphere.

"Good morning, miss, how you doing there?"

"I have a room booked. The name's Owens."

"Excuse me?"

"Owens."

"Would you mind removing your hood, miss?"

Vivian had pulled up her hood to conceal the bruising. She loosened the drawstring and pulled the hood back.

"Oh my stars!" said the receptionist. She put four heavily lacquered fingernails over her mouth.

"It's not as bad as it looks."

"Oh my goodness gracious."

"It was just an accident."

The receptionist kept staring. There was a long pause.

"So. Can I check in?" Vivian asked, finally.

The woman twitched.

"Of course. Yes. Owens. I saw your name on the booking earlier, but, you know what, I just never made the connection."

"Connection?"

Up went the receptionist's hand again, as though she'd said something she shouldn't have. Then she looked down at her computer and pressed a lot of keys, arbitrarily, it seemed.

"Do you have a credit card?"

She didn't. She didn't have any cash, either.

"I've already paid, haven't I? Online?"

"We just need it to verify your identity. Although, I guess, I can see you're... you know."

"I'm what?"

"Nothing. I'm sorry." She went back to hammering the keys on her computer. "You're in room 30," she said finally.

At this point the old man on the couch leaned forward.

"You keep her out of my room!" he yelled.

"She's not in your room, Mr Blucas."

"Is it ready yet?"

"Don't you worry, Mr Blucas, your room will be ready very soon."

"That's right! I want it good and clean."

"Cleaner's in there right now, Mr Blucas."

"You tell her to clean it inside and out."

"I have done, Mr Blucas."

The receptionist turned back to Vivian, gazed at her a moment longer, then smiled quickly.

"Here's your key," she said, handing it over. "Room 30 is up the stairs, turn right, all the way along. You have a beautiful view of the mountain up there. Do you need any help with your bags?"

The woman peered over the edge of the desk.

"No, thank you," said Vivian. She didn't have any bags.

"Okay. Well. Breakfast starts at seven-thirty and goes till ten. Unfortunately, the pool is closed because…" She laughed nervously. "Well, the pool is closed."

Vivian looked at her and didn't say anything.

"Here's a map of the town," the receptionist continued. "And would you like to make an offering to the mountain?" She gestured to a carved wooden box at the other end of the counter.

Vivian scowled. Her head was throbbing horribly now, and not just from the bruising; from the smell and the darkness and the oddness of everything.

"An offering?"

"Most visitors give an offering of thanks to the mountain."

"What kind of offering?"

"Just a few dollars."

"Do I have to?"

The receptionist chewed her lip. She turned around as though looking for support, but she was alone at the desk.

"It's just a tradition."

"I don't have any cash."

One of the receptionist's eyelids twitched.

"No problem!" she said. "Then you're all good. Is there anything else I can help you with, Vivian?"

"Can I get some ice? For my head?"

"Ice machine is right behind you there."

Vivian had to pick her way between the old man's shopping bags to get to it. He winked at her and she ignored him. She filled a paper cup with ice and held it to her forehead, but it seemed to make the pain substantially worse.

"Thanks," she said on her way across the lobby.

"You're welcome," said the receptionist, and gave another taut smile.

She was halfway to her room when she realised she'd left all her brother's posters lying on the reception desk. She sighed at the top of the stairs, turned, tramped back the way she'd come. It was incredibly hot under her coat now, and her feet were hurting, too.

When she got back to the lobby, the glamorous woman had the posters in her ringed fingers. She was looking at Jesse's face and shaking her head. Her lips were moving but Vivian couldn't hear what she was saying.

"Sorry," said Vivian, approaching from the periphery of the receptionist's vision. "Those are mine."

The receptionist whirled around.

"These here? Sure thing."

She kept them clutched to her chest.

"Can I have them?" said Vivian.

"Of course."

The receptionist handed them back very slowly.

"Thank you," she said.

"You're welcome."

"You haven't seen him, have you?"

The woman looked frightened.

"Seen who?"

"My brother. That's why I'm here. He came here about a month ago and we've not heard from him."

"No, I haven't seen him." She paused. "I'm so sorry!"

"Well. If you do, let me know."

"I'll do just that." She peered over the top of the desk at the picture of Jesse. "Say – would you let me keep one of those? So I can show it to the other staff."

Vivian gave her a poster. The receptionist traced Jesse's jawline with a fingernail and went back to muttering something.

"Are you sure you haven't seen him?" said Vivian.

"No, I have *not*," said the woman. Her eyes were suddenly wet. "And if I had, there's no way in hell—" She brought herself up short and took a deep breath. "I'm sorry for cursing. I will let you know if I hear anything."

She sniffed and smiled through her tears. Vivian watched one of them crawl down her cheek, viscous with mascara.

"Is everything alright?" she asked, though in her current state she hardly felt able to offer the woman any compassion.

"I'm good," the receptionist said. She scrubbed at her face with the heel of her hand. "Long shift. Good gracious! No one catches a break round here!"

Vivian nodded.

"Alright. Well. Thanks," she said, and she turned and went back up to her room.

The receptionist had been right about the view. The great white mountain filled the window completely, in a way that looked almost vulgar; the symmetry too perfect, the colours too bright, like a bad oil painting. Vivian closed the curtains and investigated the rest of the room. Nothing much to talk of. A bedside table with a lamp and a Bible and a magazine called *Lotus Guide Northern California*. A TV that hadn't been tuned. The bathroom smelled slightly sulphurous, and there was no difference in temperature between the hot and cold taps, so she decided not to pour herself a glass of water, despite how thirsty she was. There was nothing to eat, either, but she did open and drink four tiny pots of coffee creamer. Then she undressed, showered, dressed again, and climbed into bed fully clothed.

She lay in the sweltering darkness for some time, considering her situation. No suitcase, no wallet, no phone. "Peeled" was the term, as she'd learned from a slightly dubious young man she'd had to sit next to on the bus. His name was Lucky, and he hadn't stopped talking to her the whole way. He had open sores on his hands. He'd been "peeled" too, it turned out.

She probed at her forehead and the bridge of her nose under the covers. It was still very tender. Broken, perhaps. She remembered very little of the assault apart from the shape and the sound of the weapon her assailant had used. A bell of some kind, that made a cartoonish clanging noise when it connected with the front of her skull. The police in Lewiston had found this particular detail very funny. She could still picture them now, grinning through mouthfuls of gum. Could still hear the note of the bell, too, as she drifted into jet-lagged sleep, and the words, receding into the darkness:

"It's not him. It's not him."

2

WHAT WAS meant to be a thirty-minute nap turned into four hours sunk in blackest oblivion. When Vivian woke up a slice of late-afternoon sunshine had found its way through the gap in the curtains and was burning her cheek. She sat up, not knowing where she was, sweating heavily into her coat and hiking boots.

She got up and opened the curtains. The mountain was red and glowering, furious with her for not giving an offering, no doubt. Below her the unused pool was shivering in the shadow of the motel building. It was roped off but hadn't been covered, and its water was very dark and accruing a kind of pink scum at its edges. She closed the curtains again. She made herself a coffee, black, since she'd already drunk the free cream, and had another shower. Then she left the motel with her armful of posters to follow up her one and only lead.

Vivian's destination was the House of Telos, a school of spiritual education that promised to purge the Western capitalist mind of its ills and bring it within touching distance of the One Cosmic Spirit, through a series of online seminars that cost seventy-five dollars an hour. Jesse had never been a particularly happy child when they were growing up, but adulthood had brought with it a whole new raft of emotional and existential crises, and Vivian had watched him flounder from one to the next with a mixture of pity and frustration. When he was twenty-two he'd signed up to the House of Telos's enrichment programme, and after three years had given them so much of their parents' fortune that they'd offered him the opportunity to study at the House itself, in Mount Hookey, CA.

He'd wavered at first, thanks to a talking-to from Vivian. Then, in March, their father had died. Everyone spoke about what a shock it had been, but Vivian felt like she'd seen it coming for years, and it certainly wasn't an accident. Jesse became difficult to communicate with. Six months after the funeral, Jesse – a man who had difficulty even getting the bus by himself – had taken the flight to LA, telling Vivian he had gone to seek guidance first-hand from the Ascended Masters of Telos. That was the last they had heard of him. He'd just gone, taking his grief with him, and leaving Vivian and her mother to theirs.

The House of Telos's headquarters were at 125 Vista Street. Vivian had committed that to memory. She followed the black-and-white map that the receptionist had given her and put up half a dozen pictures of her brother on telegraph poles as she went. The reception desk at Cedar Lodge had been unattended and she'd helped herself to a roll of Sellotape. Mr Blucas had still been there with his shopping bags, though he'd moved to a different couch.

Vista Street ran parallel to the main highway. Vivian went back to the centre of town, took a left at the Earth Foods store and a right at the tea house and began counting down the numbers on the mailboxes. It was a residential street, though many of the homes doubled as businesses of a spiritual bent: psychics, yogis, healers of various kinds. In among them a video rental store and a nursery, both looking a little embattled. Outside "Mount Hookey Crystal Visions" a man in a robe and sandals was packing postcards and dreamcatchers and glass orbs into a plastic crate. He saw her and there was the same look of recognition she'd seen in the receptionist's face. He dropped the crate and the orbs went rolling all over the pavement. He stared at her as she sellotaped another poster to the mailbox outside the shop, and she turned and glared at him.

"What?" she said.

He got down on his knees and started picking up his wares.

Then he dragged his crate through the door of the shop and locked it from the inside. He watched her for another few moments from behind the glass.

"Hey. Hello? I can still see you."

Vivian took a step towards the door and the man melted into the shop's darkened interior. She stuck another poster up where his face had been.

By the time Vivian reached number 125 she was at the end of the street, almost out of the town. The road and the pavement were in bad shape, broken and split by the roots of the cedars. The address was a small, ranch-style bungalow with primrose yellow walls and a broken picket fence. The front yard was overgrown, bright plastic toys scattered in the long grass like the ruins of some lost civilisation. The garage was open and there was a child's bike lying on its side in the driveway.

Vivian went to the front door. There were two stickers in the living room window. One said: "Telos welcomes YOU!" The other said, "We heal pets."

She pulled back her hood and knocked. Somewhere inside, a toddler was screaming. Vivian heard the sound of cutlery dashed against a table, the scrape of a chair on the floor, and hurried footsteps in the hall.

The woman who opened the door was in her forties, Vivian guessed, wearing a hoodie and track pants. Her face was deeply seamed, her hair somewhere between blond and grey. She had the bluest eyes Vivian had ever seen.

She opened her mouth and made a tiny, soundless gasp. A moment of silence passed between them before she said, "Can I help you?"

Vivian looked over the woman's shoulder at the hallway strewn with toys. Back in the kitchen a toddler was smashing his tiny fists into his dinner.

"I think I'm in the wrong place," she said. She made to leave.

"Do I know you?" the woman called after her.

Vivian stopped and turned back. Someone else who seemed to recognise her.

"Why do you say that?"

"You look like someone I used to teach."

Vivian came back to the doorstep and showed her a poster. "Him?"

"Oh, Jesse!" said the woman, as though Vivian had shown her a picture of her own son.

"He's my brother," said Vivian.

"Yes. Of course he is."

"This is the House of Telos?"

The website had promised a pristine temple of the One Cosmic Spirit, with photos of jade gardens and crystal-clear pools and scores of initiates sitting cross-legged on bamboo mats, but Vivian couldn't see any of that.

The baby in the highchair threw his cup to the floor and began wailing. The woman gave a tired smile.

"He was a wonderful student," she said.

"Was?"

"He's not here anymore." She looked dejected all of a sudden.

"He left town?"

"Oh no," said the woman, "I'm sure he's still in town. With *his* energy, there's no way the mountain's letting him go."

Vivian didn't know what she meant by that.

"Then where is he?"

"I don't know. I'm sorry."

The toddler had amped up his screaming again and was rocking backwards and forwards in the chair so violently it looked like it might fall over.

"I think he's going to hurt himself," said Vivian, pointing to the kitchen.

11

The woman blinked her huge blue eyes, sighed, and said, "You'd better come in."

She led Vivian through the hall, whose walls were hung with a mixture of Christian and Buddhist and Native American bric-a-brac – crucifixes, yin and yang tapestries, strings of eagle feathers. Vivian found the combination puzzling. The House of Telos seemed to be hedging its bets, spiritually speaking. They passed the doors to the living room and another room that boomed with the bass of a stereo turned up too loud. The whole house had a strange odour of incense and cooking oil. In the kitchen the woman pulled out a chair for Vivian and then went around the other side of the table to try and coax her child into eating his bowl of pasta shapes.

"This is Chason," she said, gently probing the boy's mouth with the spoon.

"Chason?"

"Troy is in his bedroom. You probably won't see him."

"Okay."

"I'm Shelley, by the way."

"Right. Look, I don't want to take up your time—"

Chason swatted the food from his mother's hand again, and she said, "Sorry," and got down on her hands and knees to retrieve it. She was gone for some time.

"Thing is, Jesse's not been in touch."

There was no reply from under the table.

"Hello?"

"Hold on."

Vivian looked around the kitchen. More mystical bits and pieces. Crystals and tripods and strange totemic carvings, in among the microwave and the cereal boxes and Chason's fire engine. Next to the door that led out to the back yard hung a framed picture, luridly airbrushed, of a man who looked part Jesus Christ and part extraterrestrial. His face reminded her of her father in a way she couldn't grasp; but then, since March, everything seemed to remind her of her father.

"Seems someone's caught your eye." Shelley had popped up while Vivian was staring.

"Who's it meant to be?"

"That's John of Telos," she said. "The first of the Earthly Masters."

"Oh," said Vivian. "I thought maybe it was your husband."

Shelley smiled.

"No, no. He's long gone. No pictures of him anywhere. Would you like something to drink?"

"I'll take a coffee if you've got one," she said. "Black. Really black."

The last thing she needed was another coffee, but she thought she deserved it: a kind of penance for the nap she'd had earlier.

"Coming up," said Shelley. She put on the kettle and looked in the cupboards for a pot, speaking over her shoulder. "So do you know much about Telos?"

"Not really," said Vivian.

"Would you like to learn?"

"I don't think it's really my sort of thing. We're quite different, me and Jesse."

"But you're twins, right?"

Vivian nodded.

"Then you're the same. You're the same spirit."

"We're really not."

Vivian hated this sort of stuff. Everyone asking her if she and Jesse thought the same thoughts. If she felt pain when he did. The answer was always no, she did not, and she was glad of it.

Shelley fidgeted.

"Wait there," she said, "let me get you something."

She abandoned the kettle and went out of the room, leaving

Vivian with the baby. While they were staring at each other over the bowl of cold pasta, a door opened in the hallway and the throbbing bass and electronic bleeps and bloops became suddenly louder. A teenager who must have been seven feet tall lumbered into the kitchen and began rummaging in the fridge. He pulled out a can of something fizzy, turned, clocked Vivian. He kept his eyes fixed on her as he tugged on the ring-pull, drank at least half of the can, and then wiped his mouth with the back of his hand.

"Hey," he said.

"Hey," said Vivian.

He was very pale and looked like he hadn't slept. His hair was almost down to his waist, which was a long way for a boy of his size. His eyes were all pupil.

"Oh, hi Troy!" Shelley had appeared back in the doorway holding a book. She practically had to shout over the music. "This is... I'm sorry, I don't know your name."

"Vivian," said Vivian.

"She's Jesse's sister. Remember Jesse?"

The giant teenager took another swig from his can and shrugged, then pushed past his mother and went back to his room. The door shut and the music went back to sounding as if it was coming from underwater.

"Apparently he's forgotten how to speak," said Shelley, and laughed a weak laugh. Vivian suddenly found her, and the teenager, and the house, unbearably sad. It was Jesse-type sadness; a kind of disappointment with the world that made a horrible counterpoint with Shelley's hippyish positivity.

Shelley gave Vivian her coffee and sat next to the baby again, who was now squirming to be released from his chair. She handed Vivian the book she'd been holding. Vivian examined it. The cover displayed the same hyperreal figure from the portrait on the wall, thumbs and forefingers joined in a triangle just above his navel, out of which shot a beam of violet light. She flicked through the pages without reading it. It had the high gloss of a sales brochure.

"What is this?"

"Just an introduction to the Violet Path."

"What's the Violet Path?"

"The path of Telos. It's what your brother's started on."

"Oh right." Nonsense, then. She put it face-down on the table and slid it to one side. "I want to talk about my brother."

Shelley looked put out by Vivian's disinterest in the book.

"Sure. We can talk about Jesse if you like."

"When was he last here?"

"Maybe a month ago."

"A month?"

That was longer than she'd expected. He could have gone a long way in a month.

"He didn't stay very long," said Shelley. "He was with us for maybe two weeks. He outgrew this place pretty quickly."

"What do you mean, 'outgrew'?"

"Maybe that's the wrong word." Shelley frowned slightly. "He just thought it wasn't the right fit."

Vivian glanced around the kitchen.

"Maybe he was expecting something else," she said. "It doesn't look much like your website."

Shelley lifted Chason from his chair and put him on the floor. He went grubbing around on all fours, eating most of the pasta he'd thrown between their feet.

"We've had to scale things back in the last couple years," Shelley said. "There's a lot of competition around here these days." She picked at the edge of the table. Vivian saw her fingernails were ravaged. "People out to make a quick buck."

"I mean," she said, "no offence, but you've made a few thousand quick bucks out of my brother in the last three years." She took a sip of coffee. It was bitter and disgusting and exactly what she wanted.

"I've got to make money somehow, haven't I?" said Shelley. She nodded to the child under the table. Her voice had changed. "I'm not going to bag groceries when I've been given this gift. I want to help people, Vivian. I want to help people like your brother. We're trying to change the world here."

Vivian looked around the mess of the kitchen again. She drank from her coffee cup again, to stop herself from saying anything.

"We're waking people up, Vivian. To a new reality. A new peace. A new harmony. Of course, I say 'new' – it's really the old harmony. The only harmony. The oneness of Telos."

Shelley spread her fingers as if the whole thing was self-evident. She fixed Vivian with her weird opalescent eyes and for a moment Vivian thought she could, indeed, see some other reality, some deeper understanding in them; then she realised that things were probably the other way around, and that having mesmerising, otherworldly eyes recommended you for a career in spiritual charlatanism in the first place.

The baby banged his head against the table leg and started crying, and Shelley abandoned her hypnotism to pick him up again and dandle him on her knee.

"And Jesse was into all this stuff, was he?" Vivian asked.

"Jesse had committed himself fully to the Path, yes. He was always looking beyond. What I like to call a *searcher*. You know?"

That was Jesse alright. Vivian had visions of them playing together when they'd been not much older than Chason. Jesse had made a point of dismantling every one of his toys (and after that every one of Vivian's) to discover how they worked, and then always sat forlorn and inconsolable among the pieces, as if he'd expected and then failed to find the very soul of the thing. At school, his grades had been uniformly poor because he always insisted on investigating some esoteric detail way beyond the syllabus, while misunderstanding or choosing not to understand the basics. He couldn't follow instructions. He would start his maths homework when he got home at five p.m. and by midnight have filled his whole exercise book with a critique of Quantum Entanglement. He was the cleverest person Vivian knew, and the most useless. When he left school no university would have him, and he'd stayed under his parents' roof ever since, totally absorbed in his complex and futile research projects.

That was the problem with their dad's death, Vivian thought. Jesse had tried to approach it using his own unique brand of logic, as a puzzle to be solved, and had found his brain wanting. He'd taken his grief to pieces like one of his toys, and, as usual, had found nothing at the centre.

"He does think a lot," said Vivian.

Shelley nodded sympathetically.

"That was a habit we were trying to get him out of. He was making real progress, with the meditation, and the breathwork. But, you know." She shrugged. "The Path took him somewhere else."

"Where?"

"I don't know. One of the other schools, I imagine."

"What are the other schools?"

"He might have gone to the Temple of Telos. Or the Telurian Mission. Telos Centre for Spiritual Living has closed down but Glenn – he's the guy who ran it – he started the Telos Sanctuary last month, so Jesse could have gone there. Angels of Telos is cheap, that's an option. The Way of Telos has just opened, above Wing's. You know, the Chinese place? I don't know much about them but they seem a big draw."

"There's a lot of you."

"We used to get along. Some of us still do. But there's a lot of bad blood. It's hard to achieve oneness when everyone's fighting against each other, you know?"

Vivian looked down at the book again. The man on the cover stared back at her with a vague and knowing smile. The violet triangle above his groin was mirrored and expanded in a picture of the mountain itself, Mount Hookey, which served as a background to the figure of John of Telos. Incredible, she thought, that Jesse could have been taken in by such a wild fiction. Or perhaps not. He'd tried absolutely everything else. Abandoning reason altogether was perhaps the last route open to him.

"I need their names and addresses," she said.

"Sure thing," said Shelley. "Best not hang about, though. A spirit like Jesse?" She whistled. "He'll be ascended in no time. Then there's no way you'll see him again. Not unless you fancy ascending with him."

Vivian scowled so hard her forehead hurt.

"Ascended."

"Gone up the mountain. Once he's up the mountain, no point losing sleep waiting for him to come back!"

"What? Why not?"

"Well… why would he want to come back?"

"Why would he *not* want to? What's up the mountain?"

"I feel like you should maybe read the book, Vivian. It's difficult to explain from scratch."

"Can't you just tell me?"

"Bless you, there's no reason to look so worried! He won't have gone anywhere yet. I'm sure you'll find him somewhere around town. Then maybe he can explain. Better coming from him than from me."

Vivian looked into the dregs of her coffee. The hand that held the cup was shuddering slightly, and not just from the caffeine.

"I don't get it," she said.

"Don't get what?"

"This." She gestured around the kitchen, at the portrait, at the crystals. "All of this. I'm not trying to offend you. But, you know. I just don't."

"That's okay," said Shelley. "That's normal."

There was a condescending note in her voice that made the back of Vivian's head itch.

"I should go," she said. "I'll take the names of those schools if you've got them."

"You really should read the book, too. It'll help you to understand."

Vivian capitulated. She picked it up from where it lay on the table.

"They're twenty dollars," said Shelley.

Vivian stared at her. "You serious?"

"I'm not making profit from that. Just breaking even."

"I don't have any cash."

"Oh, you don't?" said Shelley. She sounded disappointed.

"Someone stole my wallet. That's how I got all this." She pointed to her bruises.

Shelley gasped. "Here? In Mount Hookey? This is such a safe town. People don't get hurt here."

"Lewiston."

"That's awful! Bless you."

"I'm okay. I'll just have to get some money, somehow. I'll work it out."

"Well. Let us know if there's anything we can do to help."

"You could let me have the book."

Shelley smiled again, but this time it seemed forced.

"Of course," she said. "Just pay me back when you can."

Vivian looked out of the window, saw a lilac dimness had come over the sky. She pushed back her chair and collected up her pile of posters with the book on top. Both were now smeared with Chason's pasta sauce. Shelley gave her the names and addresses of the various schools of Telos she had mentioned, drew her a rudimentary map, then led her back through the booming hallway to the front door.

"Vivian's leaving, Troy," she hollered through her son's bedroom door. "You want to say goodbye?"

There was no answer. She shrugged, and smiled once more, and Vivian felt that sadness creep over her again like the coldness of the evening.

"Thanks," she said. "I might be back."

"The House of Telos is always open."

"I'm going to stick some of these posters up around the street."

"It's a free country."

Vivian pulled up her hood again and tramped into the wildness of their front yard. She'd reached the picket fence when Shelley called out to her.

"Blessings, Vivian. I hope you find your brother. We all do."

Behind her, Chason had started crying again. Vivian was back on Vista Street, and had passed another three houses, before she realised how strange those last three words had been.

3

CEDAR LODGE was deserted when Vivian got back. The lobby was dark apart from a single lamp on the reception desk. The receptionist had abandoned her post and Mr Blucas had left and taken his many bags of scavenged treasure with him. Vivian checked the clock on the wall. It was only just gone eight p.m. and she apparently had the whole place to herself.

She was delirious with hunger by now and knew if she didn't eat something she'd be listening to her stomach complaining all night, thanks to a combination of jet lag and the insomnia she'd had on and off for as long as she could remember. She found the dining area at the back of the reception, chairs upended on top of the tables, and from there discovered the kitchen through a pair of flimsy double doors. It was as clean and well-kept as the rest of the motel and smelled of drains and days-old bacon fat. In the cupboards she found some tiny packets of breakfast cereal she thought she could trust, took two, and returned to her room in almost total darkness.

Inside, she lay on the bed and started reading *The Violet Path*. She ate the cereal dry, straight from the box. It was sweetened beyond recognition, and in the circumstances was the most delicious thing she'd ever eaten.

The book opened with a story. Telos, it turned out, was not a person but a place. A city, like Atlantis, that had been swallowed up by the sea and now existed alternately beneath the two icecaps. The city of Telos was populated by an ancient, super-intelligent race of beings, or Beings, who may or may not have been from outer space

(Vivian never resolved this). Some of these Beings happened to have got stranded in California before Telos had returned to the sea, and had revealed their wisdom to one man only, John of Telos, waiting, for some reason, until the late 1970s to do so. The stranded Telurians had then retreated to the inside of Mount Hookey, where they'd set up a new civilisation, a Crystal City, that could only be perceived by an Ascended Master of Telos. John of Telos was the first Ascended Master. There were others, men and women who he taught, up until his mysterious disappearance in the late eighties. It was generally agreed that he had returned to the mountain. Apparently, lots of people had met him since, while they were hiking or meditating in the woods around Mount Hookey. He appeared, it was said, in a great flash of violet light.

Vivian thought the story was idiotic, and it troubled her to think that Jesse might have swallowed the whole thing in earnest. It wasn't like him. As the foundation for a religion, or whatever the Violet Path was, it hardly stood up to interrogation, and Jesse interrogated absolutely everything.

The rest of the book was less compelling than the introduction. It was a kind of manual, written in that same highly abstract, metaphorical language that Shelley had slipped in and out of. Vivian supposed it had to be written like that. Anything too concrete and the mystery would disappear, and along with it the whole appeal of the Telos mythology. It seemed like pretty straightforward New Age flimflam. There were lots of diagrams – mostly circles and pyramids – and references to "being", and "presence", and "spirit", and "vibrations", occasionally capitalised. A chapter on "Manifesting". A chapter on "Telos and the Endless Now". A shaded box that dealt with the question of whether John of Telos and Jesus were the same person. The whole thing was seasoned with encouraging quotations from initiates, all of whom seemed to have PhDs, assuring the reader that the Violet Path was the only true way to happiness. The actual word "happiness" was almost never used, but Vivian knew that was what they meant. All these other words – oneness, wellness, peace, harmony – were just stand-ins for the big "H".

Was she happy? She banished the thought as soon as it arose. She was *better*; that was all that mattered. Better than she had been. Jesse's disappearance had, in a perverse way, been a shot in the arm. After the bleak and colourless months that followed the business with their father, it had brought Vivian back into focus, or at the very least it had given her a reason to get out of bed.

Vivian was brought out of deep rumination by the sound of feet beneath her window. She threw the book onto the bed and got up, jittering from all the sugar she'd eaten. When she opened the curtains she saw someone with a torch making their way around the swimming pool. The globe of the receptionist's hair was unmistakable.

It was later than Vivian had thought and the moon was full and high. The whole mountain glowed. There was a perfect ring of cloud over its summit, pale and rainbowed by the moonlight. The receptionist was wearing a robe like the man who had stared at Vivian outside the Crystal Visions shop. There was something tied to her back, too. Some kind of musical instrument. She was still wearing her pink jacket – Vivian could see the outlines of her shoulder pads beneath the robe's loose fabric. Vivian watched her navigate the edge of the swimming pool and then awkwardly scale the wire fence at the back of the motel. She fell over the other side and it sounded like the instrument broke. She got up and brushed leaves and pine needles from her robes, looking embarrassed. She glanced back at the motel. Vivian ducked behind the curtain. When she peered out again, the receptionist had disappeared into the dense forest at the rear of the motel, though Vivian could still see the beam of her torch flitting among the trunks and the branches.

Vivian was still fully dressed and nowhere near falling asleep. Whether it was the sugar or the caffeine or the anxiety talking, following the receptionist seemed a good idea.

She got up, left her room without locking it, and came down the fire escape to the pool's edge. It stank. Up close she saw almost all of the surface of the water was covered with detritus, like an icefloe, with a few gaps that reflected the moon clearly. Insects hopped and skated crazily across it. She made her way around the edge to the section of fence that the receptionist had vaulted, and found it bowed and easily climbable. It wasn't the first time someone had been this way.

Vivian clasped the cold mesh with her fingers and looked up the mountain. The receptionist's torch beam had disappeared. The weirdly geometric clouds were settling on the peak, and the interior of the forest was pure black, and she could well believe, after her talk with Shelley, that there was no coming back once you ventured up those slopes.

A wailing came from somewhere among the trees. More screaming than wailing. Several voices, male and female, screaming over and over again. It was wild at first, then found some kind of rhythm. The sound, Vivian thought, of a dozen people being brutally murdered, or perhaps just singing very, very badly, to the primitive beat of a drum.

She let go of the fence and ran back into the motel. Even after she'd got inside, the screaming seemed no quieter.

In the lobby there was a shadow over the desk. A night porter, perhaps? She came around the corner and saw a figure silhouetted against the lamp, feet up, reading a paperback. Vivian couldn't tell if it was a man or a woman. Their limbs were long and seemed to have too many joints.

They turned when they saw Vivian coming. It was a young man.

His legs uncurled like a spider's and he took his feet off the desk. He looked at her and then at his phone, and didn't bother taking out his earphones.

"What?" he said, scrolling through something. "You didn't want to join in?"

It was Shelley's son. His face was cadaverous in his phone's blue light, a look that wasn't helped by the length and straightness and blackness of his hair. He was grinning.

"What are you doing here?"

"This is my job."

"Can you hear that?" said Vivian. The screams sounded like they were in the next room. He finally plucked out a single earphone.

"And they wonder why no one stays here anymore," he said.

"Sounds like someone's getting hurt."

He laughed.

"Hurt?" he said. "Man, they're having the time of their lives up there!"

"Who is? What are they doing?"

"I don't know. Communing with the earth spirit. Summoning the angels of Telos. That kind of thing."

"I saw the receptionist—"

"Judy. She'll be gone for a few days. That's why I'm on shift."

"A few days?"

"Uh-huh."

"What is it? It sounds like a… ritual or something."

"Sure, you can call it that. She took her drum, right?"

"I think so."

"Makes sense."

It didn't.

Vivian listened again. The screaming had stopped abruptly. She waited a while in silence while Troy continued to fiddle with his phone.

"Aren't you a bit young to be working here?"

"I'm nineteen. And this is basically the only job I can get up here. Assuming I don't want to get into Mom's line of work."

She looked at him, and thought of Shelley and Chason, and frowned involuntarily.

"Nineteen? But your brother…"

"You trying to do the math?" he said. He took a roll-up cigarette from a little tin he had behind the desk and lit it. "I know, it doesn't add up." He laughed as he exhaled. "I'm a good old cult baby."

"Cult baby?"

"Mom had me in one of the Telos communes. She was about my age. Dad was, like, in his fifties at the time. Assuming Dad was actually my dad. Apparently one of the ways to achieve eternal peace is just to go around fucking absolutely everybody." He let that hang in the air along with his damp cigarette smoke. "You're not into all this hippy shit though, are you?"

"I don't know," said Vivian.

He took another drag.

"Come on," he said.

"I mean, no. I'm not into it. I don't think it's bad. It just doesn't make sense to me."

"Of course it's bad. It's fucking poison. Look what it did to your brother."

She gripped the edge of the reception desk until her fingernails hurt.

"What do you mean?"

"What do you mean, what do I mean? He's disappeared, right? You wouldn't even be here if there was nothing wrong with it. All the Telos stuff – it gets in here." He tapped his head with a very long finger. "Even if you don't believe any of it now, it's hard to stick to your guns when everyone else is telling you otherwise. In this town, you and me, we're the anomalies. You need to find your brother and get out, because the longer you stay here, the more this place will do things to you. Before you know it, you'll be meeting aliens in the forest and drinking mushroom tea and learning the tabla." He blew another cloud of smoke into his lap and shook his head. "There's a reason I stay in my bedroom the whole time. Just trying to limit my exposure to the contagion."

"You met him, though?" she asked. "You met Jesse?"

Troy had gone back to looking for a new song to play on his phone.

"Sure," he said, without looking up. "We talked a bit. I say *we*. He did most of the talking. Bleak stuff, too, none of the happy-clappy stuff my mom's into. Seemed like the guy needed therapy – I mean, proper therapy, not vibrational healing or whatever."

They had tried that. Jesse had been to two therapists, both of whom had told his parents that he "wasn't a good fit for them". Vivian didn't know therapists could discontinue treatment on those grounds. As often happened, her frustration had been mixed in with a glimmer of pride in the fact that her brother had somehow managed to out-think a certified psychoanalyst.

"When did you last see him?" she asked.

"Couple of weeks ago."

"Where?"

"Right here. He had a room. Mom wanted him to move in with us and pay rent but—"

"He stayed *here*?"

"Uh-huh."

"What the hell!"

"What?"

"The woman said she hadn't seen him. She took a poster and everything. Said she didn't recognise his picture."

"What woman?"

"Your colleague. The other receptionist."

Troy laughed. "My *colleague*? You mean Judy?"

"Why would she say she hadn't seen Jesse if he was staying here?"

"I mean, in *theory* they could have missed each other. Pretty unlikely, though."

Vivian chewed her lower lip.

"When's she coming back?" she said.

"Judy? Search me. Not for a few days, hopefully."

"Why hopefully?"

"I need the hours, or I'll never save up enough to get out of here." Troy took a final drag on his cigarette. "See, Judy's a case in point. She came here about six months ago. Normal, straightforward. She went feet-first into Telos and then... Well, you heard how she likes to spend her evening off."

Vivian found herself looking upon the low-lit drabness of the motel with fresh eyes. As if some clue of Jesse's whereabouts might be hanging from the wall or have fallen behind one of the sofas.

"When did you say he checked out?"

"Uh," said Troy. "We're not great at the paperwork here. Last time I saw him was about two weeks ago, I guess."

"Can you remember what room he was in?"

"Why would I remember a thing like that?"

"You obviously don't get many guests here."

He shrugged.

"I want to look in his room," said Vivian.

"I just said, I don't know which room he was in."

"Then we try all of them."

"We?"

"Do you have better things to do?"

She fixed him with a stare. He popped a bit of gum in his mouth and chewed and gave a loud, menthol-flavoured sigh.

"Fine."

He pulled a drawer fully out of the desk and upended its contents in front of her. It was all keys. Vivian thought that hotels were meant to keep the keys to the rooms on a system of little hooks, but apparently Cedar Lodge had a different way of doing things.

"You're the only guest in tonight," he said. "Go nuts."

Vivian filled all the huge pockets of her coat and left him to his book and his phone. The keys were at least numbered, and she went methodically from room to room. There were only thirty-two suites in the whole place, but there were three times that many keys. As it turned out, she'd done well on the room lottery. Most of them smelled a good deal worse than hers, especially those near the kitchen. And Troy hadn't been entirely honest about her being the only guest – the cockroaches had made themselves quite at home in several of the ground floor rooms.

The only room she didn't check was number 29, next door to hers. However much she raked through her pockets, she couldn't find the key.

"There's no key for 29," she told Troy when she got back.

"Must be."

"There isn't."

"We can't have lost all of them. There's three for every room. Two for the guests and one for reception."

"Well, it isn't here."

He sighed again.

"Let me have a look. Maybe Judy has them. Or Mr Blucas."

"Blucas?"

"Have you met him yet?"

"I think I did. Is he actually a guest here?"

"Spends half his life lurking around here, but no, he's not a paying customer. And he's pretty light-fingered."

He pushed his chair back and opened several more drawers under the desk. He began taking out handfuls of pens and rubber bands and crumpled compliments slips. He opened another, then another, building a mountain of old detritus on the leather tabletop. Decades of the stuff, it looked like. A guestbook from 1996, the year of Jesse and Vivian's birth. An antique calculator. A manual credit card imprinter. Rolls and rolls of receipt paper.

"Nope," he said. "Nothing." He poked around one last time in the bottom drawer. "Well, this is interesting."

Vivian leaned over the desk.

"What is it?"

Troy took a sheaf of paper out of the drawer and placed it on the desk, between Vivian's elbow and the reception bell.

"I take it these are yours?"

It was Vivian's posters. The ones she'd already put up around town, a dozen or so. She could tell by how creased they were. Some were missing corners, or still had scraps of Sellotape attached to them. Someone had torn them down. Not only that, but the central photograph of Jesse had been decorated somehow, in black marker pen, with glyphs and symbols. Illuminated, almost, like a medieval manuscript.

"See what I mean? She's gone."

Vivian thumbed through them.

"You think it was her? The receptionist?"

"Who else would it have been?"

He went back to rummaging in the bowels of the desk. Vivian continued staring at her brother's face, a mirror image, embellished with astrological symbols and pictograms, and the same pick 'n' mix of religious iconography she'd seen at the House of Telos. Judy had a lot of questions to answer when she came back from her trip up the mountain. If she came back.

"No, definitely no room 29 here," said Troy. "But what do you think you'll find, anyway? He checked out."

Vivian was still looking at the poster, and only half listening to him. "You're right," she said. "Thanks anyway."

"Welcome."

She left the mound of keys with him and headed out of the lobby.

"So, I've got to just clear all these away, have I?"

She didn't reply.

"Swell meeting you, Vivian," he shouted, when she was already at the door that led outside. "Same time tomorrow?"

On the way back she tried the handle of room 29, not sure why it might have magically unlocked itself in her absence. It hadn't. She passed along to room 30, went inside, and stared out of the window. She thought she saw tiny flickers of light among the trees on the mountain, but the kind of lights that were only visible when she wasn't looking directly at them. Maybe it was her concussion.

She put the posters on her bedside table and returned to *The Violet Path*. She read the book until the letters themselves drifted and merged and stopped making sense. It was six a.m., and the silhouette of the mountain was visible through the thin curtains, when Vivian finally fell asleep. Only then did the sounds of drumming and wailing return, and by that point she had no idea whether they were real or imagined.

4

VIVIAN MISSED breakfast. The motel alarm clock was broken, like everything else in the room, and its red LED display could only be read with the correct, precise application of pressure to various parts of the screen. A few minutes of manipulation passed before she realised she was reading it right. The morning was gone. It was one o'clock in the afternoon.

She put on her coat and boots and crammed *The Violet Path* into her pocket, rolling it into a tight tube so it would fit. She had no intention of reading it again, but she thought it might improve her credentials when she went to visit the other schools of Telos – they would, perhaps, be more willing to talk if they thought of her as one of their own. She found the folded piece of paper with their addresses on it, forced down a cup of sulphurous tap water, and left her room.

Down in the lobby the reception desk was unattended again. Troy was gone and Judy obviously hadn't returned, and there was an end-of-the-world emptiness about the whole place. The dining area looked as it had done the previous night. Seeing as she was the only guest, they probably hadn't even bothered opening for breakfast.

Vivian got to the entrance of the lobby and stopped. She rested her fingers on the handle, and then, seeing the parking lot was barren and knowing there was absolutely nobody else in the motel, went back to the reception desk and picked up the box of donations to the mountain. She shook it, then slid open the wooden bottom. There was a ten-dollar bill in there. She took it.

She'd get a proper breakfast, wrath of the Telurians be damned.

Outside it was another perfect, bright day. A slight chill from the altitude, despite the sunshine. Even with her body clock so askew, Vivian looked upon the town with a kind of hungover clarity. It seemed a less strange place than when she'd arrived; or rather, it seemed there was another Mount Hookey that she hadn't paid attention to the day before. She noticed regular shops and businesses – a pizza place, a realtor, a hardware store – in among the healers and the gurus. Regular people, too. Outside the gas station, two men in baseball caps and slack denims peered under the bonnet of a car. A bored-looking girl with bad skin aligned the trolleys outside the supermarket. In light of all this, the events of the previous day took on the haziness of a fever dream.

Shelley's map took her in all directions, so Vivian decided to eat in the first coffee shop she came to. It was called Steamin' Pete's and was decked out like a fisherman's shack, tackle and fibreglass fish and bits of boat nailed to the walls. Her dad had liked fishing, but had never taken her with him. There was a neat pile of *Lotus Guide Northern California* magazines on a stand near the door, but apart from that the place seemed free of spiritual trappings. It was busy, too. There was hissing and clanging from the kitchen out back, strong and delicious smells of coffee and Mexican food. Vivian joined the queue and rolled her ill-gotten ten-dollar bill in her trouser pocket.

She ordered a pancake breakfast and another black coffee, forgot about the tax for the hundredth time since arriving in the USA, and ended up spending nearly the whole ten dollars. She grimaced. The peppy waitress glanced meaningfully at the tips jar when she gave Vivian her receipt. Vivian looked at it too. It had a quirkily handwritten sign that read: "All tips go to the mountain!"

Vivian walked away with her order number on a little fishing rod and got a table to herself under a huge, fake salmon. When the waitress brought over her pancakes and coffee she asked to borrow a pen and made a list on the back of a napkin. There were other things to do besides looking for Jesse. She wanted to ring the police in Lewiston and see if they had caught the man with the bell, or at least retrieved her possessions. She'd asked them to call her at Cedar Lodge, but the chances of any message reaching her seemed slim given that the motel's reception was apparently abandoned for large portions of the day, and the Lewiston police department didn't seem a particularly motivated bunch.

If she didn't get her wallet and passport back she'd have to ring the embassy. Her bank, too. She didn't have a number for either, and without her phone she couldn't look it up. She hadn't seen a library or an internet cafe. She could go to the embassy in person, but how was she meant to do that if she couldn't pay for a bus ticket? Could her bank wire her money to anywhere in the world? Come to think of it, had she even seen a bank or an ATM since she'd got there?

That brought her to the last bullet point on her list: *Mum?* Her mother could perhaps send over the funds, but it was a call Vivian was anxious to avoid. Mrs Owens was a habitual worrier, and the combined stresses of hearing about her daughter's predicament, the lack of success on the Jesse-finding front, and the prospect of having to transfer money via twenty-first-century means would probably, literally, be enough to kill her.

Vivian went over the question mark repeatedly, until the biro had scored through to the tabletop. She realised suddenly that someone had sat opposite her. They were breathing loudly through their mouth, and each exhale was accompanied by a gust of sour coffee breath, with notes of something more grotesque underneath.

"How's it taste?"

She looked up. It was Mr Blucas. He was wearing the same

anorak and woolly hat he'd worn the previous day. He had just two shopping bags with him today, different from the ones he'd had in the motel, she noticed. One contained some women's clothes, the other a bundle of what might have been loft insulation and a fishing lure he'd obviously just stolen from one of the other tables. He nodded at the remains of her pancake.

Vivian looked around for support, but everyone else in the cafe was trying to ignore him too.

"It's good," she said quietly, and looked down at her list again as though it demanded all of her attention.

"Food's garbage here," said Mr Blucas.

Vivian shrugged. "It's okay."

"Everything's garbage here."

She glanced up. He sat back in his chair and nodded to himself in agreement. She tried to eat her last rasher of bacon but let her fork fall to the plate when she caught another mouthful of his breath.

"You come up here on the Amtrak?" he asked.

"Yeah."

"You eat onboard?"

"I'm sorry," said Vivian, "I'm just trying to do some work."

"I used to go all over on the trains," he said, ignoring her. "All over."

Vivian contemplated getting up and leaving. It wasn't fair. She'd only been here ten minutes. She wanted to finish her coffee.

"On the old Amtrak you could get a hamburger and Coke for one dollar and twenty cents." His eyes rolled back and went completely white. "Now they charge you ten dollars, twenty dollars. And you know what?"

He waited for an answer.

"What?"

"It's garbage!"

"Oh."

She looked around for another table to sit at, but the place was full.

"Who you looking for?" he demanded.

"No one," Vivian said.

"You won't find your brother in here," he said.

Vivian looked at him and he grinned a tobacco-yellow grin.

"What do you know about my brother?" she asked. She leaned forward and nearly knocked her coffee cup over with her elbow.

"They were going to put him in my room," he said. "Those sons of bitches."

"You saw him at the motel?"

"I said, 'You put him in my room and I'll get this whole garbage place closed down!' And they listened, yes ma'am. Everyone listens to me round here. I run this whole town. You'll see."

He looked around the cafe now, and the rest of the diners studied their plates of eggs and toast and tortillas. Vivian came forward again, found the smell too much, retreated to where the air was clearer.

"When you say he was in your room – do you mean you have the key to that room?"

"I got keys to every room in town. I got keys to doors folks like you can't even see. You ever seen an Ascended Master before?"

Vivian sighed.

"No."

"You're looking at one!"

He cackled.

"Do you know where Jesse is now?" Vivian asked. "Honestly?"

"My brother lived here, once," said Mr Blucas.

"Mr Blucas."

He shook his head. "Brothers. Who'd have them? Just a pain in the ass."

"Do you know where he is?"

Mr Blucas swung his head back around and his hat teetered but still refused to fall from where it was balanced on his crown. Wisps of dirty straw-coloured hair poked out from underneath.

"What do you reckon?" he said. "Do you think my brother and your brother are somewhere together? Laughing about us? I bet they are. Sons of bitches."

Vivian sat back in her chair and knew that she was getting nothing from him. She wondered if there was anyone in the whole town – the whole state – she could get a straight answer from.

"Please," she said. "If you know anything..."

"Oh, yes ma'am, you can bet he's gone to the big house."

"The big house? You mean prison?"

"They got him locked up good!" said Mr Blucas, and laughed loudly again. "You go and look in the big house. They'll be there. My brother and your brother. Two goddamn sons of bitches."

At this the waitress appeared by his side, radiant and youthful, a whole different species.

"I'm sorry, Mr Blucas," she said. "You know we can't have you cursing in here while people are trying to eat."

"I'm going already," said the old man, and heaved himself out of his chair. "Need to go and see if my room is ready. It had better be ready."

He picked up his shopping bags and turned to the rest of the room.

"You're all getting fed garbage," he said. "Twenty-four-seven. I've told you and told you. But you won't listen." He looked down at Vivian. "You got any change from that ten-dollar bill you stole?"

Vivian flushed with guilt and said nothing. How did he know? Had he been spying on her? He showed her half a mouthful of yellow teeth again.

"You're alright," he said. "You take as much as you need. They won't miss it."

Then he shuffled out of the cafe in his gigantic coat, muttering to himself. Whenever he passed a table, people put down their cutlery and pushed their plates away, as if just his presence had somehow tainted the food.

Vivian left the cafe half an hour later feeling sick and a little woozy. Her stomach was a truculent thing at the best of times, but two days of fasting followed by pancakes and bacon and heavy syrup had thrown it into great, heaving spasms. She could still smell Mr Blucas, too, regardless of how many times she washed her face and hands in Steamin' Pete's bathroom. Coffee and urine and something fungal.

What if Jesse really was in prison? That was another reason to contact the police. Before she left Steamin' Pete's, she asked the waitress if there was a police station in town. The waitress still seemed to begrudge Vivian her lack of tip, or perhaps she thought her responsible for luring Mr Blucas into the cafe, but answered her shortly: no. The nearest police station was Lewiston. Mount Hookey was a safe town, and they had no need for law enforcement.

The route Shelley had sketched took Vivian in a slightly misshapen oblong up and down both sides of the highway. The western side, further down the foothills of the mountain, seemed the more dishevelled half of town. Here the forest gave way to a kind of prairie, so dry and brittle it may as well have been desert.

In a yard of brown grass she found the "Telurian Mission", or what was left of it. It had been a converted church by the looks of things, but its spire was skeletal and the rest of the building was a charred shell. There was a wooden sign outside on which the name of the school had been stencilled, and on top of that someone had graffitied a black, inverted triangle. It seemed some kind of warning.

A man walking his shih-tzu stopped slightly too close to feel comfortable and surveyed the devastation with her. He said nothing. He was beaming.

"What happened here?" Vivian asked.

"The mission?" said the man. "They got what was coming to them!"

He made a triangle with his fingers, inverted, like the graffiti, and pointed it in the direction of the ruined church. His dog sniffed at one of Vivian's boots. Vivian guessed at what he might have meant. *A lot of bad blood*, as Shelley had said.

"Thank goodness someone's purged the negative energy, right? Can you feel that? Phewee!"

He brought his finger-triangle to his lips, blew through it, then laughed and went on his way, dragging the shih-tzu behind him. Vivian spent another few moments looking at the burned timbers of the church. She didn't agree with the man. Seemed there was a whole lot of negative energy here that hadn't been purged.

She took out her map. She crossed the Telurian Mission from her list and scanned the rest. Angels of Telos. Temple of Telos. Light of Telos. Telos Now. The Telos Sanctuary. That was just the first page.

It was tiring, demoralising work. Angels of Telos she found in a trailer park on the edge of town, an RV covered in so much neon signage it looked more like a casino than a place of spiritual learning. Vivian was met on the doorstep by the oldest, most artificially tanned woman she had ever seen, who straight-up invited her in and offered her a cup of tea and postage-stamp-sized tab of acid. Vivian declined both. She asked after Jesse. The woman said she'd never met him, but she'd seen him in a dream during one of her visits to Telos. She asked Vivian if she knew where the entrance to the Telurian vortex was. Vivian said no. She asked if Vivian would like to be shown one day. Vivian declined this, too. Vivian asked the woman – whose name sounded like "Eenoo", though she couldn't have spelled it – if she had a telephone she could use. Eenoo had thrown out her phone on the same day that John F. Kennedy had been assassinated and hadn't bought another one since.

The other schools were a series of greater or lesser disappointments. The Temple of Telos was housed in a grey, modular building that could have been the reception for a taxi rank. Its doors were closed, and there was no furniture inside. Light of Telos was a kiosk that sold organic e-cigarettes. Telos Now was another residential property, like Shelley's, but even more run-down. Its sign was a piece of A4 paper stuck to the inside of a Plymouth Voyager that was parked outside the house, all of its tyres flat. There were vague murmurings of recognition from the man in the kiosk, but he couldn't say anything definite about Jesse's whereabouts, and the woman who Vivian took to be the owner of Telos Now was asleep in the back of the Voyager and didn't look like she wanted waking.

Vivian was close to giving up when she saw the Telos Sanctuary. It seemed far more promising than any of the other schools. It was on the mountain side of the town rather than the desert side, where everything was inexplicably more affluent. It looked a little like an alpine chalet. Up some steps was a tasteful little rock garden that Vivian would have called Japanese, were it not for the totem pole centrepiece and that same childlike rendering of John of Telos that was perched on top of it. Over the front door were the words: "One Light, one Spirit."

Vivian rang the bell and heard something like wind chimes overhead. The door opened almost instantly. The man on the other side was short and bald and had a precisely trimmed white beard. He was in white robes but also wore a pair of rimless spectacles that gave him an air of approachable normality.

He smiled.

"Hello Vivian," he said. "Missing something?"

She blinked at him.

"I'm afraid Jesse is long gone. But he's not the only thing you're missing, is he?"

"I…" She started. "Sorry, what?"

"Come in, dear heart," the man said. "Come in, come in. Let's see what we can do for you."

5

THE MAN was Glenn, whom Shelley had mentioned in passing, and the Telos Sanctuary was, according to him, one of the newest and best equipped schools in Mount Hookey. He led her through the lobby, which was scattered with gigantic pebbles that Vivian presumed were for sitting on. Another reception desk here, attended by a teutonically beautiful young woman who smiled like Glenn had done, and next to it what looked like a small library and gift shop. Opposite was a great mural of John of Telos. She thought of her dad again, for some reason – something about the beard. There was a trickling fountain that was just short of relaxing since the motor that powered it was louder than the water itself. The place smelled of pine resin and incense, and there was the sound of dolphins and whales coming from somewhere.

At the rear was a circular "moon door" that led to some stairs. Vivian followed Glenn up to the floor above. The staircase was lined with more pictures of John of Telos, and some photographs of Glenn with initiates and fellow Telurians. In one of them he was embracing a famous boxer from the 1990s whose name Vivian couldn't remember.

"Is that…" she said.

Glenn just looked over his shoulder, smiled and nodded.

"I thought you'd only just opened?"

"Oh no," said Glenn, "we've been going for nearly thirty years. We had to change our name and premises, because…" He paused. "Let's just say the IRS isn't favourably disposed to us."

He had an aristocratic East Coast accent. Vivian found that reassuring, and slightly at odds with everything around him.

The floor above was one huge, long room with a vaulted roof, like a barn. In the middle of the east-facing wall was a huge triangular window, which perfectly framed the summit of the mountain. Vivian was reminded of the front cover of *The Violet Path*. There were two women in front of the window standing on coloured mats. Their hands were together in prayer. They were hardly moving at all. At the other end of the room was a fireplace and a kitchen, where a young man was stirring a pot of something. Cushions and furs on the varnished wooden floor. Crystals absolutely everywhere, but at least it was quiet, and no one was offering her acid.

Vivian looked down at her hiking boots and saw she'd trailed dirt into the Sanctuary.

"Oh," she said. "Sorry, I'll take these off."

"No, no, please don't worry," said Glenn calmly, and he put a hand on her shoulder. "Would you like me to take your coat?"

"I think I'll keep it on," she said.

Glenn smiled and nodded.

"Please," he said, and showed her a bench along the side of the room. Glenn sat opposite her and let his hands rest in his lap and looked at her as if waiting for her to begin.

"It's nice here," said Vivian, and then immediately added, "How do you know my name?"

"Your brother told me all about you," said Glenn.

"He was here?"

"Briefly."

Her heart sank again.

"Do you know where he went?"

"I do."

"And?"

"He has ascended."

She tensed.

"Already?"

"I know! Incredible, really."

"But what does that mean? He's up the mountain, right?"

He took off his glasses and cleaned them on his robe in a quiet, grandfatherly way.

"It's hard to explain. I'm sorry, I know that's frustrating for you."

The young man who had been in the kitchen came over carrying a tray with a tiny teapot and tiny cups and what looked like a plate of communion wafers. He set it down between them on the bench, and Glenn gave him another glowing smile.

"Please," Glenn said to Vivian, while the man hovered. "Help yourself."

Vivian's stomach still felt like the inside of a car battery, but she was very thirsty from traipsing all over town. She picked up the teapot and poured herself a cup. The tea was blue.

"We brew it with lichen from up on the mountain," said the young man.

"Thank you, Carl," said Glenn.

"Blessings," said Carl, making a small bow. He went back to the kitchen.

Vivian held the cup in both her hands but didn't drink from it. Glenn raised his own cup to his lips and raised his eyebrows over the rim, an expression that Vivian couldn't quite decipher. The vapours fogged his glasses and he laughed, and Vivian couldn't decide whether she liked him or not.

"Look," she said, "I don't mean to be rude, but I would really appreciate a straight answer from someone about where Jesse is. I know I'm not one of you—"

Glenn looked pained by this remark.

"—but no one wants to tell me anything. I just want to know that Jesse is okay."

"I know," said Glenn. "I know." He patted her knee in an avuncular way. It was a strange feeling. Almost electrifying. She couldn't remember the last time someone had shown her any kind of affection. She flinched and he instantly withdrew his hand. "What is it, Vivian?" he said.

"Someone said that once he's ascended, he won't be coming back."

Glenn made a shy face and looked into his teacup and said nothing.

"Why wouldn't he want to come back?" asked Vivian.

"It's difficult—"

"*Please.*"

He looked up again.

"Because he has found Telos."

Vivian winced with exasperation. She suddenly felt very tired again. Too tired to generate the heat of real anger, or anything like it. Besides, Glenn had a kind of diffidence about him that was disarming.

"Yes, sure, Telos," she said. "But what does that *mean*? I just want someone to give me a point on a map so I can go and see my brother and talk to him."

"It's not as simple as that. I am sorry."

"Why is it not as simple as that?"

Glenn took another sip of tea and set his cup down.

"Do you know anything about Telos, or the Violet Path?" he said. "This is not a test, I promise."

Vivian thought. She'd absorbed very little from the book Shelley had given her. The only thing she really remembered was the story of Telos and the Telurians, and John of Telos drifting like a purple phantom around the mountain.

"A little," she said. "I've read some of this." She pulled *The Violet Path* out of her pocket. It was a perfect cylinder now, and wouldn't unroll properly. She wondered if there was something blasphemous about this. "Sorry," she said.

Unexpectedly, Glenn's face shone.

"Aha!" he said. "You've already started!"

"What do you mean?"

"Did you order it from us online?"

"No, someone gave it to me."

Glenn frowned.

"Your brother?" he said.

"No, someone from one of the other schools." Glenn's frown deepened. "The House of Telos." It deepened again. "Shelley? She said she knew you."

Glenn's lips parted slightly in the middle of his white beard. Vivian knew straight away she'd said something she shouldn't have.

"Shelley?" said Glenn.

"Jesse signed up to her course ages ago. When we were back in the UK."

Glenn held out his hand. "Can I see that?" he said.

She handed him the rolled-up book. He looked at the back cover and flicked through the pages as best he could and handed it back.

"Shelley shouldn't really have given you this," he said.

"Oh. Why? What's wrong with it?"

"Absolutely nothing wrong with it. It's the same one we use at the Sanctuary."

"Oh. Then why—"

"Nothing," he said, smiling again. "Just boring business stuff. Carl?"

He called the young man over to him again. Glenn stood up and whispered something in his ear, and the man nodded and went over to the stairs and left. Vivian saw him through the triangular window, getting into a pickup truck and driving away. Glenn took another gulp of blue tea.

"Well," he said, while Vivian continued to look out of the window, "it seems you've already started on the path. That's good."

In front of the window, the two women had started making strange, wide twirling motions with their arms, swinging them from the shoulder, like Vivian had done when she and Jesse had fought as very young children. She brought her attention back to Glenn.

"Sorry?"

"If you're on the path, there's a good chance you might catch up with your brother."

"Catch up? Why can't I just go and see him?"

"Your brother made quite an impression on us here," said Glenn. The women sped up their arm-swinging. They started to hum. Glenn looked at them briefly, like an admiring father, then looked back. "He had a very special energy."

"Right."

"He reached the Thirteenth Stone quicker than anyone I have known."

"The thirteenth stone?"

"The Violet Path is divided into stones."

"Right."

"The Thirteenth Stone is the threshold to Telos."

"Okay."

"So, you see, a First Stone initiate like you can't possibly follow him, where he's gone. Even a Twelfth Stone initiate like Carl couldn't, and he's just a hair's breadth away from Oneness."

Vivian finally took a mouthful of tea to disguise her expression. It tasted of leaf mulch. The women's humming was very loud, now.

"But I'm not looking to follow the path, or find oneness, or whatever. I just want to find Jesse."

"Are you sure?"

"Yes," she said, and there was a weird lack of conviction in the word. "Can't you just tell me where to go?"

"I'm sorry, Vivian. Even if you were able to find Telos, they'd never let you in."

"So it is a place?"

"It is a place, and a time. But also neither of those things."

"That doesn't make any sense."

"Not to the uninitiated, no." He smiled again. "But what I *can* tell you is that now Jesse is there, he knows a greater peace than he has ever known." That didn't sound good. "So," Glenn added, "I think you can forgive him for wanting to stay!"

"Can't I just visit him?" said Vivian.

"I'm afraid not."

"Can't he come and visit me?"

"I'm sorry, Vivian. Once people ascend to Telos, they tend not to leave."

"What, ever?"

He smoothed his beard with his thumb and forefinger, but didn't say anything.

The humming of the two women reached a crescendo, so loud she almost couldn't hear what Glenn was saying. Then it died away, and the arm-twirling stopped, and they closed their eyes. When they opened them again, they each went and selected a crystal from the collection on the windowsill. They cradled it around their navel and disappeared through a sliding door at the far end of the room.

"So, I've got to go through all this, if I want to see him?"

Glenn had suddenly become shy again. He smiled and shrugged.

Vivian looked around the room at the beanbags and mats and portraits of the messianic John of Telos. She could probably grit her teeth and fake it. Besides, it was better to be somewhere like this, surrounded by incense and wind chimes and whale song, than in her motel room smelling the sulphurous drains and listening to the hum of the backup generator.

She was about to take another sip of tea when she suddenly remembered what Mr Blucas had told her. It didn't square with what Glenn was saying.

"I met someone who said he might be in prison. Do you think that might have happened?"

"*Prison?* Bless you, Vivian, who told you that?"

"Just someone who lives in the town. He said something about the 'big house', but… I don't know, I guess he wasn't all there."

"Unbalanced?"

"You could say that."

"Mr Blucas?"

"Yeah. You know him?"

Glenn hitched up his robes awkwardly.

"He was here long before me, but… Poor old Blucas is the only person who's ever come back from the mountain, you see. He went up there before he was ready. Without the right training. He had a hard time readjusting. You really mustn't go up the mountain on your own. It's dangerous."

Vivian thought of her brother, blundering around in the snows in shorts and T-shirt. She flushed hot and cold under her many layers.

"Fine. Sign me up, then."

Glenn was delighted.

"Of course! If you go back downstairs, Annabelle can get you registered, and she'll give you your initiate's rod."

"My rod?"

"It is to light your way upon the path!"

Glenn's eyes twinkled in a way that suggested his words were precisely in the middle of sincerity and self-mockery. His mouth twitched and he nudged his glasses up, like he always did, by wrinkling his nose.

"We can get you an updated edition of your book, too," he said, when she didn't offer a reply.

"When you say *registered*—"

"Just a bit of paperwork. We're trying to keep everything above board. Like I say, IRS and all that."

"And then what? Are there classes?"

"Nothing as formal as that. You can drop in when you like. There will always be someone here to learn from."

"How long before I might be able to go see Jesse?"

"That depends on how seriously you want to take it. Jesse did it in two weeks. That was highly unusual. But then you are his twin sister, so your energy is practically identical."

"We're really not that similar," said Vivian.

"Oh, that reminds me," said Glenn.

He got up from the bench and went to the sliding bamboo door at the back of the room and left Vivian alone with her thoughts. She chewed on a wafer. She hadn't properly considered the matter of payment. But what else could she do? She wasn't going to leave Jesse up there, or wait for him to come back drooling and chuntering like Mr Blucas. Besides, she might be able to make her own foray up the mountain, in the meantime.

When he came back from whatever was beyond the screen, Glenn was holding something very familiar in one hand. It was Vivian's coat. Although – and Vivian looked down at herself to check this – Vivian was still wearing her coat. And this one looked cleaner. Not hers, then. Jesse's. Their parents had long since stopped dressing them in matching outfits, but even after that, brother and sister found themselves subconsciously buying identical items of clothing. Vivian found it infuriating. It reinforced every stereotype about twins, when she had always taken pains to prove to everyone that she and Jesse were completely different people.

"He left it here," said Glenn. "Before he ascended."

He handed her the coat. It was a good coat. Warm and robust and not fashionable at all. She knew why they'd both bought it. It felt bulletproof. She squeezed the padding. It smelled of him. A trapdoor in her belly fell open and it was all black beneath and she fought to close it as quickly as she could.

"You can give it back to him when you see him," said Glenn, without a hint of irony.

"Thanks," said Vivian. She tucked it under one arm.

"I'll escort you downstairs again. You can start this evening, if you like. We're having an ecstatic dance at sunset."

She swallowed hard.

"I'll see," she said. "I've still got some stuff to… You know. I'm not quite settled in."

"Of course," said Glenn. "Whenever you're ready. We're not going anywhere. Neither is Jesse."

He led her back down to the lobby area, where Vivian filled out her personal details on a tablet and accepted the terms and conditions and asked Glenn, after the fact, what would happen with regards to payment. If Shelley had charged seventy-five dollars an hour for an online seminar, she could only imagine what the Telos Sanctuary's fees looked like.

Glenn just said, "Oh, we'll think of something."

"But you'll need paying at some point, right?"

"Not necessarily. Let's just see how you get on. Consider this a free trial. Besides, your brother was so generous I think you're already part of the family."

Annabelle went into an office and Vivian perused the gift shop. Lots of picture postcards of John of Telos and the Crystal City, talismans, dreamcatchers, nose flutes, organic soaps, organic teas, organic CBD oils. She was looking at a book on "Indigo Children" when Annabelle came back with her rod, which was just that – a white wooden stick a couple of feet long. There was a notch at one end. Vivian took it and wrapped it in Jesse's coat.

"Now," said Glenn, and clasped her one free hand in both of his, "is there anything else we can do for you?"

She thought.

"Well, actually," she said, "I really need to borrow a phone."

Glenn and Annabelle exchanged glances.

"I'm afraid we don't have any phones in the Sanctuary," he said. "They're a disruptive presence. If you know what I mean."

"Oh."

"I'm sorry."

"Then, I don't suppose you could lend me some change? There's a payphone at the motel."

"That thing's still there?"

"Yep."

"I don't know, Vivian…"

"I need to talk to my bank. And my mum. And the embassy, probably. I had all my stuff stolen."

"Your bank?" Glenn weighed this up. "Well. I suppose that wouldn't do any harm. And at least you won't be absorbing all that radiation from a cell phone. Annabelle, do you want to see if we've got any quarters in the float?"

Annabelle nodded. She opened the cash register, and it practically exploded with hundred-dollar bills.

6

WHEN VIVIAN got back to the motel parking lot she pumped five dollars in quarters into the payphone, then sat on her brother's coat on the concrete and called the number for the Lewiston police department. The phone rang for over a minute. While she waited she noticed there was a car in one of the parking spaces, the first she'd seen. It was sleek and black and looked like it belonged to a funeral cortege.

A man's voice came on the line. Irritable. It was late afternoon – she wasn't sure of the exact time – so he probably had one foot out the door. She apologised in her most English accent, but this just seemed to annoy him more. She gave him her name and case number. More minutes of silence, so many Vivian was convinced he'd hung up on her. Then the man returned, breathless. No, there was no news. No, they had not found her effects. When he was about to put the phone down for good, she quickly asked if they knew anything of Jesse Owens. She wanted to check if, despite Glenn's assurances, he had gone to the "big house", and asked if there were any recent convictions attached to his name. No, the policeman said, and besides, the Lewiston police department's jurisdiction didn't extend as far as Mount Hookey. Vivian asked: whose jurisdiction did it fall under, then, if there was no police station in the town? That was when her money ran out.

She was digging for enough change to call back when she heard shouting from inside the motel lobby. She put the phone back in its cradle and went to investigate.

The windows of Cedar Lodge were thick with dust and she could hardly see through them, but she made out the vibrant pink of the receptionist's jacket and the shape of a wiry man, perhaps in his fifties, looming over the desk.

"So you've been seeing him," the man was saying. "All this time. Behind my back. Behind all of our backs. Jesus *Christ*, Judy."

Judy protested, "I'm sorry, Shiv! It's not what you think—"

"It's exactly what I think. You'd jeopardise the whole family for your own gratification."

"But if I could show you—"

"Damn right you're going to show me," said the man. "You're going to show me right now."

"Now?"

"We're going up the mountain. Together. And you'll tell me exactly where he is."

"But he won't be there now. And – I'm sorry to say this, Shiv, I really am – I do *not* appreciate the energy you're giving off right now, and neither will he."

"My energy? Jesus *Christ*. Come on, Judy. We're going. I want to know exactly where you went on your little date last night. And if the son of a bitch isn't there, then we'll *wait* for him."

"But he'll leave if you're with me."

"Then I'll go to Telos and wait, and you bring him to me. You hear me? He *owes* us."

Vivian saw the man, Shiv, go around the other side of the desk and haul Judy out of her seat. He pulled her towards the exit and she stumbled in her heels.

Vivian backed away and loitered around the bear as the couple came out of the door and approached the black car. The man opened the door, and there was a brief exchange. No one got in. He slammed it shut again. The man was handsome, Vivian noticed, honey-skinned and silver-haired. He wore a white turtleneck and sports jacket. An unlikely representative of "Telos", but if he knew where it was then he was worth talking to. Judy was still in the clothes she'd worn the previous day and there were bits of pine tree in her hair. Vivian wanted to talk to her, too. They abandoned the car and marched off around the side of the motel to where the pool sat stinking. Vivian followed, then hung back behind the generator shed and watched until they had crossed the strip of scrub and disappeared into the woods. It was already getting cold and the sky was a deep and lonely blue. She put her brother's coat on, over her own, and zipped it up to the top. It was difficult to move her arms at the elbows, but she liked the cocoon-tightness of it.

She followed the sound of the couple's footsteps and their quiet, snippy exchanges. She couldn't hear the words but they spoke in tones that suggested they knew each other well, and argued a lot. Married, probably. They looked roughly the same age. They looked like they had the same hairdresser, too. Occasionally, Vivian got close enough to see the flash of Judy's jacket, the glint of an enormous earring, and was forced to wait in the undergrowth until they were both out of sight.

Half an hour passed. Maybe more. Vivian didn't know. There was no discernible path. She hiked up the mountain at a slight angle, through spongy, trackless wastes of pine needles and endlessly repeating ranks of mast-straight trunks. The branches overhead were black and thick and gave only glimpses of the dimming sky, the glowing mountain. She took deep lungfuls of dry air, spat flies and spiders' webs.

Vivian got tired. She worried that her panting and stumbling were too noisy, so she stopped to catch her breath and pinpoint the couple up ahead. The pines made a cool, dark cathedral around her, and the silence echoed with the rattle of a woodpecker, the rustle of some mammal on the forest floor. She couldn't hear Judy or Shiv at all.

She ran a little further up the mountain, stopped, listened again. Tracked left and right. Nothing. She sat down. Even under a fleece and a jumper and two coats, she could feel her sweat congealing. She wished she'd brought something to eat or drink. She felt foolish.

She found a fallen trunk to perch on and sat twirling her new initiate's rod and tried to gather her thoughts. She pulled up both hoods. The darkness in the forest deepened.

At some point she realised that her hands had gone numb and she thrust them into the pockets of Jesse's jacket. They were full of paper, torn and balled and folded. That was no surprise. Jesse was always writing things down. Their house had been full of his papers and notebooks, aspects of the world that he observed and questioned and figured out. He'd been like that at school, too, his exercise books and textbooks black with illegible scrawls. When paper was lacking he'd been known to write on walls, clothes, other people's hands and arms. All the other students at the school knew him and knew the signs of him – symbols and equations and questions posed to whoever happened to find his little artefacts. The sort of boy who was too strange to be worth bullying. The sort of boy who probably wouldn't even have noticed if someone had bullied him. Poor Jesse.

Vivian withdrew her hands and a few pieces of paper fell to the forest floor. She fumbled around to retrieve them, and as she squatted the slope to her right brightened suddenly. A pinkish glow among the barcode of the tree trunks. She tried to blink it away like a sunspot, but it wouldn't go. Not a torch – it was too big and had no beam. More like a streetlamp. She crammed Jesse's notes deeper into her pockets and watched as it floated here and there among the pines. For the longest time she assumed it was the product of her fatigue, until she saw it was not simply a light but a figure. Her mind went to the next likely explanation: Judy again, in her horrid fuchsia jacket. The figure emitted its own light, though, making sharp silhouettes of the bushes and branches.

She slithered down from the tree trunk and walked down the slope. It was definitely a person. A man, though the light made his features impossible to discern. He may or may not have been clothed. He walked steadily and easily, without any real purpose, as if he was out for an evening stroll and it was the most normal thing in the world. Vivian thought of the front cover of *The Violet Path*, of the man whose face had been plastered all over the walls of the Sanctuary. He was the right colour, at least.

The man drifted out of sight behind a stump. She'd had lucid dreams before, lots of them. Considerably more since the business with her father. Her usual reaction to one was to do everything and anything to make it disappear, but this felt different. Vivian was suddenly full of an inexplicable dread that it might end, that she might lose him. She ran to catch up.

It was only a handful of steps before she tripped. The ravine was definitely not in her imagination. She cracked her elbow, then her head, and there was flare of violet light and it felt like she had fallen from the summit of the mountain to its base. She caught the briefest glimpse of the stars and then the pain started and she was grateful to find herself losing consciousness.

7

WHEN SHE came to, the stars and the sky were gone and she was staring up at a ceiling, a nicer ceiling than the one in her motel room, which she was sure contained asbestos or something worse. This was the kind of ceiling she'd expected Cedar Lodge to have – sturdy wooden beams and snugly fitting boards and an oil lamp hanging from a chain in the middle. She was in a low bed, under an old blanket. She smelled woodsmoke and vinegar.

Vivian raised herself on an elbow and her whole head seemed to split like an overripe plum and she slumped back onto the mattress. It was old, too, and thin, and she felt the slats of the bed against her spine. She rolled from one side to the other.

The cabin was a little smaller than her motel room. Looking between her feet she saw a table and a single chair, and the remains of what looked like whittling. In the corner opposite the bed was a wood burner and a stove. A cupboard, open, filled with ancient cans of food. Little else besides, and no running water, it seemed. Her Telos rod was leaning against the doorframe as if it was the owner's walking stick.

She touched her forehead. The lump was enormous, and a little sticky. Combined with her black eyes she must have looked a complete ruin. She flexed her elbow and got a jolt of pain and sucked her teeth.

There were footsteps outside the cabin, a crunch of pine needles, and the door opened. There was a flood of mountain air, chill and dusty. With it came Mr Blucas.

He looked quickly at Vivian, then stomped around the cabin in his heavy boots, stoking the fire, opening a can of something. Vivian drew the bedclothes around her and waited for the smell to hit her but it never came. He looked different. Cleaner shaven, and slightly thinner. He was wearing his woolly hat properly, pulled down over his ears. And his bags – where were all his bags? Perhaps this was what a sober Mr Blucas looked like, first thing in the morning.

He emptied the can of beans into a pan and then turned to face her properly.

"How you feeling?" he said.

Vivian didn't know what to say. She was surprised by how much stronger his voice sounded.

"You're welcome," he muttered, when she made no reply.

He went back and prodded the beans.

"If I had a dollar for every damn hippy I saved from dying on this mountain, I'd be a millionaire." He made a noise that might have been a cough or a laugh. "Again, I mean."

"Mr Blucas?" said Vivian. She still wasn't sure it was him.

He turned and glared at her. "So what if I am?"

"You live up here?"

The glaring intensified. "So what if I *do*?"

She held her tongue, and her head throbbed some more. He emptied the beans into two chipped bowls and brought one of them over to her. She ate them too quickly and scalded her tongue but didn't mind.

"What time is it?" she asked.

"*Time is just a construct*," he said in a sarcastic voice with his mouth full of beans, twirling his spoon in mock reverie. "Isn't that right? Isn't that what the Telurians say?"

"The what?"

He put his bowl down and wiped his mouth and went over to the door. He hefted her initiate's rod in one hand, then in both, then spun it between his thumbs and forefingers.

"No crystal, huh?" he said, looking at the notch at one end. "You're a real newbie, then."

"I don't understand..."

"I'll help you understand," he said, and he cracked the rod over his knee and tossed each half into the wood burner. "Forget all this crap. There's no Crystal City up here. There's no John of Telos. There's no goddamn salvation, no matter what anyone tells you. You hear me? Here is my teaching, and Telos's blessing be upon it: go back to town, pack your bags, and get the hell out."

Only when he mentioned John of Telos did Vivian remember the figure she'd seen in the woods. The sunlight from the grimy window, the burn on her tongue, Mr Blucas's brusqueness – it all made it much harder to believe what she thought she'd seen. She hadn't slept enough. That was the truth of it. Too much time in the presence of people like Shelley and Glenn and Eenoo. Maybe there really had been something in the blue tea. Maybe she'd touched something she shouldn't have in Eenoo's trailer.

"I'm not like the others," she said. "I mean, I'm not a hippy-type person."

"Sure you're not," said Mr Blucas. "You're just keeping that rod for a friend."

"I'm looking for my brother."

Mr Blucas pointed his spoon at her.

"Don't talk to me about brothers."

"What did you mean when you said—"

"You done with that?"

He nodded at her bowl. She handed it back.

"You're *welcome*," he said again.

She watched him go back to the table and pick up his whittling knife. Her heart convulsed for a moment, then he took his seat and start working on a half-carved spoon. His hands worked strongly and steadily. They were clean. His fingernails were pared. He'd tidied himself up to the extent that he looked a completely different person.

He looked up from whittling and met her gaze.

"What are you waiting for? Dessert?"

"No. Sorry. I just—"

"You just?"

"You've changed."

"'Course I've changed. What do you expect?"

"I don't understand—"

"I don't have any answers for you, hippy. Not anymore. Now git."

"Git?"

"Go! You'll live. Now get out of here."

Without getting out of his chair he kicked at the door and it opened.

Vivian swung her legs out of the bed, stood up, nearly fainted. The wood burner had made the cabin uncomfortably hot, and she was still wearing both her and her brother's coats. She was thankful for that. The injuries to her elbow and forehead would have been a lot worse without the padding. She steadied herself, hands on knees, swaying in time with her pulse. Mr Blucas glanced at her but made no move to help.

When her head had cleared she went to the door.

"Well," she said. "Thank you."

Mr Blucas grunted.

"What's the best way back to town?"

"Down," he said.

"Down?"

He sighed and threw his spoon on the table and gave her a weary stare.

"Just go straight out the door and down the mountain. Fifteen minutes you see a creek. If you don't get yourself in some hippy trance on the way. Follow the creek all the way to the bottom and you'll get yourself on the 55."

"The 55?"

"The highway. My God, they really melted your brain, didn't they? Or are you concussed?"

He folded his arms. Vivian took a step sideways, and then went out into the woods. She felt a pleasant thrill in the cold breeze. A jay scampered in the undergrowth and tossed some leaves and flew up into the branches. It beat the Cedar Lodge parking lot as the first sight of the day. After a moment or two she turned back to the door, which Mr Blucas was trying to close with his toe again.

"Wait," she said.

"What now?"

"Have you really seen my brother?"

"I see a lot of people around here. I just try and make sure they don't see me."

"But yesterday, you said—"

"Yesterday?"

"When you spoke to me in the cafe."

"What cafe?"

"Steaming Pete's. The fishing place."

"My God, you are half gone. You poor, stupid girl."

Vivian flushed.

"What?"

"I don't know you. We've never met. First time I saw you, you were lying on your back in the creek with blood pumping out of your head."

"But—"

"Git! I'm done with you. And don't go telling anyone I'm up here, because I can whittle this into something sharper if I have to."

He slid down in the chair, kicked the door, and it slammed in Vivian's face. What did he mean? Perhaps he had been drunk, and really didn't remember meeting her. Or maybe she'd imagined that whole episode, too.

She started down the mountain and touched every tree trunk as she went, pinching the bark. The coldness and hardness reassured her. She licked the moss and dirt from her fingers. This was real. The mountain was real.

Ten minutes had passed and she was nearly at the creek when she thought, suddenly: his teeth. The Mr Blucas she had just left behind had a full set of teeth.

8

AFTER ANOTHER hour's hiking, Route 55 appeared out of nowhere. A lost highway, reclaimed by the forest. Vivian didn't see a single car on her walk back into town. The clouds rolled in and Mount Hookey was completely concealed. By the time she rounded the last bend and saw the stoical bear of Cedar Lodge and his neon sign – from the other direction, this time – the sky seemed impossibly low and claustrophobic. It started to rain. She hurried into the lobby as if escaping the cloud of an erupting volcano.

Troy was on reception, even though it wasn't the night shift. She heard the hiss of his earphones before she saw him. Judy hadn't come back.

Vivian went over and stood at the desk. He obviously knew she was there but he didn't look up. She dinged the bell but he just raised his purple-ringed eyes at her and shook his head, and went back to looking at his phone. Today he was wearing a T-shirt that said "No Future", over the top of a second, long-sleeved T-shirt. He smelled of marijuana and deodorant.

"Judy still not here?" said Vivian.

He didn't reply.

"You weren't wrong," she said. She paused. "About this place. Getting in your head."

She saw and heard him raise the volume on his phone. She took a step backwards, formed another word with her mouth, but didn't say it. He clearly didn't want to talk.

"Well," she said. "I'll see you round."

"You didn't have to tell them about Mom," he said suddenly, when she was halfway across the lobby. She stopped and came back.

"Tell who? About what?"

"You know who."

She thought for a moment. She remembered Glenn, whispering to Carl. Carl, hopping into his pickup.

"The thing with the book?" she said.

"See," said Troy. "There you go."

"What happened?"

"Mom got screwed, that's what happened."

"What do you mean?"

He didn't reply while his thumbs hammered the phone screen. A few messages came and went. He finally plucked out his earphones and leaned forwards in his chair, arms jointed like a praying mantis.

"How much money do you think your brother spent here? How much do you think he's *still* paying?"

"I don't know," said Vivian, and she genuinely didn't. At least as much as the university fund his father had set aside for them both. That was the deal to begin with, since he didn't go to university. But she was pretty sure he'd exceeded the cost of his education by now. If her parents had been anything less than obscenely wealthy, they would have cut off the payments years ago. Chances were, though, they probably didn't even notice the money leaving the account. Especially not now Dad was gone.

"You don't know because you don't know, or you don't know because you can't even imagine how much he's pumped into this place?"

She shrugged.

"This is something you've got to understand about Mount Hookey, Vivian. They're hippies, yes – but *free* love? Forget it. You've got to *pay* for communion with the Great Spirit. And when there's that much money flying about, people get competitive. Everyone's out to screw everyone."

Vivian thought about the burned-out church. *They got what was coming to them.*

"So what happened to your mum?" she asked.

He smiled at her pronunciation, but only briefly.

"Mom's been operating *off-radar*, you could say."

"Off-radar?"

"Illegally. The Telos thing is kind of a franchise, and she's not meant to be teaching."

"A franchise?"

"Sure. You can teach yoga or meditation or hypnotherapy or whatever the fuck, but you can't use the word 'Telos' unless you've been approved."

"Approved by whom?"

"I don't know. John of Telos?" He sniffed hard. "He's probably got an office on the Upper East Side somewhere."

"And your mum wasn't approved."

"She was once, but she lost the franchise because she wasn't profitable."

"Did I get her in trouble?"

"Yep," said Troy matter-of-factly. "Some guy gave her a good talking to. Said they'd tell the boss, and there was a good chance she'd get sued. Took away all her books. They were the only thing that made money."

"Why does Glenn care, though?"

"'Glenn'—" he made inverted commas around Glenn with his fingers "—cares because Mom is taking potential clients from him when she's not supposed to. But there's something else you've got to understand, Viv." Viv? No one called her Viv. She liked it. "These people really *believe* this shit. Glenn probably thinks Mom is some kind of false prophet who's leading people off the purple path."

"The Violet Path," said Vivian.

"Right," said Troy, and he rolled his eyes and looked at the replies on his phone.

"I'm sorry," said Vivian.

"What for?"

"For getting your mum into trouble."

He looked up, seemed to be formulating a reply, then said, "What happened to your head?"

Vivian touched the lump gingerly.

"I fell over."

"You fell over?"

He sat back in his chair and folded his giant spider-arms and looked over her coat. It was smeared with mud, sap and pine needles clinging to the shoulders and elbows.

"You been up the mountain?"

She didn't reply.

"Man, they got to you quick. You find enlightenment or what? Hmmm? What's the secret?"

"I didn't find anything. Well, nothing like that. I was following Judy. I thought she might lead me to my brother. Glenn said he's somewhere up the mountain—"

"That's no good."

"—and she was with this other guy—"

"Shiv?"

"Yeah. You know him too?"

"He's her husband."

"What does he do?"

"Don't know. Some kind of salesman."

"Oh."

"And?" said Troy.

"And what?"

"What happened?"

"I fell over. Like I said."

"Did you meet your brother?"

"I met—" She thought of her vision of the violet man. She decided not to mention it. It was embarrassing. She could imagine Troy's mockery, and she was too tired to tolerate it. "—this guy."

"An Ascended Master!" cried Troy. Seemed she was going to get mocked anyway.

"No. A guy living in a kind of shed." She looked over her shoulder at the lobby's grimy sofas. "Has Mr Blucas been around here lately?"

"Blucas?"

"Yeah."

"Not seen him for a couple of days."

"Has he got a brother? He told me he did, but…"

"I don't know. I don't think so. But I try to avoid having conversations with him. Why?"

"Doesn't matter."

Troy frowned at her.

"I think you need a lie down," he said. He sounded suddenly gentle. She felt like crying.

"So do I," she said.

She stood and he sat and they said nothing for a moment.

"Well, I'll see you later then," said Vivian.

"Sure thing."

"I'm sorry."

"About what?"

"About the book thing. About your mum."

"Forget it. It was going to happen at some point. And I should have told you. *She* should have told you."

"Well… Sorry anyway."

"You Brits love apologising."

"Yeah. Sorry."

She left the desk and crossed the lobby. A couple of paces from the side door, Troy yelled at her.

"Oh shit. Wait. Shit. Should have said. *Your* mom called."

Vivian felt something like a premonition. A cold sensation at the base of her skull.

"She did?"

"Earlier this morning."

"What did she say?"

"She wants you to call her back."

"Right."

"She didn't sound great."

"Right."

"Just passing on the message."

He put his earphones back in. Vivian turned and set off for her room with a whole new kind of headache.

Back in the room Vivian took off all of her layers and couldn't believe the depth and complexity of the stench that had evolved underneath. She stood under a boiling shower for close to an hour, thinking. She was still no closer to knowing anything about Jesse's whereabouts, other than he was somewhere up the mountain, in some subterranean alien civilisation, or in a state of bliss outside of time and space, or in prison, or dead in a ravine, like had almost happened to her. That led her to thinking about the vision of the violet man, and the other Mr Blucas. And now there was her mother to consider, too. There was just no way Vivian could ring home, not with so many things unresolved. But then she needed money from somewhere. That brought on a rush of guilt and she started sweating all over again, right there under the showerhead.

It seemed the Sanctuary was the best place to be, right now. She could ask after Jesse as much as she liked. The meals were free. She remembered the smell of the place with some fondness.

She got out of the bathroom and dressed herself. Both coats again. She tried to tune the TV while she was getting ready, thinking it might be good to remind herself of the outside world. She found a documentary about the Old West, just visible through the snowstorm. Someone was talking about smallpox and the picture came into focus just as they showed a photograph of a Sioux tribesman covered in sores and she decided to turn it off. What a country.

In a few minutes she was standing at the door to her room patting her pockets. She realised suddenly: Jesse's notes. She hadn't looked at them properly since she'd got back from the mountain. She turfed out all the scraps of paper he'd secreted inside and laid them out on the table at the foot of the bed.

She didn't know what she'd been expecting, but there were no more clues to go on. It was all nonsense, the usual noisy and impenetrable mental contortions. Numbers and symbols and algebraic functions that were so complex as to look almost alien, like the ideograms that Judy had added to the posters. There were words, too. Questions and theories with little or no punctuation. On the back of a receipt from a Mexican restaurant, from which it seemed he'd bought six identical bags of tortilla chips and nothing else, he'd written: *lambda-CDM model of cosmology puts dark energy 68% of total energy in the observable universe mass/ energy of dark matter and ord matter 27% and 5% other e.g. neutrinos photons negligible density of dark energy very low (~ 7 × 10–30 g/ cm3) much less than the density of ordinary matter, so what if dark energy/telos energy/violet energy essentially cognate...* It trailed off where the paper had been torn. A piece of legal pad folded in four asked, over and over: *what is the thing what is the thing what is the thing WHAT IS THE THING.* And, in among these, most lucid and miserable of all the notes, a page from a diary, 19 March, that just said: *Where is Dad?*

Even when their father had been alive, that had been a difficult question to answer. He had been "away on business" for most of their lives, coming back maybe once or twice a week to sit at the head of their enormous dinner table and do his beneficent paterfamilias thing. Neither she nor Jesse had ever really known what he did for a living. The closest they got to a job description was "consultant", and that was second-hand from their mother. What the word actually meant, Vivian had no idea. He could have been a management consultant, or a consultant podiatric surgeon, for all she knew.

That was the day he'd died: 19 March. Their mother said he'd had a heart attack in the car, but what she hadn't mentioned was that the car had been parked in the garage, and the garage door had been closed, and the engine had been running for a good three quarters of an hour before someone phoned an ambulance. Vivian had heard it from her bedroom window.

Her stomach gurgled.

When she got up to leave, Vivian found another piece of paper on the carpet by the door. She assumed it had fallen from her pocket or blown from the table, but on closer inspection it wasn't as grubby or dog-eared as any of Jesse's notes. She picked it up and unfolded it. The paper was crisp and the writing was in neat, clear capitals. It said:

WING'S. 1900HRS. ALONE. J.

9

VIVIAN LOOKED out into the parking lot. There was nobody there. The message must have been delivered some time ago, while she was studying Jesse's scribblings, or while she was in the shower, or watching TV. Jesse never called himself "J" to her knowledge, but it was just like him to say "1900" instead of "seven o'clock". Then again, if it was him, how had he known she was here? And why not just knock on her door instead of doing all this spy stuff? What other "J"s did she know... Judy? John of Telos?

After a lot of frustrated screen-prodding, the alarm clock told her it was two minutes past seven. She was already late. The thought of missing her brother gave her a sudden nauseous spasm. She pictured Jesse sitting in the Chinese restaurant, small and alone, checking his watch, picking at the basket of free prawn crackers.

She ran down to the lobby, where Troy saw her over the top of his book.

"Something up?" he said.

"Did someone come through here?" she said, already on her way to the door.

"When?"

"I don't know. Last few hours."

"I don't know," he said. "I don't think so."

He still had his music on full blast and probably wouldn't have noticed any visitors unless they came right up to the desk. Besides, it was easy enough to get up to the motel's rooms straight from the parking lot via the fire escape.

"Why?" he called after her, but she didn't reply.

It was still raining half-heartedly outside, a warm mizzle that found its way through all her layers. She kept up her half-walk, half-run. The two bars in the centre of town were open, neon beer adverts reflected in the wet pavement. They were blaring country music at each other across the street, but from a quick look inside it seemed they didn't have any customers.

Wing's shutters were open for the first time. Vivian looked through the window. No Jesse. There was an elderly couple eating in one of the booths. The man was holding a pair of chopsticks in both hands like a knife and fork, and the woman was searching for a way to approach a mountain of plain-looking noodles. There was no one else.

She went to the restaurant door and saw two handwritten signs stuck to the inside of the glass. The top one said:

> Dishwasher/waitress/chef/accountant wanted.
> Hardworking, experienced, "smiley". Start immediately.
> No time-wasters.

The one below said:

> We do NOT accept crystals, heart-stones, Telurian
> opals, etc. as payment!!

She made a mental note of the job advert. If there was no way of getting to her bank account – and she still refused to ask her mother for help – then some casual work might be useful. She wasn't particularly "smiley" and she'd never had a job in a restaurant before. Had never had a job before, period, but maybe now was the time. (Her father's legacy: twenty-five years old and not so much as a paper round to put on her CV.)

She took a seat on the opposite side of the restaurant to the old couple, facing the door. She opened a menu and flicked through its laminated pages without reading them, glancing up whenever someone passed in the street. There was music playing, though, a flutey dirge that she suspected had been composed by someone who had never been to China, and who perhaps hadn't studied music at all. The restaurant was decked out in lanterns and Chinese characters and bright red good-luck knots. No pictures of Telurians or John of Telos.

A young man materialised at her shoulder. He was not much older than Troy, she thought. He seemed nervous.

"Good evening," he said. He wiped his palms on his smart black trousers. "Can I get you started on some drinks, maybe?"

Vivian still didn't have a dollar to her name. She hadn't been expecting to actually eat here – though, if "J" had offered to treat her she wouldn't have turned it down.

"Uh," she said. "Just tap water, please."

The young man winced and said, "Alright, no problem." He took two paces towards the kitchen, then came back. "You had any thoughts about food?"

She'd had a lot of thoughts about food.

"I'm still deciding," she said, and tried to smile.

"Sure thing!" the man said, too loudly. "I'll get you some crackers while you wait."

He ducked away. Vivian felt the rising tide of anxiety. There was no escaping payment once the prawn crackers were in play.

She took out the secret note from her pocket and read it again and only felt more confounded. The lettering was neat, the message concise. Not like something Jesse or Judy would write, in appearance or tone. But then, after her meeting with Mr Blucas on the mountain, she was starting to learn that people weren't necessarily who they seemed to be.

"Excuse me, miss?"

She crushed the paper in her hand and looked up. The old man from the couple in the booth was standing next to her, a little stooped, a tired but easy smile on his face. He wore a thick plaid shirt tucked into blue jeans. He looked like a cowboy, or at least an extra in a film about cowboys. Vivian thought about the Sioux tribe and their infected blankets. Behind him, his wife stuck a fork in her mountain of noodles and raised it and the whole thing, including the dish, lifted off the table.

Vivian looked back at the man and said, "Hi." The message felt like it was dissolving from the sweat on her palm.

"My wife and I couldn't help noticing you were eating alone over here, and we wondered if you'd like to join us."

Vivian glanced at the door. The old man did too, and their eyes met again.

"That's very kind," she said. "I'm actually waiting for someone."

"Well, that's too bad," the old man said. He scratched behind one of his large ears but didn't leave. Vivian's eyes burned a hole in the menu.

He fidgeted for a moment and then said, "Well, say, how about you join us for a drink, anyway? We can talk, and when your friend gets here y'all can go back to your table. Or he can join us too, if he likes. How about that?"

Vivian opened her mouth but didn't say anything, trapped between the need to be alone and the need to be polite. Before she could reply, there was a clatter from the couple's table and they both turned to see his wife's dinner slopped over most of the tablecloth.

"Oh for goodness sake, Jerome!" she said. "Enough with the cloak and dagger nonsense, just get her over here and help me with this!"

"Jerome?" said Vivian.

He sighed and nodded.

"With a J?" She opened the fingers of the hand holding the note.

"Were you followed?" he said quietly.

She'd not really paid attention to that part of the message. "I don't know. I don't think so. Why would anyone want to follow me?"

"Why don't you come over and keep us old folks company, and maybe it'll come up in conversation. That's all this is. Just three folks, talking 'bout the weather."

He went back to his booth rubbing the top of his head. Vivian followed him. He had a slight limp, and again she couldn't help picturing him in a saloon, or leaning on a hitching post, chewing and spitting tobacco.

She slid into the booth opposite him, next to his wife.

"Hello, dear," she said, and gave the same kindly smile as her husband, and went back to shovelling her dinner onto her plate. Vivian helped, and the old woman looked up in delight. "Well, you're very nice," she said.

Jerome tucked his napkin into the top of his shirt like a bib and began to skewer bits of chicken with his chopsticks. No one said anything for a while. The waiter came over to Vivian's empty table with a glass of water and the basket of crackers and looked mortified, before Jerome hollered, "She's over here," and the young man sagged with relief.

The waiter left. Vivian sipped her water. Jerome dabbed at his mouth.

"I'm sorry to bring you here," he said. "But it's a safe place."

"Safe?"

"I mean, they don't care about the mountain," he said. "It's just a restaurant. Period."

"Oh."

"We want to talk to you about… your problems."

Vivian looked at them both.

"Who are you?" she said.

He extended a strong, long-fingered hand over the table.

"Sheriff Jerome Carter," he said.

"Retired," said his wife.

He looked at her, tutted, and then echoed, "Retired." He paused. "My wife, Minnie."

Minnie shook Vivian's hand too.

"It's a pleasure, miss," she said. "You're from England?"

Vivian nodded. "From London."

"Well, I think that's wonderful. How do you like California?"

"Uh," said Vivian.

"I hope my husband didn't scare you."

"Come on, Minnie," said Jerome. "There wasn't another way I could have done it."

"I'm not saying there was," said Minnie.

"It's fine," said Vivian. "I wasn't scared. I just thought the note might have been from Jesse."

"That's your brother, right?" said Jerome.

"Right."

"Jesse Owens. Now there was an athlete."

Vivian didn't comment. Of course she knew about the other Jesse Owens, and she knew that her brother was as unlike his namesake as it was possible to be. It was something his teachers had pointed out all the way through school, incessantly and with great hilarity.

Jerome seemed to sense her discomfort. "He's missing, isn't he?" he said.

"How do you know all this?"

"You told the police in Lewiston."

"Did I?"

"You did. I read the report."

She couldn't remember doing that. She thought she'd deliberately kept it to herself when she'd spoken to the sergeant, because she thought getting the police involved would scare Jesse off. It had probably been the concussion talking.

"How did you find me?"

"You told the police where to contact you, right?"

"I did but—"

"You're the only guest at the motel. Wasn't hard."

"Oh." She frowned. "So are you here to talk about what happened at Lewiston, or about my brother?"

Husband and wife looked at each other.

"Both, I think," said Jerome, and impaled another cube of chicken on his chopstick.

The nervous waiter came back and asked her if she was ready to order. When Vivian hesitated Minnie touched her hand and said, "It's okay, dear, this is on us." Vivian asked for a bowl of "special fried rice". The waiter looked pained again, then realised what expression he was pulling, and yanked his mouth up into a smile. He went back to the kitchen and there was the sound of muttering and slamming cupboards. It seemed he was running the whole operation himself.

Jerome leaned forward on his elbows.

"You're not the first person to come here looking for someone who's gone missing," he said.

"I'm not?" said Vivian.

Jerome shook his old head slowly.

"I may be ten, eleven years out of the force, but I still like to keep an ear to the ground, you know?"

"Still sleeps in his office sometimes," Minnie interjected.

He ignored her.

"In the past few years there have been dozens of people come looking for friends and relatives around here. But under the new sheriff the police just don't want to get involved. They think this whole town is just bums, hippies, drug addicts, all kinds of lost souls—"

Minnie started shaking her head at this.

"—and far as they're concerned there's no point wasting time and money looking for anyone. But there's something else going on. I don't know." He rolled his chopstick between thumb and forefinger. "The cops in Lewiston, they don't even send patrol cars up here. Like they think this place just looks after itself. Wasn't like that on my watch. We knew the place was crazy, but that didn't mean we just forgot about them. You know?"

Minnie sniffed. She wiped an eye with her greasy napkin.

"I'm sorry," she said.

Jerome reached out and clasped her hand.

"It's going to be alright, Min," he said.

Vivian looked at both of them, baffled. Jerome turned back to her and continued.

"Fourth of July this year, our son Nathan didn't come home like he usually does. We found out from one of his old school friends, after the event, that he'd got into this stuff with his girlfriend and he'd come up here. One of the schools, or sanctuaries, or whatever they call them. We haven't had a single call from him, and it's been months. Now Nathan, he's a clever kid. Bit older than you, but not much."

"He went to Brown!" said Minnie, suddenly.

"He was a real clever kid," said Jerome again. "He graduated top of his class. He was a lawyer in LA for five, six years. And then... I don't know. I tried to call in favours at the sheriff's office in Trinity and Siskyou, but no one wanted to lift a finger. Even old friends. It's like they were scared or something."

They fell silent. There was a *whoosh* of gas igniting from the kitchen, and more cursing.

"So what do you want from me?" asked Vivian. "Sounds like you probably know more than I do."

"At the moment, yes, I think I probably do."

"At the moment?"

"Listen: I heard about what happened to you in Lewiston. Like I say, I've kept a hand in the department, not that they like it. I know you're looking for your brother up here. And I know you said you got beat up by some clown with a bell. Right?"

"Right…"

"Look at this." He took out a pair of glasses from his shirt pocket, held his phone at arm's length from his face, and typed something with one finger. He scrolled around and then showed her a photo. It was a semicircle of grinning men and women in robes, gathered around a fire. She could see their shoes poking out from beneath the robes – brogues and sneakers and plimsolls. Each of them was holding a decorative handbell.

"Who are they?" asked Vivian.

"It's one of the communities they have here. This one's called the Telos Centre for Spiritual Living. But there's hundreds of them, I guess you know that."

Vivian couldn't quite remember where she'd heard that specific name before.

"You think someone was trying to stop me looking for my brother?"

"Doesn't make sense any other way. How many perps do you think there are whose weapon of choice is a prayer bell?"

Vivian thought about this. She remembered the last words she'd heard, before her cheek hit the dirty linoleum of the bus station waiting room: *It's not him. It's not him.*

"Could be the other way around. Could be they thought I was Jesse, and they thought he was trying to escape. I mean, we are pretty much identical." She quickly added, "Physically, at least."

"Well," said Jerome, "either way, these Telos folks aren't your friends."

Then why, Vivian thought, had Glenn welcomed her with such open arms?

"Okay," she said. "Was that all you wanted? To warn me?"

Jerome was on the cusp of replying when Minnie interjected. "We just want our boy back."

Vivian looked in her tired eyes and suddenly thought of her own mother, at home, waiting for Vivian to return her call. It had been almost a week. She swallowed another lump of guilt.

"But how—"

"Tell her, Jerome," said Minnie.

"There's no point trying to get questions answered from the outside," he said. "We need someone to sign up with these folks and see just what in the heck is going on in there. Someone to just, you know, go through the motions – ring your bell and pray to the great spirit or whatever it is you do – and see where it takes you. A lot of these websites talk about going up the mountain. I can't help thinking there's another *place*, you know? Where you graduate to."

"There is."

"There is?"

"Apparently. It's called Telos."

Jerome sat back.

"Huh." He studied Vivian. "Well, see now, they'll know I'm a cop so I can't join. And we're both too old, anyway. But we were thinking, maybe you could—"

"I've already signed up," said Vivian.

Jerome and Minnie looked at each other. "You have?"

Vivian nodded. "I'm not sure it's the same one as your son signed up for. But I think they all go in the same direction. It's a franchise, you know. Like McDonald's."

"So you're already a card-carrying Telurian?" Jerome laughed.

"I've got a rod and everything," said Vivian. "Well, I did have one, but I... Doesn't matter."

"And you're paying for the whole thing yourself?" said Minnie.

That question again.

"Not yet," she said. "I don't know how I'll pay for it. At the moment I'm on some kind of free trial, I think."

"No such thing," said Jerome. "They'll get you to pay up one way or another."

"I can't," said Vivian. "I still don't have any money. Not since what happened in Lewiston."

"Nothing at all?" said Minnie.

Vivian shook her head.

"Isn't there someone you can call? Your mother or father?"

"I don't want to worry them," said Vivian, as though her father were still alive. She didn't want to get into all that now.

"What about your phone? Your passport?"

Vivian shrugged. "I guess I've been distracted. I'll get around to it. I suppose I need to go to an embassy but—" But what? "Well, I'm here now. I don't want to just abandon Jesse again now I've got a lead. Anyway, I don't have the money for a bus or a train ticket."

Minnie put her hand on Vivian's arm again and looked imploringly at her husband.

"Give it to her, Jerome. Poor thing needs a proper meal or five."

"Alright. I was going to give it her anyway, Minnie."

"Then give it, there's no one here."

He looked over her shoulder. The owner was still clattering about in the kitchen. He produced a brown envelope from his calfskin jacket, which was bundled up beside him in the booth. He put it on a clean bit of the table.

"Me and Min been moving some money around so we can pay someone to take the course. If you're already enrolled, then… Well, how about you see how far you can get. Stay on it as long as you can, ask some questions. When you find Nathan and Jesse, you call it in."

"Call it in?"

"He's being dramatic," said Minnie. "He means *let us know*."

"I can do that," said Vivian.

The envelope still sat on the table between them.

"Go ahead, dear," said Minnie. "Take it."

Vivian picked it up. It felt vulgar to check the contents, but she could tell from the weight and thickness that there must be several hundred dollars in there. A lot of money, but definitely not enough to pay for more than a week of the Violet Path. Not enough to get her to the Thirteenth Stone, or even the Third Stone. Minnie squeezed her arm and gave an encouraging smile. Vivian wondered how much of their combined pensions was in that envelope, then wondered what percentage of her own family's wealth it constituted. The kind of money her mother might spend on a scarf that she never wore.

"I'll pay you back," she said.

"Don't even think of it," said Minnie. "You're the one putting yourself at risk." She looked at Vivian seriously. "If it gets too much you just stop right away. They stop you thinking straight, these people. A boy like Nathan. Such a smart boy." She started welling up. "He went to *Brown*, for goodness sake," she said again.

The waiter finally emerged from the kitchen and Vivian hid the envelope on her lap. He placed the bowl of fried rice in front of her, hovered for a moment as though expecting a comment, or a tip, and then slunk away. Vivian looked over the dish. The rice was speckled with lots of brightly coloured morsels that looked like M&Ms. She picked out two, an orange one and a green one. They both tasted of chicken.

The rest of the dinner was quiet and awkward. They spoke as if their first conversation had never really happened. They talked about the weather, then Nathan, then about the rest of their families. Vivian kept up the pretence that her dad was still alive, for expediency's sake. No point getting into it. She told them he was retired, like Jerome, and had worked in finance, and Jerome looked at her and nodded like she was speaking a language he didn't understand. That was fine because Vivian didn't understand either.

She finished her bowl of multicoloured rice, and Jerome insisted on paying, and they went out into the street. The waiter almost followed them out of the door, as if, even after settling the bill and putting on their coats, they might decide they wanted dessert after all.

"Well, thank you, Vivian," said Jerome. He looked up and down the 55. It was still raining. "I hope this works out for all of us."

"You're very nice," Minnie assured her again.

"When you want to get in touch," said Jerome, "use this."

He gave her what looked like a small plastic egg with an LCD screen.

"What is it?"

"Pager. Two-way. I prefer to use them. Got a bad feeling about using phones around here."

"Okay. I'll figure it out."

She pocketed it, next to the envelope of cash.

"We'll see you soon then, I hope."

"I'll let you know."

"Where are you going now?" asked Minnie. "Can we give you a ride?"

"I was actually already on my way to the Sanctuary."

"Really?"

She shrugged. "May as well."

"Cedar Lodge not all you hoped for?" said Jerome.

"Something like that."

"Alright." He shook her hand. "Well, be safe. Goodnight Vivian."

"Goodnight."

He loped off into the night with his wife and Vivian watched them disappear around the corner. Minnie was fussing with her husband's collar. Vivian found them very sweet, and very sad.

Her coat felt heavy now, with the money and the pager and the handfuls of Jesse's notes. Her head felt heavy, too. She didn't move, as if weighed down by some terrible new burden. She was still standing there in the deserted street when the electric shutters of Wing's began to grind and complain, and then jammed, and the young man who'd served her came out with a stepladder and began jimmying around in the mechanism with a fork.

10

THE TRIANGULAR window of the Telos Sanctuary shone out like a lighthouse through the rain. Vivian climbed the steps and found the door open. Glenn was inside, perched on one of the colossal pebble-chairs, talking with Annabelle. He turned and got up when she came through the door, but Annabelle continued gazing at the spot where he'd been sitting, a half-smile on her face, as if in some kind of blissful trance. Vivian's conversation with Jerome suddenly seemed a distant thing. The music, the warmth, the scent of the place — it was hard to imagine the Sanctuary as anything other than benevolent once you were actually inside it.

"Vivian," Glenn said, almost with relief. "We were just talking about you."

"Really?"

Her face grew hot.

"We were worried perhaps you weren't going to come back," said Glenn. He pushed up his glasses in that familiar way and looked her over. He frowned. "Has something happened? You look like you've been in the wars, dear heart."

Vivian looked down and saw that her coat was still smeared with mud from her tumble into the ravine and torn at one elbow. There was the shiny egg on her forehead, too.

"Oh," she said. "Right. No. I just went for a walk."

"A walk?"

"Yeah, just up the…" She waved a hand in the direction of the mountain and then stopped, already thinking she'd said too much.

Glenn looked puzzled, or was at least pretending to.

"Up where?"

"Up the road. To the gas station. Someone had been washing their car and I slipped. Onto my head."

"Slipped onto your head."

"Yeah."

"I daresay your mind was on higher things," said Glenn.

Vivian was saved from her embarrassment by the arrival of three more initiates, who came through the door in coats and robes, the hems soaked and dirty with rainwater. Two of them were young women she'd never seen before. The other was the man from the Mount Hookey Crystal Visions shop, the one who had stared at her while she was putting up posters of Jesse. He stared at her some more now while he took off his mackintosh.

"Blessings," everyone said to each other, and they bobbed their heads like seagulls. The man from the shop didn't say anything. The trio went upstairs.

"Do you have your rod?" said Glenn.

"Oh," said Vivian. "I was going to say. I forgot it. I left it in the motel. Sorry."

"Don't tell me you're staying in Cedar Lodge, too?"

"It was the only place I could find."

"That's what Jesse said. Do you like it there?"

"Not really…"

"We couldn't get Jesse out of there!"

Vivian thought of the locked door to room 29.

"Get him out?"

"There was always the offer of staying in the Sanctuary, but he said he was happy where he was. Well, not happy, but… You know. No accounting for taste, I suppose." He chuckled again. "Maybe they do a better breakfast there."

"I can guarantee they don't."

Glenn laughed and did a strange wink, that might have been involuntary. "You know you can stay here," he said. "Sleep here, eat here. I told you, you're part of the family now."

"Really?"

"Of course!"

Vivian thought. She ran her tongue around the inside of her mouth. She'd make a far better undercover operative if she was actually a resident at the Sanctuary. She'd have more opportunity to ask questions. It was also just so very *nice* here.

"Maybe," she said, at last.

"No pressure at all."

"I'll think about it."

"Good."

"What about the rod thing?"

"Oh, don't worry," he said. "Plenty of them lying around. Annabelle?"

She came out of her hypnotised state and got up from the big pebble.

"Another rod for Vivian, please." He turned back to her. "And did we give you a robe? We didn't give you a robe! Let's get you disrobed, then re-robed, then we can get started."

"Started on what?"

"Your first session."

"I'm not sure—"

"Chop chop!"

"I wanted to ask—"

"Save questions till afterwards!"

"But—"

"The spheres won't wait for you, Vivian!"

Fifteen minutes later Vivian was sitting cross-legged on a circular mat in the big room. The session was something that Glenn had called "violet flame meditation". She sat in a ring of ten other initiates, her new rod lying on the floor next to her. She noticed that everyone else's rods had a jewel affixed to the end. The only light came from the wood burner at the far end and several dozen candles that Carl had lit around the place. The candles were purple, both the wax and the flame.

When everyone was settled, Glenn hit a big bowl of water with a mallet and brought one of the candles into the centre of the circle. Everyone was told to focus on the flame, but Vivian couldn't help noticing the glances she was getting from the other people seated around her. They knew, somehow. Knew about her meeting with Jerome, knew she was a fraud.

"...Vivian Owens."

She heard her name and came to attention. Everyone was smiling at her.

"I'm sure you remember her brother Jesse, who ascended last month," said Glenn.

They nodded enthusiastically.

"Vivian will be joining us on the path, starting today, so I ask that you send any positive thoughts and energies her way in this session. As you know, Vivian and Jesse lost their father this year, so perhaps you would like to make that the focus of your healing prayers."

They all nodded again. Vivian stiffened, and tasted something acidic in the back of her mouth. Jesse must have told him. Why bring it up here, now, in public? The exposure was horrifying. By the time she'd made up her mind to leave, the session was already under way.

The first half seemed to involve just sitting still for a long time, staring at the candle and listening to Glenn hit the bowl at regular intervals. Vivian never found it easy to relax but after Glenn's little revelation it was an impossibility. Her knees, hips and the small of her back ached. From time to time, just when she was starting to get used to the silence, one or other of the initiates would gasp, as if they had experienced a revelation, or a small fright, or had just realised they'd forgotten to do something important.

By the mid-point of the hour, Vivian was acutely aware that everyone was doing the gasping apart from her. Again she felt the urge to get up and leave. Glenn was walking around the outside of the circle, and their eyes met while she was looking over towards the stairs. He smiled indulgently.

"At this meeting of the spheres, let's try and expel everything that isn't serving us…"

Vivian glanced at the initiates on either side of her. They were practically in convulsions. It didn't look like much fun, but she wasn't going to get far if she didn't at least try to play along. She inhaled and exhaled sharply. Something flew out of her nose, but apart from that, nothing. She felt stupid.

She tried another two, three, four times with clear nostrils and began to feel pleasantly light-headed. She kept going. Yes, it felt good. Her fingers and toes drifted away from the rest of her. She felt airy, and bright, and hot; a mirror of the candle in the centre of the circle.

Once she'd started, she found it impossible to stop. The gasping and snorting became percussive and rhythmic. The room began to slant and pitch, and the candles brightened and melted into one another, and for a brief and ecstatic and extraordinary moment she was outside of herself and looking down from somewhere way up in the rafters. Vivian watched herself rock backwards and bang her head on the floorboards, just beyond the soft edge of her mat, and then she was suddenly, painfully back in her old lump of a body and her vision was dull and her lungs were raw.

She felt a hand under her back, and a bearded face appeared above her. A mural on the ceiling.

"Dad?" she said.

"Vivian," said a man's voice.

"*Dad?*"

"It's just me, dear heart."

Her father's features swam in front of her for a moment, then came into focus.

"Where am I?" Vivian said.

"You're exactly where you're meant to be," said Glenn.

She blinked a few times and saw the faces of the other initiates huddled around her. They looked at her with a kind of wonder. She hadn't moved from her mat.

"Are you alright?" said Glenn.

"I think so," said Vivian.

"Sure?"

"I'm good."

"I'm sorry. Maybe it was too soon for breathwork."

"Really. I'm fine. I'm probably just hungry or something. I feel…"

She didn't finish the thought. Glenn looked at her with concern.

"I think poor old Vivian is tired, everyone," he said finally. "Let's give the girl some space, shall we? Up you get, dear heart."

The other initiates parted. Someone said something complimentary about her aura. Glenn extended his hand and helped her to her feet. She wavered for a few seconds, from tiredness, from too much air in the blood, from the alternating throbs in the front and back of her head.

Glenn led her to the back of the hall. Vivian could hear a lot of excited chatter from the others. Through the kitchen and the bamboo doors were a bathroom and a laundry room, and beyond that a dozen or so bedrooms. Glenn helped her into one of these and down onto a futon.

"You should stay here, at least for tonight. Until your head's better."

She thanked him and he nodded. When he reached the door he turned back again.

"I am sorry, Vivian," he said.

"It's alright," she said. "It doesn't hurt that much."

"No, not the breathwork. I mean I'm sorry about your father."

"Dad?" said Vivian, for the third time that night.

"You know, I'll always remember something Jesse said about him."

Vivian didn't reply. She was furious with Jesse in his absence for even mentioning their home life. Glenn pushed on.

"At Telos we talk a lot about making a connection with the *infinite*. You read that in the book. Right?"

Vivian still said nothing.

"But Jesse used to say, while the universe is *infinite*, it contains a finite amount of positive energy. And if the energy of the universe is finite, then it's constant; and if it's constant, then your father never really went anywhere. His energy is unchanged. You see?" He put his hand over her heart. "He's still with you, Vivian. He's still here."

He smiled and got up. Vivian looked at him and couldn't help feeling he'd misunderstood what Jesse had been getting at. Knowing her brother, he had probably been thinking about mass and volume and spacetime and dark matter, while Glenn had heard the word "energy" and interpreted it in only the vague, quasi-spiritual terms that came so easily to him and the initiates.

But then, was there any difference in the end? Whether you called the thing "Oneness" or a unified theory, hippies and physicists were working towards the same thing, really. They were just approaching it with varying amounts of thoroughness.

"Look at you, dear heart," said Glenn. "Your mind is going a mile a minute. Let me get you some tea."

He left and came back with a cup of the blue, mulchy infusion. She drank it all, more because she was thirsty than because she needed calming.

"Don't worry yourself," said Glenn, watching her finish the tea with satisfaction. "You've just taken your first steps into a great, deep ocean of understanding."

He smiled again, and Vivian began to feel pleasantly sleepy. She remembered thinking, as she got into bed and someone who she couldn't see tucked her in, that if you stepped into the ocean you generally drowned.

11

VIVIAN SPENT the next three days at the Sanctuary, loitering on the fringes while the other initiates whiled away the hours twirling around and sitting still and twanging instruments. She was terrified of trying the "breathwork" again. Every time she saw the lurid picture of John of Telos she thought she saw her father smiling inscrutably back at her. Everyone else was very kind to her. They spoke about her and Jesse with a kind of quiet reverence, and kept giving her compliments about her aura, which she accepted with a mixture of bewilderment and gratitude. Apparently it had a colour that no one had a name for, just like Jesse's.

She shared a room with a girl called Forrest – two Rs, and definitely not her real name – who was from Louisiana. She had six older brothers who had all been in the marines, and she had bug eyes and a lot of scratches on both forearms. Glenn hadn't been able to find a robe small enough for Forrest and she drifted around the Sanctuary looking like a child in one of her parents' dressing gowns. She ground her teeth all the time, and spoke a lot when she was both asleep and awake, mostly about how she was feeling. Vivian didn't say much at all. Perhaps Glenn had thought that made them good roommates.

Vivian observed the rituals and pretended to meditate and ate a lot of seeds and salads but started to feel like she was wasting her time. She was no closer to understanding where Jesse was – or Nathan, for that matter. The nature of "Telos" still escaped her, too.

When she'd asked Forrest what she thought, the slip-thin girl had just laughed and said, "I don't know! Isn't that the point? If we knew *where* it was, there'd be Greyhound buses headed there morning, noon and night, and if we knew *what* it was, then, well, we'd already be enlightened and one with the Spirit, wouldn't we? We all just got to keep faith with the Path, and it shall surely lead us unto Telos."

She had a habit of slipping into this strange Old Testament vernacular, which Vivian suspected was a vestige of her Christian upbringing. Nor was this any obstacle to her advancement along the Path. One thing that Vivian learned in those first few days was the school's insistence that all other belief systems were simply lesser manifestations of the one truth of Telos. Whether you were a Catholic or a ufologist or a Native American shaman, Telos welcomed you without judgement.

On the third day Vivian decided to go back to the motel. She wanted to use Troy's phone, and thought there might be a map of the mountain somewhere in among the trash of the reception desk. If he wasn't there, she still wanted to talk to Judy. She also just needed a break from Forrest, who had become a sort of unofficial disciple of hers.

Troy was on duty after all. He watched her come through the front door and stood up. He was drumming his long, skeletal fingers on the desktop. For once, he was the first to speak.

"You didn't leave anything valuable in your room, did you?" he said.

"What?" said Vivian.

"I mean, like, you had all your valuables stolen, didn't you? So you wouldn't've had anything important in your room."

The only things she'd left in her room were the posters of her brother and the notes she'd found in Jesse's coat pocket. Which, yes, were valuable in a way.

"Why do you say that?" she asked.

"Ah," said Troy, and leant awkwardly to one side like part of him had snapped. "Mr Blucas has been tidying up again."

Mr Blucas. She wanted to see him, too.

"Tidying?"

"Yeah. Like I said before, he sometimes takes the keys. He has this habit of going into other people's rooms and… cleaning. And by 'cleaning', I mean stealing. He doesn't just do it here. He does it everywhere. He empties all the trash cans, too. I don't know what he does with all of it."

Vivian went straight up to room 30. She opened the door and turned on the light, and in the brownish, nicotine haze of the old light bulb she saw the place was spotless. The bed was made. The coffee-making area was tidied. The posters and the scraps from Jesse's pockets had gone.

She came out and tried 29 again. It was still locked.

Troy came up behind her, stooping under the motel roof, hair swaying like some great black willow.

"Is anything missing?"

"Yes," said Vivian.

"Anything important?"

"Kind of."

It wasn't that the content of the notes was important – that was nonsense, decipherable by Jesse alone – but it was good to have physical evidence of his presence in Mount Hookey, however fragmentary. She also felt a kind of embarrassment on Jesse's behalf. The notes were a private matter for her brother, whatever they actually meant. It was as if someone had stolen his teenage diary.

"Ah shit," said Troy. "Sorry. Expensive?"

"No."

"What was it?"

"Just some things Jesse left behind. Some things he'd written."

"Oh. So. No big deal."

Troy perched on the railing outside the room, practically folded in half under the roof, and began to roll a cigarette. Vivian came out of the room and stood next to him, facing in the opposite direction, out into the parking lot.

"When did this happen?" she said, looking down the street.

"What? Blucas? Dunno. He probably left twenty minutes ago."

"Where did he go?"

"I haven't got a homing device on him, Viv."

"Does he have a house nearby?"

"I don't think he has a house, period. Anyway, he was on his bike, he could be anywhere by now. If you want to get your stuff back, it's not going to happen. You've seen all the crap he carries around."

"Isn't that him?"

Vivian pointed down the 55, away from town, where something with wheels was labouring up the hill in the heat haze.

"Huh," said Troy, taking a drag on his cigarette. "Yup. That's him."

Mr Blucas's bicycle was more of a wagon, one huge wheel at the front and two at the back with an open-topped wooden box between them. The box was piled high with his carrier bags full of newspapers and other assorted trash.

Vivian waded through Troy's cloud of smoke and ran back down to the highway. By the time she'd got down there Mr Blucas had pedalled past the motel and continued through the intersection, ignoring the red light, and Vivian came out of the parking lot to a chorus of car horns.

She followed him up onto Vista Street, and he got further away while she waited for a chance to cross the road. He was pedalling furiously and she had to run to catch up. It seemed suddenly imperative that she speak with him. Jesse's notes were a precious thing. And she wanted to talk to him about the other Mr Blucas she'd met, the Mr Blucas who was gruff and neat and had saved her life up on the mountain. And he might have had the key to Jesse's room. She shouted for him a couple of times, but he either ignored her or didn't hear.

She followed him all the way along Vista, past Shelley's house. Mr Blucas turned left at the very end of the street and disappeared, and Vivian was walking by the time she reached the junction. The road to the right was asphalt and led back to town. To the left was a rough dirt track that led into the forest. He could hardly be going any speed now, looking at the ruts and troughs in the dry earth. She might catch him yet.

She walked for ten minutes and saw nothing but trees and birds and the occasional abandoned item on the roadside – a shoe, a hubcap, the grill of a barbecue. It was late afternoon and the sun was low and warm and the forest seemed preserved in amber. The scent and the stillness reminded her of the Sanctuary. She wondered if Glenn and the others were missing her. She wouldn't progress very far along the Violet Path if she was absent for half the sessions. She considered turning back.

The road started to climb and she saw someone coming around the switchback at the top of the hill. It wasn't Mr Blucas. Vivian squinted and the figure came towards her almost stumbling, animated like a plasticine miniature. It was the woman she knew as Eenoo. She was wearing a broad-brimmed felt hat, sunglasses and many hundreds of beaded necklaces. On her feet were a pair of high heels that were in no way suited to the terrain.

"He's coming back!" said Eenoo from afar.

"Sorry?" said Vivian.

"The moon is ascending and he is returning!"

"Who is?"

Eenoo spun on the spot and her handbag was flung outwards and orbited around her. She looked up into the sky and laughed. She was still spinning when Vivian was a few feet away.

"Did you see someone come through here?" Vivian asked.

"Oh, I've seen him!" said Eenoo.

"On a sort of bicycle?"

"On a what?" The woman came to a stop.

"An oldish man. On a bicycle with a trailer on the back. Mr Blucas."

"Blucas?" Eenoo's mouth went slack. She spent a moment conjuring a mouthful of saliva and then spat in the dust. "Fuck him."

"Oh."

"That's what happens to you when you betray Telos."

Eenoo rummaged in her handbag and produced what looked like a luridly coloured raffle ticket. She offered it to Vivian. Vivian suspected what it was and shook her head.

"Did you see him, though? Blucas?" she said.

"You go up the mountain tonight, girl, you'll see the real thing."

"The real thing?"

"You bet, gorgeous!"

Eenoo dragged the raffle ticket across her tongue and it made a sound like sandpaper. Then she laughed loudly and stumbled off down the track in her stilettos, turning her ankle every three or four steps.

"*Bless you!*" she hollered when she was almost out of sight.

Vivian decided she would walk as far as the next bend. Here, a second, smaller track peeled off and went down into a gully that the sun no longer reached. There was a building at the bottom, a barn or a warehouse of some kind. All the windows were broken, and a large portion of the roof had fallen in. Outside were rusted hulks of farm machinery, the chassis of a car, wheel-less, nettles and weeds growing up through the bonnet. In among it all was Mr Blucas's tricycle. When Vivian stopped to catch her breath she could hear him talking, his voice amplified and distorted by the dimensions of the warehouse.

Vivian scrambled down. The wagon had been unloaded of its cargo already. The warehouse had a huge sliding door that was as big as the end wall, with a smaller door built into it. The smaller one was wide open. She held her nose and went inside.

There was a disorientating mixture of light and darkness thanks to the missing panels in the warehouse's roof. It threw off Vivian's sense of perspective. As far as she could see there were steel shelves two storeys high, and the shelves were packed with hundreds, thousands of garbage bags. There were ladders on wheels to allow someone to reach the very highest shelves. The contents of the bags were overflowing, and there were scraps of paper and plastic and clothing spilling onto the floor, but the bags themselves were arranged in such a way that suggested there was some incredibly complex filing system here that only Mr Blucas understood.

She couldn't see Mr Blucas, but she heard him muttering somewhere at the back of the warehouse. At the end of the aisle of shelves she could see a mattress and standing lamp and a desk, also piled with paper. Vivian inspected one of the shopping bags closest to her, whose plastic was colourless and had a powdery residue that suggested it could have been decades old. She pawed through its contents. It was mostly newspapers, but also contained some paperwork from a car body-shop, a few receipts, a menu from a restaurant whose name Vivian didn't recognise. There was scribbling on all of them. It looked like Jesse's torturous note-taking.

"Still looking for him?" said Mr Blucas from the other side of the shelves.

"Mr Blucas?" she said.

"Well he's not here, I can tell you that!" he said.

He cackled. She couldn't see him through the bags, but she heard the sound of his saliva and his missing teeth.

She went to the end of the aisle, where the desk and the mattress were. On the desk was an ancient shotgun, too rusted to be of any use, a rabbit carcass and the remains of a can of dog food with a spoon sticking out of it. The mattress was crawling with lice. She shut her eyes and turned away as if faced with a crime scene. In the next aisle she opened them and saw Mr Blucas swapping bits of paper in and out of different bags. So there was a system, apparently.

He took out a newspaper and tied the plastic bag's handles in a knot. He shuffled towards her and thrust the front page in her face.

"This country is going straight to the garbage heap!" he said. "See that?"

It was an article about an arson attack, dated March 1988. The paper was a local one, the typesetting so inexpert that it looked like it had been made on a home computer. There was a photo of a burned-out house and a headline that simply read: *We Got Him!* Vivian didn't know if that referred to the arsonist or the victim.

"What is that?" she asked.

"I tried to help, I asked to help, but they wouldn't listen, and now look." He stuffed the newspaper back in the bag before she could read more of it and gestured around the warehouse. "What's the point, huh? Just a lot of garbage."

He laughed loudly and Vivian smelled the dog food on him. She looked at his face in the darkness, saw the ruined mirror-image of the man who'd taken her in on the mountain.

"Excuse me, Mr Blucas," she said. "I think you took something that was mine from the motel. Well, not mine. My brother's."

"You still looking for him?" he said again, in an identical cadence to the last time. "I told you, I don't have him. I collect a lot of things, but I don't collect people no more! Too damn hard!"

"I'm not looking for him, I'm just looking for his notes."

"That garbage from the room?"

"Yes. Someone said you... tidied it."

"Had to tidy it. It's my room. Where am I meant to stay if the room's all full of dirt? I'm not paying full price for a room full of dirt, don't care how good the breakfast is."

"Do you have them?"

"Do I have what now?"

"They're just pieces of paper with some writing on. And some posters. Of my brother."

He frowned and looked very serious for a moment.

"Oh they'll be here somewhere, sure, sure."

"Do you know where?"

He shrugged.

"You don't know?" said Vivian.

"Haven't got around to archiving them yet. There's a lot of backlog, see? Got to do it properly. If I'm going to work it all out. Got to do it properly. See, people nowadays, they cut corners. I'm out to do a good job. Going to work it all out." He tapped the side of his head, then stopped and wagged his finger at her. "You know, you look a lot like a guy I used to work with…"

Vivian held in a sigh. She looked up through the hole in the roof. The tide of the evening had turned, now – the sky was pink and the earth was giving back its warmth and the air had turned cool and damp. She thought of the Sanctuary again, with a certain amount of longing.

There was something else she had to ask before she plotted her escape.

"Mr Blucas," she said.

He was looking at the front page of the paper again and tutting.

"Mr Blucas, you've got a brother, haven't you?"

He looked up sharply and his eyes were wild and frightening. He said nothing.

"When you were in the cafe. You said you had a brother. And you said my brother and your brother might be together somewhere. In the big house. Or wherever."

"I don't have a brother," he said.

Vivian paused.

"Are you sure? You said you did… and I think I met him. I met someone who looked a lot like you. Maybe a twin. Like Jesse."

"Son of a bitch."

"He was living up the mountain —"

"I don't have a brother."

"Then why—"

"If I say I haven't got a brother, I haven't got a brother!" roared Mr Blucas. Vivian felt his spittle fizzing on her cheek. "Dumb son of a bitch is dead to me! And good riddance!"

"Mr Blucas—"

"Get out of here, stupid girl. Go on, git!"

He tried to hustle her out of the warehouse but didn't need to. She'd seen his long nails and dirty fingers and didn't want them touching her. She backed away and hurried around the end of the aisle, and he continued to yell at her, about brothers, and garbage, and sons of bitches. She ran for the door and just before she reached the outside world she tripped on her own too-large feet and tumbled onto the dirt floor of the warehouse.

She didn't get up at once, even though Mr Blucas was still coming at her with his thunderous limp. She stayed on the ground on all fours, looking at something she'd seen on the very lowest shelf. There, in a shaft of evening light that shone through the broken roof, were hundreds of mouldering copies of *The Violet Path*.

12

IT WAS nearly dark by the time she got back to the Sanctuary. She met Forrest coming down the steps and braced herself for a torrent of questions. Forrest pushed past her and said nothing, though. She was holding her rod in one hand and seemed purposeful. Vivian watched her small, ghostlike form disappear into the evening, and even after she'd turned her back could still hear the slap of the girl's bare feet on the concrete as she hurried down to the highway.

Vivian showered and slipped into freshly laundered robes and felt glad to be back. Glenn wasn't there but the other initiates were happy to see her. They'd been worried about her. They plied her with tea and stew and offered her a tincture to help her relax, because her energy seemed all askew. They were right about that. They lay her down and administered drops of the stuff to her forehead and her palms and her tongue. One of the girls crouched down, pursed her lips, and blew up Vivian's nose. Wasn't that what you did with horses? Whether it was the tincture or the blowing or just the gentleness of her fellow initiates, Vivian was ready for bed before it was even nine p.m. She wasn't thinking about Blucas. She wasn't even thinking about Jesse. Forrest's futon was still empty when she crawled into hers.

The following morning there were raised voices from the main room of the Sanctuary. The light seeping into her bedroom was a watery, dawn grey. It was the first time she'd been awake before midday in months. She got to her feet and put on her robes. They were lavender scented and very soft. She zipped up her coat over the top of everything and went out to see what was happening.

Forrest was in the main room, and the centre of a scene. Vivian could hear her but not see her, since she was so much smaller than everyone else in the Sanctuary. There was a wildness to her voice that sounded like she was about to laugh or cry or some combination of the two.

She came to the edge of the crowd and stood next to a young man with shoulder-length hair who called himself Peace, but who Vivian had been calling "Pete" for the last two days after mishearing him when they were introduced. Peace turned to look at her. He was beaming.

"She saw him," he said.

"Saw who?"

"John of Telos. She actually saw him."

He was looking at Vivian's face but his eyes were focused somewhere beyond that. Peace had come to the Sanctuary from Colorado, via a tribe in Brazil. He'd undergone dozens of Kambo toad cleanses while he was there, and had the wide, black, bottomless pupils to prove it.

Vivian frowned and raised herself on tiptoes. Forrest was regaling the rest of the initiates with her story. Her feet were filthy, and her robes had the telltale mixture of leaves and pine needles stuck to them.

"I just remember the clouds over the mountain," she was saying, "and they parted, and I saw the two moons, the earthly moon and the Telurian moon—"

Her audience gasped and clasped their hands over their hearts.

"—and I heard this beautiful sound, like a choir of angels, and there was this *warmth*, like a *wave*—"

"And it was him?" said one of the other girls at the front of the crowd.

Forrest nodded. "I looked down the mountain and there he was, praise be to God, just taking a walk among the trees, and there was an incredible light, a beautiful light—" she was starting to cry, now, and the girl put an arm around her and her eyes started shining too "—and I *understood*, you know? I knew, I just knew that all would be well, that we would all find our way to Telos in the end, and we would be *one*, and all would be well."

"What did he say?" said the man standing next to Vivian.

"Oh, he didn't speak," said Forrest, wiping one cheek with her palm. "He didn't need to. Why would he?"

Lots of the initiates nodded in agreement.

"Did you see his face? What did he look like?"

"It was just *pure light*, and Lord have mercy it was the most beautiful thing I have ever seen in my life. And he just looked at me, and turned his head, and he went into the woods. I thought we'd been together for hours, days, but it wasn't even dawn, and my heart, my *heart*, it was just full of joy and peace and I just know that we will be together again when I have reached the threshold of the Thirteenth Stone."

She made a triangle shape over her chest and then, inexplicably, the sign of the cross. Vivian looked around and noticed Glenn standing on the opposite side of the crowd, an inscrutable expression on his face.

She didn't know what to think. Forrest's vision of the violet man was virtually identical to hers. The girl seemed more deeply touched by the experience, certainly, but everything else was the same. What was it, then, that made them both see and feel these things? Group delusion? The tea? Everyone else at the Sanctuary gulped down gallons of it. And if it was a delusion, or a hallucination, or whatever, did it even *matter*, if it gave people joy?

"I just can't wait for y'all to meet him," Forrest was saying. "I can't wait for you to feel that energy. Praise be! What a blessing. What a deep, deep blessing. Maybe we can all go up the mountain together?

Maybe he will come unto us? Glenn?" She turned to him. "Can we go up the mountain tonight? The Telurian moon is still ascendant, isn't it?"

Glenn's look of disappointment was chilling.

"Did you go up the mountain on your own?" he said to Forrest.

Forrest wrung her skinny hands.

"I did," she said. "I was called. It called to me, Glenn."

"It's dangerous up the mountain," said Glenn. "None of you should really be going up there on your own. I don't think any of you are ready. *I'm* certainly not ready."

For reasons she didn't understand, Vivian suddenly said, "I saw him, too."

The group turned to her.

"Saw who?" said Glenn.

"The guy. The violet… John, whatever."

Forrest's eyes lit up and then immediately dimmed. Her mouth went to a pinprick.

"You weren't there," she said.

"Not last night. But a few nights ago. I thought I imagined it, but…"

But what? She looked at Glenn. He still seemed disappointed by something. Angry, even. She felt suddenly ashamed, for reasons she couldn't explain. He was about to speak when there was the sound of shattering glass and his head jerked sideways and something heavy clattered onto the floorboards. He staggered sideways and put a hand to his temple, then fell to the floor himself. His glasses were broken, and where he lay sprawled on the floor his robe had opened to reveal a thigh the colour and consistency of soft cheese.

While the others yelped and cowered or went to help him, Vivian bent down and picked up the object that had struck him. It was a black and red crystal. She examined its surface and a second one came flying through the broken triangular window, and the initiates scattered again. Then came a third, and a fourth, followed by a stream of profanities from outside in the street.

Vivian went to the window and looked down. It was Shelley.

"Glenn Schultz you fucking bastard! You come down here if you want to talk Telos! Fucking coward! Send your fucking lackies round to intimidate me, then grass me up to your boss!"

She'd been drinking and was wearing the same sweatpants she'd had on when Vivian had first visited her. She had Chason suspended from her neck in a kind of papoose, and his legs and arms drooped out on either side and his head was so big and so high he was getting the full force of his mother's tirade. He was crying uncontrollably.

Shelley drew her arm back to launch another missile at the Sanctuary, but stopped when she saw Vivian in the window.

"Well," she shouted, "there she is. Thanks a fucking bunch, Vivian. I was trying to *help* you, and you come here and stab me in the back. I've got nothing, Vivian! Nothing!"

She hurled another crystal and Vivian had to duck to avoid yet another head wound.

"I didn't realise..." she said weakly, but there was no chance Shelley could hear her over the crying of her child.

"You hear that, Glenn?" she shouted. "You hear my boy crying? That's all on you. When he starts crying because I can't put food on the table, or he's crying because his mom's working her second fucking job and won't be home till midnight, that's *your* fault. What am I going to do? Huh? Glenn? It wasn't enough taking all my students from me?"

Vivian turned round. Glenn was still on the floor and couldn't hear any of this. The man called Carl came to the window carrying the black crystals and threw them, one by one, so they landed just at Shelley's feet.

"Go home, Shelley," he said. "You knew the rules."

He was about to throw the last one when Vivian held his arm.

"Don't," she said.

"What?" said Carl. He looked at her. He had the face of a male model, with very precisely buzzed hair and sideburns. His eyebrows were perfect. He looked like he'd just come from a photoshoot.

"Don't do that."

"Why not? Look what she did."

He pulled his hand from hers and lobbed the last crystal at the woman and her child. Shelley had to hop back, and in her drunken state she staggered slightly and went to one knee, clutching Chason in his sling like he was a priceless vase.

"That's right, Glenn! Stay up there in your Sanctuary, get your kid to do all the dirty work, as usual!"

She came up the steps into the peace garden just in front of the door and splashed into the shallow, circular pond. There she began kicking at the totem pole at its centre until it fell over. Then she marched back down the steps into the street, found a garbage can, hauled it with one arm into the garden, and emptied it into the pool.

Another five or six initiates, including Forrest, had gathered at the window to watch her ploughing her trail of destruction.

"She's going to come inside," said Carl.

"Do we call the police?" someone said, and everyone else looked daggers at her.

"I'll deal with her," said Carl.

"No," said Vivian, "I'll go."

Vivian ran downstairs and through the lobby and into the peace garden. Shelley was by now throwing the remains of the totem pole through the windows on the ground floor. Vivian held up her hands in surrender, and Shelley frisbeed the picture of John of Telos in its golden frame at her head. It arced past Vivian's ear and skittered across the floor of the lobby.

"Come on, Shelley," said Vivian.

"Don't touch me!" Shelley swatted away her hand. There was the sweet and sour smell of cheap liquor.

"You're going to get yourself in more trouble."

"I don't care."

"Yes, you do. Think about your kids."

"These *bastards*. They ruined me! *You* ruined me!"

The other members of the Sanctuary had started jeering at Shelley from up in the triangular window. "Telos is ashamed of you!" screamed Forrest. The man called Peace or Pete was making the inverted triangle sign with his fingers and humming loudly.

The fight seemed to have gone out of Shelley now. She sat on the edge of the pond and rocked back and forth slightly, though whether this was for Chason's benefit, Vivian wasn't sure. Vivian went and stood awkwardly next to her while the insults continued to rain down from above.

"Let me take you home."

"I don't want you to take me home."

Chason cried and cried.

"What about Troy?" said Vivian. "Shall I get Troy?"

Shelley continued gently rocking her child and seemed to be considering this. Then she reached beneath the papoose and into the pocket of her hoodie and took out her phone. She handed it wordlessly to Vivian.

"You want me to call him?"

Shelley didn't reply, which Vivian took to mean yes.

Vivian hadn't held a phone for almost a week, and after so long without one it felt like an artefact of immense power. The screen was mesmerising. Shelley had chosen a predictable image as her background – John of Telos, robed and bearded and, in this particular artist's impression, surrounded by woodland creatures like a Disney princess. Vivian had to swipe up into his crotch to open the phone. She went to the address book and found Troy and called him three times before he picked up.

"I'm at work, Mom," he said.

"It's Vivian," said Vivian.

"Who?"

"Vivian."

"You? How come?"

"Your mum gave me her phone."

"Why?"

"She asked me to call you."

"Where are you? Are you at the house?"

"We're outside the Telos Sanctuary. Up on…" She squinted. "… Quail Hill. I think you need to come here. She's… not feeling well."

He paused and listened.

"Is that Chason?"

"Yeah."

"What happened?"

"Can you just come?"

There was a long, crackling exhale from the other end of the phone.

"Jesus," said Troy, and hung up.

Vivian looked down at Shelley.

"He's coming," she said. "I think."

Shelley eventually got to her feet and Vivian helped her down to the highway. On the corner of Quail and the 55, right where Shelley had stolen the trash can from, they found a bench that was out of earshot and throwing distance of the other members of the Sanctuary.

Perhaps ten minutes had passed, and Chason had finally quietened down, when Shelley turned to Vivian and said, "Did you find him?"

"Jesse? No." She paused. "He's gone up the mountain. That's why I'm, you know…" She gestured to her robes.

"Good for you," Shelley said, sadly. "I'm sure you'll ascend just as quickly as your brother. I've been doing this for twenty years and no one has ever invited me up the mountain."

"Why do you even need to be invited, though? Couldn't you just go up there?"

"Oh Vivian. Do you know how silly that sounds?"

"Take a map."

"The Crystal City isn't on any maps."

Shelley's eyes still had that blue, alien iridescence that made Vivian want to look away, for fear of being sucked into them.

"I'm sorry about the book thing," she said. "I didn't know I wasn't supposed to show anyone."

Shelley shook her head.

"I had hundreds of those. They were a good earner." She added, "My boys… What am I going to do about my boys?"

"I can pay you back for my copy," said Vivian. She patted her robes. The cash from Jerome and Minnie was back in her room, folded up in Jesse's coat. "Not right now. But I've got the money."

"It's not just about the money, though," said Shelley. "I really felt I was helping."

"Can't you help, but just not do the Telos thing?" Vivian suggested.

"What do you mean?"

"I don't know. You can still teach people yoga or something, but just without the brand name."

"It's not just a brand name, Vivian," said Shelley, sharply.

"Sure, I get that, but—"

"It's the Violet Path or nothing. It's the one true Path. And now they've cast me out." She stared in front of her, and spoke half to herself. "They told *Shiv*."

"Shiv?" Vivian sat up. "Which Shiv?"

Before she could say any more she heard Troy's voice from further along the road.

"You know I could lose my job too, if I just leave the motel in the middle of the day. Then where would we be? We need that income."

"Troy!"

Shelley stood up and staggered and tried to hug him. This started the baby grumbling again.

"What did you do, Mom?"

"She took matters into her own hands," said Vivian, and jerked her head back towards the Sanctuary.

Troy looked up.

"Great, Mom. Just great. As if we didn't have enough trouble." He flicked his eyes back down to Vivian. "Nice robes," he said.

"It's not..." said Vivian. "I mean, I'm not..."

"You're not what? Totally, hopelessly indoctrinated?"

He grinned.

"I just joined to find Jesse."

"Sure you did. It's okay. Don't worry, I don't judge you. Happens to everyone."

"I mean it."

Troy just kept grinning and turned to his mother. "Come on, we're going home and you're going to bed. You've got your shift tonight. Remember? Mom? You want to impress your new boss, right?"

Shelley groaned.

"Wait," said Vivian. Too many thoughts tried to exit her brain at the same time and got jammed there like the Marx Brothers.

"See you, Viv. Hope it all works out."

"Please, Troy..."

He already had his back to her. Shelley leaned heavily on her son as he led her down the street. He was so unbelievably tall – he bowed like a bamboo pole where his mother clutched his waist.

He was nearly round the corner when he stopped and called back to Vivian, "Your mom called again, by the way."

He was too far away for Vivian to bother replying.

"You ever going to call her back?" he shouted.

She watched them both take an alley up to Vista Street, and they were out of sight before she realised that she was still holding Shelley's phone, and she honestly couldn't say whether she'd stolen it on purpose or not.

13

WHILE THE others were still cleaning up, Vivian crept back up the stairs to the dormitories. Glenn had regained consciousness by now and was propped up under a blanket in the corner of the room, glasses still slightly askew, a bag of ice on his head. He didn't look well. The initiates fussed over him, bringing him water and tea and scented candles, but he waved them away, smiling indulgently. He caught Vivian's eye again. Vivian pretended she hadn't seen and slipped into her bedroom.

With one ear on the sounds of sweeping glass, Vivian lay on her futon and took out Shelley's phone. She found her way to the Telos Sanctuary website and spent half an hour looking at photos of her room, of the big room, of Glenn and his grinning followers. She found nothing of any specificity when it came to Telos and the Crystal City – just the same vague references to ascension and the Thirteenth Stone and so forth. She searched for "Shiv" and "Telos" in various combinations but found nothing.

Out of interest, she checked the prices for a residential stay at the Sanctuary. They were eye-watering.

She put the phone on the bed and fetched the envelope that Jerome and Minnie had given her. It contained two photos of Nathan Carter, one a passport photo, the other taken at his graduation. A smart, young African American. It also contained three thousand dollars, which according to the list of fees would cover one week's residence at the Sanctuary, with not quite enough left over to pay for her First Stone ceremony and certificate. If Glenn decided to call in his debts, Vivian would be out of money again in four days.

She rang her bank and spent half an hour listening to options and pushing buttons and getting nowhere. When she finally spoke to an operator she was told her account had already been frozen due to irregularities in spending, and there was some special number she needed to unfreeze it, a special number she couldn't remember. All this took much longer than expected because Vivian knew she wasn't supposed to be using a phone in the Sanctuary, and was speaking in almost a whisper, and the man on the other end kept asking her to repeat everything two or three times.

Vivian hung up in frustration. She'd have to beg from her mother if she wanted to stay on at the Sanctuary. And of course she wanted to stay on at the Sanctuary.

She slipped out of her room and went to the bathroom down the hall. It didn't have a lock – none of the rooms had locks – but she closed the papery door and turned on the taps in an attempt to conceal her voice. Everyone seemed busy with tidying up, anyway. She sat in the stall (which, far from having a lock, had no door at all) and dialled her home number and hung up before it started ringing. She did this three more times. Her heart was thumping so vigorously the mouthpiece shuddered beside her lips. She didn't know if this was from fear of being caught, or pre-emptive adrenaline at the prospect of speaking to her mother.

On the fifth attempt, she let the phone ring. Her mother answered almost immediately. She must have been perched by the phone. Perhaps she'd been like that for days.

"Hello?"

She sounded tired and faint.

"Hi Mum," said Vivian.

"Jesse?"

"It's Vivian," said Vivian.

"Oh." She was disappointed. There was a pause.

"How are you doing?" asked Vivian.

"What's that noise?"

"It's the taps."

"The what?"

"I'm in the bathroom."

"Why?"

"I just am."

"You're just what?"

She was having to shout over the noise of the water anyway so she came out of the stall, turned the taps off, and went back in.

"Better?" she said.

"I called you at the motel and you didn't call back. Why didn't you call back?"

"Sorry, Mum."

"I called you three times."

"I'm sorry."

"What time is it?"

"I don't know. About midday I think."

"I thought it was later than that. It's dark outside already."

"That's the time here. You're eight hours ahead, Mum. Remember? I'm in California. It'll be about eight o'clock there. In the evening."

"Oh yes. Yes, yes. I'm being an idiot. I'm sorry, Vivian."

"No, it's confusing."

"It *is* confusing."

This was her mother's take on most of the world, and it had only got worse since her husband had died. Vivian never knew whether to humour her or correct her. Both seemed equally patronising.

"You've found him then?" her mother said, hopefully, and Vivian's heart broke a little.

"Sort of," she said.

Silence.

"What's that?"

"I said, sort of. I think I've found him."

"I don't understand."

"I know where he is. I just don't know how to get there. I mean, I do, but… It's difficult to explain."

She sounded like Glenn, deliberately obfuscating.

"I don't understand. Is he at his summer camp or isn't he?"

"It's not a summer camp, Mum. It's a…" What the hell was it? After so long in Mount Hookey's spiritual microclimate, she found it impossible to describe it to an outsider. "It's a sort of course. Sort of self-help course."

"Oh right."

The way she said that made it clear that "self-help" meant nothing to her. The very ideas of self-help, self-care, mindfulness, wellness, perhaps even happiness, were completely alien to her mother. Her husband's money had kept her insulated from all that.

"I've joined the course, now," said Vivian. "So I think I'll see him soon. He's just in a different… class."

"But he's okay?"

"I think so." She honestly had no idea.

"I'm confused. You haven't seen him or spoken to him?"

"No, but other people have. Other people on the course."

"Oh right."

"I'm sure I'll see him soon."

Shelley's phone beeped with the arrival of a text.

"What was that noise?" said her mother.

Vivian heard the tones of buttons being pressed at her mother's end of the line. When she had trouble hearing, she had a tendency to press the handset very close to her face and mash the buttons with her cheek and jaw.

"It's nothing, Mum."

"I heard a noise."

"It's nothing. Just a message."

"From Jesse?"

"No."

Her mother sighed.

"Why hasn't he called home? I wish he'd let us know."

"I know. I think the course is quite intense. That's why I haven't called, either. Sorry. I'm just quite busy. There's a lot going on here."

"Oh well."

"How are you, anyway?"

"Oh, you know."

"Are you sleeping alright?"

"Not really. You know I don't sleep when you and Jesse aren't here."

"I'm sorry, Mum. I should have called earlier."

"I had an appointment for my eye."

"Your eye?"

This was another habit of her mother's: she would name a body part, and tell Vivian she was seeing someone about it, without ever explaining what was specifically wrong. It was a generational thing, Vivian thought, an attempt to minimise fuss. She compared it to Jesse, to Forrest, to all the other initiates, whose whole lives were spent examining and analysing and explaining everything that could be wrong with them, both physically and spiritually.

"You know, my eye thing. Anyway I missed the appointment. I just completely forgot about it. I am a stupid woman!"

"No you're not, Mum."

"I gave the doctor my urine, for my blood thing."

"Your blood thing?"

"You know, the thing with my blood."

"I'm not sure you told me."

"Well, he's got my urine now, so we'll know soon enough. Couple of weeks, he said, but you know what they're like, could be months in reality. I saw Mrs Holmes in the surgery. Do you remember Mrs Holmes? She made that jam you liked. Her husband died. Just like that. She looked awfully thin."

There was another patch of silence. From where Vivian was, under the shadow of the mountain, looking at the bear holding its neon sign, the concept of sitting in a North London doctor's surgery talking about jam seemed unfathomably alien; as alien, no doubt, as Telos would have seemed to her mother.

"So you'll be seeing Jesse soon?" her mother said.

"Wait, Mum, this blood thing..."

"How soon?"

"I don't know."

"Tell him to call me, please."

"I will."

"When are you coming home?"

"I'm not sure. Once I've found him and made sure he's okay."

"I thought you said he was okay?"

"He is, I think."

"You think?"

"Yes."

"Are you okay?"

"Me?" Vivian didn't know how to answer that. "I'm fine," she said. "I've lost my card though."

"What card?"

"My credit card."

"Oh Vivian... That was silly. How did you lose it?"

"I don't know." She definitely wasn't going to tell her mother about the mugging in Lewiston.

"Then how are you paying for things?"

"I've got some cash. But, actually, I was wondering if maybe…" There was a taut silence from the other end. The purpose of the call was unavoidable now. "…maybe you could send me some more?"

"I don't know how to do that, Vivian. It was your father who knew how the money worked. I'll just make a mess of it, you know I will. I'll have to use the internet, won't I?"

"You could maybe just post some cash to me?"

"I don't know."

"I know that's not really the right way to do things."

"I don't think I can get you any more money, though. The bank have been sending me letters, Vivian."

"Letters? What kind of letters?"

"They're very confusing. And the writing is so small! Why do they print them like that?"

"What do the letters say?"

"I've been writing back to them but I never got a reply. I suppose they want me to email or something."

"Mum? What do the letters say?"

She eventually convinced her mother to fetch one of the bank's letters, along with a handful of recent statements. Her mother read it aloud, slowly, cursing her eyesight. It made for sobering listening. The account was frozen. It was gone. All of it. Courtesy of a variety of direct debits to the House of Telos, the Telos Sanctuary, Telos Multimedia Productions, Telos Outreach, Telos Pharmaceuticals. It wasn't just the Telos franchise, either. In the last year, Jesse had signed up for every wellness and self-help course he could find. He was a member of countless secular and religious groups, from the Stoic Fellowship to the Hare Krishna Temple to NASA, each staking a claim to their parents' apparently limitless wealth, and each slowly but surely draining it dry.

Vivian felt a renewed sense of urgency and wanted to get off the phone, but her mother was warmed up now and wanted to talk. They got onto the subject of Vivian's father. Vivian wanted to discuss the practicalities of the frozen bank account, but her mother had become suddenly sentimental. She had bought back a lot of her husband's clothes from a charity shop, it turned out. "I thought Jesse might want them," she reasoned. She told Vivian that she'd found an old dressing gown from the seventies that Vivian might like. Vivian told her that she didn't think that was a good idea, and it would be healthier to clear the house out properly. There was silence at the other end. Vivian tried to say it again, more kindly.

"But I miss him so much," her mother said.

Vivian said nothing. She could hear someone coming.

"Don't you?"

Frantic little footsteps.

"Vivian?"

She hung up while her mother was still calling her name and stuffed the phone deep into her pocket.

14

FORREST WAS outside the bathroom.

"Happy now?" she said.

"About what?" said Vivian.

It looked like all of Forrest's features had been gathered into a couple of square inches in the middle of her face. The sinews of her jaw twitched.

"You're already Glenn's favourite, honey. You don't have to try so hard."

"I don't know what you're talking about."

"You just couldn't let me have my moment, could you? My one little bit of joy. Well, Vivian, the Lord does not look kindly upon the likes of you."

"The Lord?"

"God forgive me for saying so, but you're some liar. You ain't seen John of Telos. I seen him. I had the vision. Me. But you couldn't bear not being centre of attention for once."

"I did see him, actually," said Vivian. She couldn't believe she was arguing the point.

"Then what's he look like?"

Vivian shrugged. "He was like you described him, I guess."

"That's convenient. When you see him?"

"I don't know. Three nights ago. Maybe four. Can't remember." She genuinely couldn't.

"She can't remember. Been here less than a week and thinks she's seeing Ascended Masters already. You got some nerve, Vivian." She suddenly stuck her tongue out and smacked her lips like she could taste something rancid. "What is that?"

"What's what?"

"Something in the air. It ain't right. Why you in here by yourself, anyways?"

"I just needed the bathroom." She paused. "My energy's all shaken up by what happened with that woman. That's probably what you're feeling."

Forrest squinted.

"Aura looks fine to me," she said. There was no fooling these people at their own game.

"I don't know what you want me to say," said Vivian.

A few tense seconds passed. Forrest jerked her head around like a bird, as if listening for something.

"You seemed awful friendly with Shelley," she said at last.

"Oh please, I barely know her."

"What did you tell her?"

"I didn't *tell* her anything. I just made sure she was okay, and got her son to come and get her."

"Made sure she was *okay*?" Forrest was smiling incredulously. "Well, good for you. That won't last long."

"Forrest, I'm sorry if I've offended you in some way. I really am. But—" She stopped. "What do you mean, it won't last long?"

"You think Shelley's going to get away with a verbal warning?"

"What are you going to do?"

"Why you want to know? You want to tell Glenn you came up with the idea? I told you, Vivian, you don't have to butter him up none."

"What's the idea?"

Forrest mimed sealing her lips. Vivian remembered something.

"Wait," she said. "That other school. In the old church. The one that burned down. Was that you?"

Forrest gave a gleeful shrug.

"That's awful. You can't do that, Forrest. You could have killed someone."

"You got a problem with it, you better come out and make yourself heard." She turned to go and then turned back again. "And if you don't tell Glenn about your little ruse back there, then so help me God I will."

As if summoned by her, Glenn himself came hobbling past the bathroom door, supported by Carl. Forrest tried to get his attention.

"Glenn, sir, I'm sorry, but I think Vivian would like to say something."

Carl waved her away.

"Go help clean up," he said. "Glenn needs a rest."

Forrest looked put out.

"Yes sir. Only—"

"Later, Forrest."

"Yes sir. Shelley won't get away with this. All shall be well! In Telos's name!"

She gave Vivian a final bitter glance and went through to the main room. Glenn limped back to his office at the rear of the Sanctuary and didn't say a word.

Vivian decided she should go out and be with the others for a while, at least until Forrest's suspicions were abated. There wasn't much left to do upstairs. The floor had been swept clean and someone had hung a large black tarpaulin over the broken window. It snapped and rippled in the wind and the noise of the traffic from the 55 was loud. The Sanctuary felt cold and sad and very different.

She busied herself tidying up the lobby and the gift shop. She tried to fix the totem pole. The other initiates were keen to talk to her about her vision of the violet man, but after what Forrest had said she only threw more doubt on it. Besides, it was probably in her interest to deny it now, since Glenn hadn't seemed at all happy with the idea of her going up the mountain in the first place.

In the evening she came up the stairs to find a small group of initiates sat around the dining table. Forrest was at the centre of things again. She glanced up at Vivian and went on talking very quickly.

"You can see it from the bus route," she said. "Those big round things. We can just take a pickup and jump the fence."

"Can we though?" said one of the other girls.

"Sure we can."

"Isn't there security?"

"Can't be that much. Why would anyone want to steal from it?"

"*You* want to steal from it."

They laughed. Vivian went to the kitchen to get a glass of water.

"Has Glenn come out yet?" she asked.

The others shook their heads sadly. Forrest ignored her.

"And the cops never come up that stretch," she continued. "Ya'll know that."

"What are you talking about?" said Vivian. "Is this about Shelley?"

There was a brief pause while it seemed everyone was weighing up whether to tell her or not. In the end it was the man called Peace or Pete who answered.

"We just want to restore the balance," he said.

"The balance?" Vivian looked around at their faces. "I think Shelley's already had a hard enough time. I don't think she needs punishing."

"You seen the window?" Forrest cried. "You know what kind of crystals she was throwing in here?"

"No. A bad kind, I imagine."

"The *worst* kind, Vivian. Malachite! Do you have any idea what that would have done to the alignment of the Sanctuary? After all Glenn has done for us?"

"What are you going to do?"

"Sewage works on the 55."

"Sewage works?"

"She wants to throw her shit in here? We'll throw it right back."

"You mean real, actual sewage?"

"She's got to learn."

"Aren't you a Catholic or something?"

"Methodist. And no! And who cares anyway?"

"She's a single mother, Forrest. It's not exactly Christian. Anyway, Glenn wouldn't want you to do it."

"You sure about that?"

"Pretty sure."

"Shows how much you understand about Glenn. Thought you two were in each other's pockets?" She folded her arms as if this had conclusively won the argument. "This is *exactly* what he would want. Whose idea do you think it was to burn down the Telurian Mission?"

"Glenn told you to do that?"

"He didn't need to."

"But did he?"

Forrest left the question hanging. Glenn, an arsonist? She couldn't square it with the glasses and the wrinkled nose and the grandfatherly chuckling. Then again, he was the one who'd told Carl to put Shelley out of business in the first place.

"I need to speak to him," she said.

"Oh no," said Forrest, wagging her finger. "No you don't. You are not spoiling the surprise."

"The surprise?"

"He'll love it!"

Vivian got up and made for the stairs.

"Where's she going now?" said Forrest, to no one in particular. "Vivian, you come back here!"

Vivian didn't stop. She went through the lobby and out of the door and started off into town. When she was halfway to the 55, Forrest unpinned the tarpaulin that covered the broken window and screamed at her.

"The lowest circle of Hell is reserved for traitors, Vivian!"

15

AS SOON as she was out of sight of the Sanctuary, Vivian tried to call Troy to warn him. He wasn't picking up. He'd mentioned his mother was on shift that night, so she went through Shelley's texts to try and decipher where she might have started working, but this turned up no clues – they were mostly from Troy, asking what was for dinner, or where his bandana was, or if she'd seen his phone charger. Vivian went to their house on Vista Street and then the motel, but found them both dark and empty. She spent the next hour or so wandering around town, peering into shops and bars to see if she could find Shelley at work. It got dark.

In an alley that ran parallel to the main highway she saw a woman struggling with two large black garbage bags. She was wearing shapeless overalls and dragging the bags over the concrete and one of the bags had split, leaving a trail of something that looked like chicken carcasses behind it. Vivian crossed the road to pass her by. Only when the woman moved under a cone of orange street light did Vivian recognise her.

"Shelley?"

Shelley hefted one of the bags into a dumpster that was chained to the street light. She tried to lift the other one and its split widened and the entirety of its contents fell onto the pavement and her shoes.

"Ah shit…" she muttered.

"Shelley?" said Vivian again, and crossed back over the street. "It's me. It's Vivian."

Shelley shook the chicken bones from her feet and trousers and looked at her.

"Hey," she said. And then, very quietly, almost embarrassed, "Blessings."

"Where are you working?" she asked. She looked along the alley and saw the dusty back entrances to the shops that lined the 55. Fire escapes and air conditioning units and piles of garbage.

"The Chinese place."

"Wing's?"

"Said I could start straight away. So here I am."

"Listen, Shelley…"

"I'm sorry about earlier," said Shelley.

"It's about that. I need to tell you something."

There was a yell from the back of the restaurant.

"I'm busy, Vivian."

"It's important."

"Tell me while I work. I don't want to start and lose a job in the same evening."

Shelley looked despondently at the mess she'd made of the pavement, then clutched at a gemstone that was hanging around her neck, whispered something, and turned to go back up the alley. Vivian followed her.

In the kitchen of Wing's, the owner was trying to monitor three different pans at once while the microwave's alarm went on and on. Something was definitely burning. There was a wailing sound, too, almost the same timbre as the microwave. Vivian pursued Shelley to the pot-wash area and found Chason, the child, attached to the sink by a kind of leash. He'd pulled the rope tight and Vivian nearly tripped over it and swore.

"Sorry," said Shelley. She began scrubbing at the dishes. "I couldn't leave him at home by himself."

Vivian looked down at the miserable creature. He blubbed at her under a thick fringe of black hair. She undid the harness on him and picked him up. She was surprised by how heavy he was.

"Where's Troy? I couldn't get through to him."

"Smoking in his bedroom, I think."

"Oh." She let the child tug at her hood. "I have your phone by the way."

"You do?" said Shelley, and she brightened slightly. "Oh, bless you. I thought I'd dropped it somewhere."

Vivian fished for it with one hand and put it on the counter.

"You know," said Shelley, "you really shouldn't have that. The radiation. It's the wrong frequency. It disrupts the Violet Waves."

"Uh-huh."

Chason pulled on the hood so strongly it nearly choked her, and she had to prise his little hands from it.

"Wait, how come you have a phone?" said Vivian. "If, you know, the frequency is so bad for your energy?"

Shelley stared at her with her mouth half open. She was spared having to reply by the owner, who was now plating up the contents of the various pans with great dexterity.

"Take these out," he said. "Couple at table four."

"Me?" said Shelley.

"You work here, don't you?"

"But look at me."

She gestured down at her grubby overalls.

"Just take it. I've got to start cooking the next order. And who's this?" He nodded at Vivian. "Weren't you here the other day?" His face made a series of grotesque contortions. "Wait: do you want a table? Are you here to eat? I don't... I don't get it."

"I'm just here to see Shelley."

He frowned. The microwave beeped again, sounding like a fire alarm. He whirled around.

"I don't need this," he muttered.

Vivian spoke to Shelley quickly.

"I should go, but I thought you should know: some of the people from the Sanctuary are planning on doing something to your house. To pay you back for breaking the window."

"Planning on doing what?"

The owner shouted again.

"Shelley, take that *out*."

"I'll be back in a sec," said Shelley. "Watch Chason, would you?" She ruffled the boy's hair. "Mommy will only be gone a little while, angel."

Shelley dried her hands on her filthy apron and picked up a tray of meat and vegetables so red and glossy they looked like they had been lacquered. She disappeared around the corner of the kitchen while the owner continued to count on his fingers and mutter to himself. Chason looked at Vivian with his huge, wet eyes. Vivian felt suddenly awkward to be holding a baby and have nothing to say to it.

Shelley came back into the kitchen almost immediately, still holding the tray of dishes.

"What is it?" said the owner. "I told you, table four. Two of them. Man and a woman."

"I can't," said Shelley. She put the tray down on the side.

"What do you mean you can't?"

"I can't go out there."

"Why?"

Shelley looked at Vivian, as though she should already know the answer.

"It's Shiv," she said.

"Shiv?" said Vivian.

"And his wife."

"Who the hell is Shiv?" said the owner.

"He runs the whole show!" said Shelley, as though both of them should know what that meant. "He's the one who cast me from the Violet Path!"

"Hey," said the owner, suddenly very serious. He stabbed a finger at her. "You told me you weren't into all that. This isn't one of your Telos places, you hear me? Never has been."

"Is he from up the mountain?" asked Vivian.

Shelley nodded. "He's the one who looks after all the schools. Glenn reported me to him. Oh, it's too much, I don't want to see him again, not like this…"

"Can someone just take him his goddamn food?"

"I'll take it," said Vivian.

"You?" said Shelley.

"I want to talk to him."

She handed Chason to his mother and picked up the tray and went out into the red and gold décor of the restaurant.

Shiv and Judy were sitting in the exact spot where Vivian had met with Jerome and his wife. They weren't talking. Shiv had his head down and was typing on a laptop. Judy had her back to Vivian, and was looking around the restaurant as though her eyes were following the path of a fly. Her globe of bronze-coloured hair quivered. She had changed out of her fuchsia trouser suit and was in a cardigan of the same colour.

Vivian watched them both for a moment, wondering whether it was a good idea to confront them or not. But her blood was up, after the talk with her mother, and her talk with Forrest, and her suspicions about Glenn.

Judy started speaking.

"I don't like this place," she said. "You know I don't like it. My chakras are all over the place, Shiv, and you don't care one bit."

He didn't reply.

"Why couldn't we have gone to the teahouse? With everything that's happened we could at least have gone somewhere to calm you down. Look at you. You're on that thing twenty-four hours a day."

"Another three sightings last night," said Shiv, not looking up. "We're going to have to go back up there. Charter a helicopter or something."

"Again? Oh Shiv, please, can't you just let him be."

"Let him *be*?" said Shiv.

He looked up at his wife, then noticed Vivian. He stared at her.

"Shiv?" said Judy. "Honey?"

She turned in her seat.

"Oh my stars!" she said, and placed her fingers over her heart.

Vivian came forward with the tray and unloaded the dishes onto the table one by one. Husband and wife looked at her, and each other, in astonishment. Both of their mouths were slightly open.

"Hi," said Vivian.

Neither said a word.

"Was that everything you ordered?"

Still nothing. A slight frown was creeping over Shiv's forehead.

"I want to talk to you about Telos."

"Excuse me?" said Shiv. He looked like he'd been confronted with a ghost.

"You're a high-ranking Telurian. Right?"

Shiv looked at his wife again, then back at Vivian. Judy was playing nervously with her necklace, a string of pearls as big as cocktail onions.

"Who are you?" Shiv said.

"I'm Vivian Owens."

"What are you doing here? In Mount Hookey, I mean?"

"I'm looking for my brother. Jesse. That's what I wanted to talk to you about."

A tiny pause.

"I don't know any Jesse," he said.

"That's what your wife said." Vivian turned to Judy. "Why didn't you tell me he'd stayed in the motel?"

Judy tugged on her necklace so hard that it broke, and the pearls flew onto the floor, and into the rice and the sticky red sauce.

"You two have met?" said Shiv, and he gave his wife a look that was unequivocally murderous.

Judy disappeared under the table to retrieve her lost pearls.

"Do you know Glenn?" Vivian asked. Shiv turned back to her but didn't reply. "He told me that Jesse had gone up the mountain. He said he'd gone to Telos. But no one wants to tell me what or where Telos is. I'm not here to cause any trouble. I just want answers, and I don't want to have to do your bullshit wellness course. Not anymore. You nearly got me. Nearly. But I think I'll pass. Tell me where to find my brother."

Shiv looked at her a while longer, seeming to weigh up what to say. He ran a hand through his silver hair. His wife still hadn't emerged from under the table.

"You're at the Sanctuary, are you?" said Shiv. "With Glenn?"

"That's right."

"And he knows you're Jesse's sister?"

"Of course he does."

"And you haven't heard from your brother at all?" His eyes were very steady all of a sudden.

"No. Nothing."

"He hasn't tried to contact you?"

"No."

"And you haven't seen him anywhere?"

She shook her head. It troubled her, when he said that.

Shiv sat back in his seat and studied her a while longer. He looked at his phone, typed something quickly, then closed the laptop and grabbed his sports jacket from the seat next to him.

"We need to go, darling," he said. He threw a handful of dollar bills onto the table and grabbed his wife's arm and hauled her upright. She was muttering something about the purifying effects of pearls.

"Wait, where are you going?"

Shiv shrugged on his jacket and left the booth. The owner of the restaurant suddenly appeared at Vivian's shoulder.

"What happened?" he said, looking at the table of untouched food. "What did you do?"

Just as Shiv reached the door he turned and said in a loud voice, "You."

The owner pointed at himself. "Me?"

"Send your tips to Telos or I'm closing this place down."

Then he pushed through the door and into the street, watched by two other diners. Vivian went after them, but by the time she was out of the restaurant Shiv and Judy had got into the back of their black car and been driven away. They had a *chauffeur*. That didn't seem very Mount Hookey at all.

"Oh Christ," said the owner. "*Shelley*." She appeared in the double doors. "Did you bring him here? Did you tell him?"

"I didn't! I swear!"

"Seems like an inside job," he muttered. "Did you tell him?" he said to Vivian.

"Not me," she said, still staring after the car as it disappeared down the highway and took a right at the intersection.

"Well," the owner said. "That's that, then."

He slumped into the booth and began to eat the couple's leftovers with his fingers.

Vivian didn't particularly want to go back to the Sanctuary but she needed to pick up the Carters' envelope. She didn't know what she'd tell Jerome, because the plan to complete the course undercover was plainly doomed, but she wasn't going to just abandon the best part of three thousand dollars in cash.

When she got back the main room was half empty and the tarp that covered the window had come undone and was flapping over the floor like an injured bird. Forrest wasn't there. Those who hadn't gone with her watched Vivian uncertainly. She went through the bamboo door behind the kitchen and reached her bedroom, but stopped when she heard Glenn's voice. He was in his office at the far end of the corridor. It was the only room that had a proper door, with a handle and a lock. He was talking to someone on the phone.

"I think you're overreacting," he said.

A pause. Vivian could hear the voice coming out of the phone was apoplectic about something. Glenn was bouncing a ball while he paced around his office.

"I understand that. But if you'd told me about the situation in the first place then perhaps I would have done things differently... Anyway, I think *threat* is rather an overstatement. If anything, she could actually help us out."

More bouncing. Something getting knocked off a desk.

"I don't know. They *are* twins... Oh come on, I don't sound like one of *them*. It's not hippy-dippy to suggest twins might have some kind of a connection. That's science... And she said just this morning that she saw *him*..."

They were talking about Vivian, then.

"Yes really... No, I don't think so, she's not like that... Alright, alright. I'll ask. But I don't think we really have to..."

The voice on the other end got quieter.

"Because I like her," said Glenn.

Another couple of quiet words.

"I don't know, Shiv. I just like her. She's cute."

Vivian wanted to disappear into the hood of her coat and never come out again. Shiv – for it was he – raised his voice to such a volume that he sounded like a bird squawking.

"Okay, I'll do it!" said Glenn. "Jeez Louise! Listen, while I have you, you know Shelley from House of Telos nearly killed me this— Hello?"

Glenn sighed heavily. There was a lot of shuffling around behind the door and Vivian retreated to her bedroom. He opened his door at the same time as she closed hers. She rolled onto her futon and lay in the dark, pretending to sleep as he wandered past. His footsteps were muffled. He must have been wearing slippers. The sound of her father, padding up and down the landing on his way to bed.

Glenn went past her room and out into the kitchen. Vivian pulled the covers up to her chin and felt her whole body shuddering in time with her heart. She had no idea whether she should stay or go. A minute passed. Then another.

Glenn pulled back the door. She yelped.

"Vivian?" he said. "Everything alright, dear heart?"

He was carrying a cup and saucer.

"I've been worrying about you all day," he said. "After everything that happened this morning."

She didn't reply.

He sat on the futon next to her again. He placed the cup and saucer on the floor and took the sleeve of her anorak in his thumb and forefinger.

"You never take this thing off." He leaned forwards so his face loomed in front of hers. "When I look at it, it makes me think of a chrysalis. You know what I mean? This is the old Vivian, isn't it? You're a beautiful butterfly under this."

He jostled her playfully with his shoulder. She didn't say anything.

"Listen to me!" he said. "Getting schmaltzy in my old age. Say, have you seen Forrest? I wanted to talk to you together, really. About what you said this morning. About this business up the mountain."

Vivian sat perfectly still, unsure of the direction this was heading in. He looked at her over the top of his spectacles.

"You know, I *should* be angry with you. You're not supposed to be up the mountain at all, given you're only an initiate. It's for your own safety, really. One glimpse of an Ascended Master will turn your mind and spirit to scrambled eggs. At least, it should. But then, here you are. That's why I'm curious. Tell me, Vivian: what did you see?"

A few moments passed.

"I overheard you just now," said Vivian.

"Excuse me?"

"Overheard you. On the phone."

He furrowed his brow in disappointment and Vivian couldn't help feeling that involuntary squirm of shame again.

"You were eavesdropping?"

"You were talking about me and Jesse."

"Well, yes, if you must know, I was talking about you. I was talking to one of my superiors. We were discussing the possibility of accelerating your progress along the Violet Path, in light of everything that has happened."

"You were talking to Shiv."

"Talking to who?"

"Don't lie to me."

"Maybe you misheard. Sieve? Was I talking about a sieve? Or maybe the *sheriff*? I think I said something about a sheriff."

"No, it wasn't that."

He smiled sympathetically. "Don't worry, Vivian. I know the first few days of the Path can be disorientating. There's a lot to take in, a lot of readjusting to do." He paused. "That's why I really want to get to the bottom of this John of Telos story that you and Forrest were telling. It may well be that you were *yearning* for ascension so much that you imagined something."

"I didn't imagine the phone call. I thought you weren't allowed phones in the Sanctuary?"

"Didn't stop you, did it, dear heart?"

Glenn kept smiling. How did he know? He tried to brush a strand of hair from out of her eyes and she slapped his hand away. He recoiled.

"I understand, Vivian. I do, really. You poor thing. You've had a heavy few days. That's the only reason I'm here, really." He nodded to the cup and saucer. "Drink your tea and get a good night's sleep and we can discuss it in the morning." He put the backs of his fingers against the cup. "Quickly," he said, "it's getting cold!" Then he squeezed Vivian's shoulder, stood up, and left the room.

Vivian sat and didn't move and didn't drink the tea. She could feel things closing in around her. Where to next? Back to the motel? Up the mountain? The plan was ruined. To escape Glenn she'd have to leave town, maybe the country.

She waited for an hour until the Sanctuary was completely silent, then got changed and tucked the Carters' envelope inside her coat and opened the door.

"Oh," said Glenn.

He was still waiting outside the bedroom. He looked different somehow, in the way he was holding himself. She took a step back and squinted. For the first time since she'd arrived, he wasn't in his robes. He was wearing dark slacks and a leather motorcyclist's jacket, zipped to the top. Someone else was standing next to him in the darkness. Carl, she suspected.

Glenn looked at Vivian, then at the teacup still on the floor. He sighed.

"Still awake?"

She blinked at them.

"You're not making this easy, dear heart."

They stepped into the room and Glenn slid the door closed behind him. Carl produced something that looked like a tea towel, took a couple of paces forward. Before Vivian could do or say anything it was over her head and she smelled lavender, like the Sanctuary's washing detergent, only much stronger and with a sweetness that was almost rotten, and the darkness of the hood was quickly replaced with a deeper darkness, which blossomed inside her head and rendered her numb and blissfully thoughtless.

16

SHE WAS in the back of a truck. Carl's, she assumed. Her head was right next to the top of the wheel arch, and the noise was like an angle-grinder boring into her skull. The cargo bed of the truck had a tarp over the top and smelled of oil and cigarettes and a savoury, hotdog-type smell. There was a long, hard object sticking into her back; a crowbar, perhaps, or a tyre iron. Her hands and feet were tied.

It was almost a relief, Vivian thought, to finally be sure of something. To know, without doubt, that Telos really was as bad as her worst suspicions. But then: what did this mean for Jesse? Were they doing to her what they'd already done to him? And what *were* they doing to her?

The radio was on in the front of the truck. It was playing some classical music, the orchestra only just audible over the growl of the engine. Someone tried to change the station and there was a short argument and the truck wavered slightly on the road. She could hear Glenn's raised voice, his clear and aristocratic diction. The truck straightened itself again and they went quiet.

They drove for a long while without turning. Light began to creep in around the edges of the tarpaulin. After an hour or so they swung sharply to the right and there was the crunch of dirt and gravel, and the truck started to bounce and creak. The suspension was shot. There were more cries of consternation from Glenn, who was apparently unhappy with the way Carl was handling the vehicle.

The rope around Vivian's wrists had not been tied very tightly, but the fibres still bit into her skin when she tried to pull her hands out of the loop. She wriggled around underneath the tarp, banging her poor, tired, throbbing head on the truck bed every time they went over a pothole. She discovered the thing stabbing her in the back was an initiate's rod. There were dozens of them rattling around in there with her.

At her feet she found a can of motor oil. She managed to unscrew the cap and tip it over, and she smeared her hands and wrists in the oil that pooled on the bed of the truck. It stung where it met her raw skin, but with a little more teasing she was able to slip her hands out of the rope, and then undo the bindings around her ankles. Next she slithered to the cab end of the truck and felt with her oily fingers for a way to undo the tarpaulin. She heard Glenn in the passenger seat again.

"Listen to this," he was saying. "Glorious."

He turned up the volume on the radio and the voice of an opera singer wobbled raucously out of the cab's open windows. Then it went quiet.

"What are you doing?" said Glenn.

"Why'd you put it up so loud? It's embarrassing."

"It's not like anyone's going to hear us out here," said Glenn. "Your reputation will remain intact. Listen, this part—"

They fought over the volume again.

"My truck, my radio," said Carl.

"I'm your boss."

"I'm a Twelfth Stone initiate."

They both had a good laugh about this. They drove on for a few moments in silence, and then Carl tuned the radio to something more modern.

"This is atrocious," said Glenn.

"Why are you here, anyway?" said Carl. "Shouldn't you be back at the Sanctuary?"

"Just thought I'd come along for the ride."

"Bullshit. You never get your hands dirty."

"Shiv wants me to get some answers from her."

"You don't trust me to do that?"

"I trust you, my sweet."

"Then what?"

"The questions are of a very specific nature. Also, when we're done with the questions I thought I might…"

"Thought you might what?"

"Oh, I don't know."

Carl tutted.

"Glenn, you are a fiend."

Vivian waited for Glenn to reply to that, head pushed up against the tarp roof, making a gap of just a couple of inches where she could see them in the cab. Glenn didn't say anything. The truck rumbled on.

She fiddled with the hooks and eyes that held the tarpaulin down. Once she'd undone the two front corners it flapped backwards and suddenly she was exposed to the cold air and the red light of dawn. She sat up. They were in the middle of dry prairie grasses and ridges of low, bronze hills, like sand dunes. She could see Mount Hookey in the distance but it was such a colossal thing she had no idea how far away it was. Fifty miles? A hundred? Two hundred? There were a few barns and bits of farming machinery scattered around the prairie. They could have been thousands of years old. It felt like they were traversing the surface of some abandoned alien planet.

"Shit, she's awake!"

Carl was looking in his rear-view mirror. Glenn turned in his seat to look at Vivian. Then Carl turned, too, and the truck swerved on the dirt track.

Glenn smiled at her and spoke through the glass of the cab.

"Just relax, Vivian. It's going to be fine. This – all of this – is part of your ascension. You've been chosen. Do you understand?"

She crawled to the back of the truck and looked down at the road as it sped under and away from them. Carl seemed to be accelerating.

"What's she doing? Glenn? She going to jump?"

"No, she won't jump."

"What am I doing, here? Am I stopping?"

"Keep driving, and calm down," said Glenn. "And keep your eyes on the damn road!"

Vivian was still watching the stones and grasses whizz past. A barn and an outhouse and the desiccated corpse of a tree. The truck threw up great clouds of yellow dust. Could she jump? She might survive unscathed – she was still in Jesse's indestructible coat, after all.

"Vivian? Dear heart?" Glenn called to her. "Don't do anything to hurt yourself."

"Why's she awake anyway? I gave her enough to knock out an elephant."

Carl was trying to look over his shoulder again.

"Watch the *road*, Carl."

"Didn't you tie her up?"

"Carl, watch the—"

As if trotting in from the wings of a stage, a skinny horse and foal appeared from behind a farmhouse and stood in the middle of the road. Carl spun the wheel. The truck hit the back end of the foal, and its mother screamed, and Glenn screamed too. They lurched off the road, the windscreen already cracked, and drove straight into the farmhouse. The truck obliterated the front porch and then struck something harder in the building's foundations. The nose drove down towards the earth and the tail bucked and Vivian was thrown down the length of the truck's bed into the rear window of the cab, and it felt as if all of her ribs shattered at once and the air was snapped out of her like someone beating the dust from a rug.

Vivian's ears rang. She lay on her back, looking up at the sky, which was somehow brightening and darkening at the same time. The engine made tortured, irregular ticking noises, and there was steam hissing from somewhere. A beam fell from the remains of the farmhouse and landed on the cab. Then all was quiet, save for a mournful whinnying coming from the horse a few hundred yards back.

Vivian picked herself up and prodded her sides. Jesse's coat still held her together. She crawled painfully to the side of the truck and climbed down into the ruins of the farmhouse's veranda. She went around to the front of the cab. The noise from the horse was unbearable. She didn't want to look behind her.

The bonnet and everything beneath it was crushed like a paper bag, and the windscreen was gone. It was an old truck – no airbags or anything like that. Carl was slumped over the steering wheel, pinned between it and the seat. There was a lot of blood coming from his forehead and nose and mouth. He wasn't moving. Glenn was bloodied, too, but breathing. The rafter that had fallen from the roof was lying at an angle across his lap.

Vivian just looked at him for a while, and he sat with his eyes closed as if he was having a nap. He didn't seem to know she was there. She leaned into the cab and undid his seat belt and ran a hand over the pockets of his leather jacket. She felt the edges of his phone and took it out. The screen was cracked and blank and no amount of button mashing would make it turn on. When she looked up, she saw Glenn had opened his eyes.

"Vivian," he said, "dear heart, let me explain."

"Where's Jesse?" she said.

"I can't say."

His eyelids fluttered when he spoke, and he seemed to be in a lot of pain. His voice was quieter than it had been. The horse was still stamping and moaning back in the road, and Vivian finally turned around and saw it nosing at the broken body of the foal and decided she had to leave as quickly as possible, or her heart might just go black and die from the horror of it all.

She left Glenn in the cab and went to check quickly if there was anything of use in the back of the truck. If she was going to walk back to civilisation she'd need food and water. There was none – just the half-empty oil can, some tins of paint, a bag of cement, and the bundles of initiate rods. She picked her way through the debris of the farmhouse, thinking it might have a kitchen, perhaps a bicycle leaning against a wall out back, but the place had been abandoned for years and contained only dust and rat droppings.

When she came back past the truck, Glenn flopped out of the passenger seat and stumbled towards her.

"Wait, Vivian," he said.

He grasped at her coat and she tried to shrug him off but he sunk his fingers into her arms.

"It's not at all what you're thinking," he said.

He clung to her like a child. She looked down and saw him, his broken glasses still somehow attached to his face. He nudged them up his nose in that familiar gesture. She pushed him back into the tailgate.

"Where's Jesse?" she asked.

He sagged and said nothing. Vivian reached into the truck bed and pulled out one of the initiate rods. She hefted it like a baton in one hand.

"Careful, Vivian," he said, "that's a sacred rod. Violence is not the way of Telos."

"Where's Jesse, Glenn?"

"I can't tell you."

She struck his elbow and he howled.

"I'm serious, Vivian! For God's sake! I *can't* tell you because I don't *know*."

"Not privy to the secrets of Telos, right? Why don't we just phone Shiv now, then?"

"He doesn't know either," said Glenn. He put his uninjured arm out and came forward slowly, as if approaching a wild animal. "None of us do. We thought maybe you did. We thought maybe you could help us."

Vivian watched him and took several dry breaths.

"Are you trying to tell me that no one in top brass actually knows where Telos is?"

"Be calm, Vivian. We know your brother is up the mountain. We know he has ascended. *Truly* ascended. Only..."

"Only what?"

"There are certain truths here that need to be shared. I'm willing to share them, Vivian, only because I know you are ready. So put down the rod. If you please, dear heart. Let us talk. Let us commune. Two souls, together."

He tried to put a hand to her cheek, and she flinched and raised her weapon. He caught the rod in mid-air and tried to yank it from her, but she held on and pulled it out of his fingers and he went for her throat. They spun like that, three or four times, and she couldn't prise his hands off her. He started hissing.

"You fucking horrible cunt," he said, and his voice sounded like someone else altogether, and she felt his nails on the soft skin behind her ears.

Her knee made contact with his groin and when he doubled over she cracked him hard on the side of the head. He swayed and looked up at her sadly, and she hit him again, and he fell to the floor.

Vivian looked at him sprawled in the dust. She nudged him with a toe.

"Why would I know where Jesse is?" she said. "Why would *I* know?"

He didn't move. Vivian checked his breathing. It was very shallow, not much more than a flutter. He might have been dying. She dragged him around the other side of the truck and leant him against the wheel arch; then she changed her mind, hauled him to the cab, and propped him up in the passenger seat. She took off through the prairie grass, giving the horses a wide berth, and joined the road where Carl had first lost control of the truck. She was still holding the rod, for some reason, its tip now bejewelled with a deep red.

To begin with Vivian worried she would die from thirst or exposure, but after an hour's hiking she was half-convinced that she was already dead. Under the high sun the prairie was a kind of purgatory, a dusty and bleached wasteland that she wandered through like a lost soul. If she was not dead then she was at least asleep, and dreaming an endless, colourless, dreadful dream.

Even though it was nearly November the midday sun was oppressively hot. She thought she could feel her hair sizzling and shrinking under its rays. When it became unbearable she took shelter in an old outhouse, so old it didn't smell of anything, though it did still have a pin-up tacked to the wall, the shape of the woman's naked body now just a whiteish, irradiated outline. Vivian waited on the seat for half an hour or so, hoping that the door would open on someplace completely different, but the weird dead land was all still there when she left. She found a small, broken-down tractor whose tyres had mostly disintegrated but which still had a key in its ignition. She got in the seat and tried it, not really knowing what she would do if it started. She hadn't had a driving lesson in her life. It didn't start, at any rate. The key wouldn't even turn.

It was nearly evening when the dirt track met the highway – whether it was the 55, she didn't know. She was too thirsty to swallow. Her mouth hung slightly open like a dog's. At the turning was a bar and restaurant called Dos Amigos, which on the face of it didn't look very different from the abandoned farmhouse the truck had destroyed, except for the neon sign of two sombreros over the entrance. There were a couple of pickups and a motorcycle parked outside. Vivian realised she was still clutching her bloodied rod. She threw it in a ditch by the roadside and covered it with dirt and gravel and approached the entrance of the bar.

Dos Amigos was a Tex-Mex place, even though it was halfway to Oregon, and leaned far more heavily towards Tex than Mex. It had saloon doors that flapped noisily when Vivian entered. Inside, the walls were hung with a mixture of buffalo heads and plasma TVs and signs that made goofy but also threatening jokes about trespassing and gun ownership and what you should expect from your wife. The barman and the clientele looked up in silence when she came in, as if she were a newcomer in some frontier town; a lone gunman.

Vivian took a stool at the bar. The barman came over to her.

"Evenin'. What can I get you?"

"I just need a glass of water."

"Say again?"

"Just tap water."

He stared at her, then looked at the other men at the bar. She wasn't sure if he was having trouble with her accent, or if he was offended that she wasn't buying a drink.

He said nothing. Then he turned, filled up a shot glass from the tap, and set it on the bar in front of her.

"That's twenty bucks," he said.

He looked at her seriously, then the other men at the bar started laughing, and he joined in. Shoulders still shaking, he filled another, larger glass with water and slammed it down and walked away without saying anything.

Vivian emptied both the shot glass and the larger glass and

looked up at one of the TVs that was hanging from the wall. It was showing a hunting programme of some kind. Some men in fatigues were chasing pigs with an anti-aircraft gun attached to the back of a truck, and having a great time by the looks of things. The pigs didn't stand a chance. When she looked away she saw that the men at the bar were watching her, not the TV, and she peered into the depths of her glass.

The barman came back and leant on one elbow.

"Look, I'm sorry, miss, all joking aside, but you're gonna have to buy something if you want to sit there."

It wasn't that she couldn't afford it – she still had all of Jerome and Minnie's cash in her coat, bound in a rubber band. The real problem was her stomach, which after all that had happened was clenched like a fist and itching from the inside out. Any kind of alcoholic drink was out of the question.

"Can I get a juice?" she said.

"A juice?"

More sniggering from the other drinkers.

"Or a milk?"

The barman laughed again and shook his head.

"I can do you a glass of milk, no problem. Something to eat? Hot wings are good."

"I can't do spicy."

"Can't do spicy," he repeated.

"Do you have any nuts?"

"Sure do." He shook his head and laughed. "Milk and nuts, coming right up."

His guffaw turned into a strange, lingering whine and he disappeared into a room behind the bar that she presumed was a kitchen.

"That's some accent you got," said one of the drinkers.

Vivian just looked at her empty, dirty glass and nodded.

"You British?"

She didn't respond to that. She didn't want to tell anyone anything about herself.

"Lot of Brits on the road these days. Come out to Cali looking for God knows what and it just chews 'em up and spits 'em out."

"Lot of Americans, too," said another man.

"That's true too," said the first.

Vivian suddenly saw what she looked like in the mirror behind the whiskey bottles, dirty and bruised, padding sprouting like white hair from the tears in Jesse's coat. Her hands were still black from where she'd covered them in motor oil.

"I'm not a tramp," she said.

"A tramp?"

"I mean, I'm not homeless."

The first man held up his hands to protest his innocence. He was wearing a Stetson and bolo tie with a silver star.

"I ain't judgin', I'm just sayin' it's a shame is all."

Vivian turned away from him again.

"Where are you headed?" he persisted. "You headed north, I can drive you. I can tell you're alright."

She didn't know where to look. Not at him, not at the TV, not at herself in the glass behind the bar.

"Where you comin' from? You walk here? Must of walked here, ain't no buses or nothin' that come by here."

She could have told him she'd been drugged and kidnapped and was possibly on the way to being murdered, but for some reason couldn't say it. Some complex of guilt and fear. The distorted, nightmare vision of the crashed truck came back to her. Carl pinned in his seat and covered in blood, Glenn sprawled in the dust with his eyes rolling up into the top of his head. The rod was buried only a stone's throw away from the bar. If someone found the scene and followed her tracks it wouldn't look good for her at all. The only witnesses were Carl and Glenn, and the whole Telos machine would rally around them if people started asking questions. Besides, it seemed the police wouldn't even get involved if it was Telos business, not according to Jerome.

"I need to get back to Mount Hookey," she said to the man in the Stetson, just as the barman reappeared from the kitchen. He was holding a packet of nuts and a litre of milk in a cardboard carton. Everyone looked at each other.

"Hookey?" said the man at the bar. "Ah. No, miss, that's one place I ain't going."

"You don't want to go to Mount Hookey," said the barman. "That's some whack-job, druggy amusement park. You're better off staying around here." He put the nuts and litre of milk on the bar. "You can keep that," he said. "We'll call it five."

Vivian reached into her coat pocket and pulled out the roll of notes and gave him ten. His eyes widened and narrowed at the sight of so much money. One of the other drinkers whistled.

"If I let you keep the change," she said, "can I use your phone?"

She didn't know who she wanted to call. Her mother was both the first and last person she wanted to speak to. Troy might have been old enough to drive, perhaps he could come and pick her up if she got through to the motel. The police weren't going to help.

"Are you in some kind of trouble, miss?" said the barman.

"Do you have a phone here?"

He scrutinised her and the oily roll of bills in her hand and shook his head.

"Depends what you want to use it for."

She turned to the other drinkers.

"Do any of you have a phone I could borrow?"

They rustled like hens on their stools. She looked at the man in the Stetson and the bolo tie and the plaid shirt and suddenly thought of another faded, retired cowboy: Jerome. She patted the many pockets of her coat and felt the large plastic pebble of the pager he'd given her.

"Listen, I'm sorry, miss," said the Stetson, "but I don't want to get mixed up in anything here…"

"Forget it," she said.

"Say what?"

"It's fine. I know someone. What road is this?"

"This here's the Old Stage Road south."

The Old Stage Road! She really was in a Western.

She took out the pager. This was another intriguing development for the barman and his customers.

"Say, what is that?" Stetson asked.

She didn't answer. She looked at the dull screen and had to angle it just-so to read what was written there. The thing must have been twenty years old. It was like dealing with her motel room alarm clock all over again. She hadn't checked the pager for days and already she had two messages from Jerome. One just said: *Anything?* The one after that had arrived the previous night, and said: *You okay?*

She let the barman keep the change anyway. Then she emptied the nuts into the large exterior pocket of her coat, swigged from the milk carton, and went back out into the cool, pink evening.

She sat on the ridge of the ditch where she'd thrown the rod and composed a message to Jerome. It was only two letters, in answer to his second question. It said: *No.*

17

BY THE time Jerome arrived – with Minnie in the passenger seat – Dos Amigos had closed and it was freezing. One by one the other customers had come outside and gotten in their trucks and on their bikes and driven away with no idea that she was perched there in the darkness. Then someone had switched off all the neon and turned down the music and the world was all silent and starlit and Vivian had only the crickets for company.

Jerome's Buick emerged like a submarine, headlights cutting through the pitch black, and pulled up on the other side of the ditch. It stood there ticking. Vivian got up and felt the blood rush back into the bottom of her legs. She slid to the bottom of the ditch, dug up the rod she'd used to batter Glenn, then went up to the car and opened one of the rear doors and got in. Jerome turned on the interior light and twisted in his seat.

"Jesus, Mary and Joseph," he said.

Minnie reached between the two front seats and put a hand on her knee.

"We are so sorry," she said, shaking her head. "If we'd known…"

"It's fine," said Vivian. "It's not your fault."

"I brought you some coffee." She took a thermos flask out of a basket between her legs. "The top is also the cup. Just screws off like that. No, other way. That's right."

The coffee was hot and sweet and delicious. Vivian sat in the back seat and warmed her filthy hands on the plastic cup and they drove through the night in silence. Occasionally Minnie would rustle in her seat, turn, and give Vivian a lingering, sympathetic smile over her shoulder. Then she'd go back to staring at the endless highway.

Once she looked at her husband and said, "If they did this to her, what have they gone and done to Nathan?"

But Jerome didn't reply.

After an hour's driving they arrived at a township called Gazelle. The Buick's headlights illuminated the sign as they entered, "Population: 4", but it was more likely it was forty-something, and the second number had fallen off. It was just one road of neat and modest bungalows. There were a couple of empty wooden barns among them, though it didn't seem like a lot of farming went on in Gazelle. They pulled into the driveway of a house with a picket fence – blindingly white in the car's headlights – and a veranda with a swinging chair.

"Alright," said Jerome, "this is us."

They got out and Minnie led her to the front door.

"Watch your step here," she said as they went up onto the veranda.

Jerome fumbled for a moment with the keys. A dog barked somewhere down the road. Minnie blew on her hands.

"Getting cold," she said.

Inside the house was warm and smelled of coffee and roasting meat. The living room seemed old-fashioned, all brown and orange furnishings, a fringed lampshade hanging from the centre of the ceiling. Bookshelves and chairs and a coffee table that were all varnished to an unnatural gloss, or perhaps weren't real wood at all. They also had a pale stone fireplace filled with coals that were perhaps also artificial. Vivian saw an enlarged version of the photo of Nathan at his graduation, in a gold frame in the centre of the mantelpiece.

"Well," said Jerome. He put his thumbs into his belt loops and sagged like a question mark. "I suggest you get yourself cleaned up, and get yourself fed, then you can tell us what's what. Minnie, do you want to get her a towel and all the rest?"

Vivian nodded and followed Minnie down the hall to the bathroom, which was clean and neat but also looked like it hadn't been redecorated in thirty years or more. Minnie started the taps for her, tested the temperature three or four times like she was drawing the bath for a baby, and then let it run. She gave Vivian a towel and a nightie and a heavily perfumed bar of soap, whose scent reminded Vivian so much of her mother that she had to leave it on the corner of the sink, diametrically opposed to where the bath was.

Jerome and Minnie were waiting for her when she returned. The nightie was like a hair shirt against her skin. She sat with them at the kitchen table and Minnie gave her some meatloaf that was cold in the middle and scalding on the outside, but didn't taste bad.

They watched her eat, still in silence, and when she finished the last mouthful and put her knife and fork together Minnie said, "There. Better?"

"Much," said Vivian. "Thank you."

Jerome took her plate and dumped it in the sink.

"Now," he said, coming back to the table. "What in the hell happened to you?"

Vivian began by talking them through everything that had happened since she'd left the Chinese restaurant – about the course, and the initiates, and Glenn, and Shelley, and Shiv – but apart from names and specifics of the rituals of Telos, she couldn't tell them anything they didn't already know.

"Has anyone mentioned Nathan at all?" Minnie interrupted.

"She's getting to that," said Jerome.

"No," said Vivian, looking at Minnie. "No one's said anything about him."

But then, she'd hardly been asking after him at all. She wriggled uncomfortably under the nightie. She was getting a rash around her shoulders. A hair shirt, indeed – she'd earned it.

"These two, Glenn and— what did you call him, Shiv? They brought you out here?"

Vivian told them about the kidnapping, and the accident, and, eventually, what Glenn had said to her.

"They've lost him?" said Jerome. "They don't know where he is?"

"Seems like that."

"But he thought *you* knew where he was?"

"I don't get that either."

"Didn't you ask him?"

"I didn't get that far…"

She told him what she'd done to Glenn. There was a pause. The Carters had a very loud carriage clock next to the photo of Nathan, whose ticking filled the silence.

"You left him there?" he said.

"Glenn? Yeah."

"Was he…" He interlaced his fingers. "Was he alive?"

"I don't know."

"And that stick you've got. You used that to…"

"Yeah," said Vivian. The rod was still on the back seat of their car.

The muscle in Jerome's jaw twitched.

"This is not good," he said.

"I know."

"If he's alive and he walks out of there…"

"I know."

"And if he's dead…"

"But she was defending herself, Jay!" said Minnie. "Won't that hold up?"

"Maybe, but it looks damn suspicious, not reporting it," he said. "And this is Telos people we're talking about. You know there's something going on between them and the cops. That's why we're in the mess in the first place."

"What do you think they wanted with you?" asked Minnie.

"I don't know," said Vivian. "When I was in the truck, the guy, Glenn, said he had some questions for me. About Jesse, I guess. Don't know why he needed to ask me out in the desert. I think maybe he was angry with me, too."

"What for?"

"For going up the mountain when I wasn't supposed to."

"You went up?"

"I'd already been up when you left me my note."

"And?"

"I didn't get far. I had a bit of an accident." She pointed out the bruise on her head.

"Oh you poor thing," said Minnie, and squeezed her knee under the table.

"Did you see anything?" said Jerome.

John of Telos, Vivian thought. *I saw John of Telos. Praise be!*

"No," she said.

Jerome's fingers made a sandpapery noise as he rubbed his chin. He was thinking hard about something.

"This man, Shiv," he said. "What's his story?"

"I don't know, exactly. Seems like he's someone high ranking in the whole Telos setup. I think he calls the shots. He was the one who excommunicated Shelley—"

"Excommunicated?"

"Barred her from the franchise. And I think he was the one who wanted me removed from the picture. He seemed pissed-off that I was looking for Jesse. Then Glenn and Carl took me out in the truck, same night."

Jerome wordlessly left the table and went into the hallway while Vivian was finishing speaking. She watched him go.

"And you don't know anything about our Nathan?" said Minnie.

"Not yet," said Vivian. "Sorry."

Minnie folded her hands in her lap and sighed.

"I can't help thinking, did we do something wrong? I always thought me and Jerome brought him up as best we could. Nathan, I mean. I thought this was a happy home. But then it turns out he's so unhappy he's got to run off and join these crazy folks – excuse me for cursing." Vivian wasn't sure what was meant to be the curse-word. "Did we get it all wrong? Was his life really so bad? He had a good job, a lot of money. He had everything."

Maybe that was the problem, Vivian thought.

"What about your mom and dad?" said Minnie.

"Mine?"

"You're a nice young woman. They must have brought you up right. They must have loved you and your brother. What happened? Why do you think your brother ran out on them?"

There were a few assumptions there that Vivian wasn't sure she agreed with. She was excused from answering by the return of Jerome, who came back into the kitchen carrying two large box files. He set them down on the table next to each other.

"What's this?" asked Vivian.

"This is everything I've dug up on Telos since Nathan went missing. It's not a lot, but it would maybe make sense for us to have a look over it. See if there's anything there that's interesting. Something that might match up with what you've seen and heard. I don't remember the name Shiv coming up in any of it."

Vivian opened the box file on the left. She hefted the contents in both hands. Most of it was screenshots of the website that Jerome had printed out, but there were also a few newspaper cuttings and promotional flyers and pamphlets for various schools of Telos.

"I've got bits and pieces going back to the mid-1970s, when Telos first came here. A lot of hippies kind of gave up after the whole Summer of Love thing didn't work out, but some of them doubled down, if you know what I mean. Like world peace was still achievable if they just got weirder."

Vivian thumbed through them.

"There's nothing about Shiv in here?" she said.

"Not that I know of," said Jerome. "And I've read that whole lot back to front."

She put the documents in front of her and straightened the pile and frowned.

"Aren't you going to look at it properly?" said Jerome.

"What we really need to know," said Vivian, "is where everyone goes when they're up the mountain. What everyone means when they're talking about Telos."

"Right."

"I mean… can't we just look at a map? Isn't there one online or something? Must be visible from a satellite."

"Well sure, that would be just dandy," said Jerome, and gave a little laugh that suggested Vivian hadn't been keeping up. "There's nothing on any map, though. Either they've got it good and hidden, or they've found a way to keep it off the map. Or, it might not be up the mountain at all. Not literally. You know the kind of hokum they all talk. Could mean something totally different."

That was a desperate thought – that all the talk of "ascension" and "going up the mountain" was pure metaphor, and that Jesse was nowhere near Mount Hookey.

"I don't think Shiv would tell us anything, even if we found him again."

"He sounds like bad news," Jerome agreed.

"His wife might."

"His wife?"

"She works as a receptionist in the motel. Or she did. She'll know something." Vivian thought of the posters of Jesse, covered in symbols. "Yeah," she said, "we need to talk to her."

"Alright," said Jerome. "Maybe we can do that, then." He massaged his temples. "There's still this business with the truck, though. If your guy Glenn doesn't wake up, then…" He paused. "And if he *does* wake up… I think we're going to have to try and straighten this out. Tomorrow. I'll take you back there. Then we can figure out what's what."

Vivian didn't want to revisit the morning's nightmare under any circumstances. She wondered if the horse was still there, grieving. But she supposed Jerome was right: she couldn't just leave the crime scene as it was.

"You sure you don't want to look through that?" Jerome said, nodding to the pile of documents on the table.

Vivian drew it towards her and flicked through the pages. There didn't seem to be much of interest. A lot of promotional materials she'd already read, photocopied pages from *The Violet Path*, topographical sketches of the mountain that just showed hundreds of square miles of forests and scree and nothing else besides. At the very back of the pile was a yellowed newspaper from August 1976, the same local edition that Mr Blucas had thrust in her face. She turned the pages carefully.

"Why's this here?" she asked.

"He stole it from Lewiston library," said Minnie, shaking her head. "A police officer!"

"That's the first time Telos gets mentioned anywhere," said Jerome. "Look in the classified bit."

She turned to the back and found, there, circled in pencil amid the lonely hearts and adverts for old cars and damaged coffee tables, a call to action:

JOIN THE INTERNATIONAL CHURCH OF TELOS!

Followed by questions:

DO YOU FEEL UNFULFILLED?
DO YOU SEEK GREATER CONNECTION?
DO YOU WANT TO GET TO KNOW YOUR TRUE SPIRIT?

And then an invitation to attend the Church of Telos's first meeting at the veterans' hall in the centre of Mount Hookey.

"Who started it?" Vivian asked. Although everyone seemed so deferential to him, it couldn't have been Shiv. He was grey-haired, yes, but was probably only in his fifties, and too young to have been starting cults in the 1970s.

"Some guy," said Jerome. He raised his eyebrows. "Usual, bearded, Charles Manson type. There's a picture of him somewhere."

Vivian waited while he sifted through the other box file. He dug out an edition of the *Lotus Guide*, this one from the early 1980s. He opened it to the centrefold and spread it on the table. The article was called "A Message for the Arrival of the New Moon". On one side there was a "sermon" from John of Telos, accompanied by a photograph of the man himself. There he was, surrounded by his flock.

Vivian blurted something unintelligible. She recognised him instantly, despite the gulf of nearly forty years, as her recently deceased father.

18

VIVIAN'S MOTHER had occasionally made off-colour jokes about her husband visiting his "secret family". Vivian wondered, now, if they had been jokes at all; or rather, the truth spoken in jest. She looked at him, spread-armed behind his followers, hair and beard darker than she remembered but otherwise unchanged. Of course, she'd recognised her father the first time she'd seen his picture in Shelley's kitchen; recognised him over and over again in the Sanctuary's garish portraits and murals. The image was stylised just to the point where her brain had refused to make an explicit connection. It was so deep in the uncanny valley she hadn't even thought of John of Telos as a real person.

"What is it?" said Jerome, when she hadn't spoken for a while.

"That's my dad," she said.

"Your *dad*?"

"Mm-hmm."

Her father's name was Graham, not John. Had John been his middle name? She honestly couldn't remember. It didn't matter a great deal – he would hardly have used his real name if he was in the business of founding a cult. Or perhaps his real name *was* John, and he'd taken on an alias just for the sake of marrying and having children without his initiates catching up with him.

"Did you know?" asked Jerome.

"Of course she didn't know!" said Minnie.

Vivian laughed flatly, picturing the circular economy their family had created. All that money getting pumped straight back into the

Telos franchise, passed from father to son to father again. And, on top of that, an even sweeter layer of irony: would Jesse have even signed up for the course in the first place if his father had been around a little more, and if he hadn't been just *swimming* in cash since the day he was born?

"Vivian?" Jerome was saying. "Are you okay?"

She didn't answer and kept scrutinising the photo. There were two more faces she knew among the group of initiates, two faces that were practically identical to each other. The brothers Blucas.

"Look," she said. "I've met these two. At least one of them might give us some answers."

"Sure," said Jerome, though he looked unconvinced. "But, I mean, Vivian… If it's a family business, couldn't you do some digging of your own?"

"How do you mean?"

"Can't you speak to your dad?"

She'd forgotten the lies she'd peddled.

"Oh. No. Dad's dead."

But then she thought: the violet man. Everyone said that was what John of Telos looked like when he appeared. And she remembered Glenn's words about finite energy and infinite space and the idea that, *yes*, her dad was still with them, though perhaps in a form she wouldn't recognise. Surely not? She'd seen the ambulance, and she'd smelled the fumes, and she'd been to the funeral and seen the box disappear behind that horrible, inexorable, mechanical curtain. And Glenn, well, Glenn had wanted to kill her, or worse. She pictured him hissing and swearing.

"I thought—" said Jerome, but Vivian cut him off.

"I need some sleep," she said, and pushed back her chair.

"But—"

"Leave the poor thing be," said Minnie. "We don't have to talk right now. I'll make you up a bed."

Vivian stayed on a sofa in the "den" but didn't sleep. The sofa creaked all night and every half hour or so the refrigerator made a sound like a hovercraft starting up, which startled her out of whatever doze she'd managed to fall into. The faces of her family were on heavy rotation behind her eyelids, her father's in particular. In the morning, the squirrels and the birds were up at the same time as the sun and she lay listening to them cavorting on the roof, her eyes wide open, until Minnie came out of the Carters' bedroom and tiptoed into the kitchen. Vivian rolled over so her face was pointing into the crack at the back of the sofa. The frame creaked again.

"Oh, I'm sorry!" called Minnie from the other room. "I didn't want to wake you."

Vivian rolled back again.

"It's alright," she said. "I was up."

Minnie was concealed by the refrigerator's open door. A coffee machine gurgled somewhere. The smell of it made Vivian feel even more strung-out. The knowledge that the coffee was going to drag her through the day, no matter how tired she was.

Minnie came over and handed her a mug.

"You sleep good?" she asked.

"Okay," said Vivian.

"Poor soul. A lot on your mind, I'll bet."

Vivian nodded and hid behind the mug when she drank from it.

When Jerome got up the three of them sat at the table again and ate dry, over-sweet muffins and drank more coffee. Jerome and his wife hardly spoke, and when they did it was about the weather or local news. The files containing all the Telos material had been removed to a side table next to the phone.

They finished and sat in silence. Jerome sat back in his chair, warming his fingers on his mug but not drinking from it.

"So," he said. "What you want to do?"

"I need to talk to my mum."

"Okay." He paused and waited for her to continue, but that was as far as Vivian could get. "Anything else?"

"I guess I need to go back to Mount Hookey. Talk to the receptionist. Have a proper look up the mountain. Find one of the Blucases maybe."

"The Blucases?"

"The men from the picture. The twins. They might know something about what's up the mountain. At least, one of them might."

"Okay." He paused again. "But if Glenn and the others don't know where he is, he might not even *be* on the mountain anymore."

"Then what do you suggest?" she said, and she was angrier than expected, and the words came out with a good helping of spit. Jerome looked contrite.

"You're right," he said. "You're right. Got to start somewhere. Maybe he told someone up there where he was going."

Vivian had to admit that was clutching at straws. If he'd left Mount Hookey altogether, why hadn't he rung home? In all likelihood they were looking for a body.

"I'll run you in," said Jerome. He ran a finger around the handle of his coffee cup. "But we still need to think about what happened yesterday. The truck. Glenn. I don't know... I think we should go back."

At this point Minnie got up from the table, as if she didn't want to hear about it. Vivian didn't want to hear about it either, not on top of everything else.

"Do we have to? Maybe it'll just look like an accident."

"You said you beat the guy half to death, Vivian."

"I hit him once. Maybe twice."

"You said you didn't know if he was breathing or not."

"Maybe it'll look like he injured himself when the truck crashed."

Jerome sighed.

"Vivian, come on. No one's that stupid. Even in the police force. And like I said, even if it did look like an accident, pretty damn strange you just walking away and not telling anyone."

She hung her head.

"And you've got witnesses at the bar. You think about that?"

"No," she said. "I didn't."

She imagined the man in the Stetson bringing her in like the outlaw she was, hog-tied on the back of a horse.

"So," said Jerome. "I think we've got to go back there on our way to Mount Hookey. See what's what."

It took them half an hour to get ready. Minnie gave her a packed lunch of dry, yellow carbohydrates – cornbread, crisps, more breakfast muffins – and let her borrow the thermos for coffee. Jerome and Vivian got in the car and drove out the way they had come. Gazelle was a little more lively in the morning. Someone mowing a yard, someone washing a car. People just getting on with things.

She called home on Jerome's mobile while he drove. Same deal as before – just one ring before her mother snatched up the phone.

"Hello?"

Vivian hadn't thought about how this conversation might go.

"Jesse?" said her mother.

"No, Mum," said Vivian. "Just me again."

There was a very long pause.

"Is he there?" said her mother.

"No," said Vivian.

"Have you—"

"Can we talk about Dad?" Vivian interrupted.

"If you're going to nag me about taking his clothes back to the charity shop, I'll hang up, Vivian."

"It's not that." Another long pause. "You met Dad, when? '89, was it?"

"Why are you asking? Put Jesse on, would you."

"Jesse's not here. Mum, quickly, I just need you to tell me something. It'll help me find him. Jesse, I mean."

"I thought you'd found him?"

"*Mum*. When did you meet him?"

She sighed.

"I met your father in 1988. We got married in 1989."

The same time John of Telos disappeared, Vivian remembered from *The Violet Path*.

"Do you know what he did before that?"

"He was a consultant. You know that."

"But what do you mean by that?"

"What I say!" Her mother sounded angry. There was flutter in her voice. "He was a consultant. People consulted with him. About business and things."

"'Business'? Was that all he told you?"

"He didn't go into detail, no. He knew I didn't understand all these sorts of things."

"But when he went away, Mum. When he was away for all that time. Did he tell you where he was going?"

"Why do you have to bring this up now, Vivian? I'm *tired*." She was crying, Vivian could hear, but it was the kind of dry, restrained crying that she'd only ever heard her mum doing. "Put Jesse on," she said again.

"I can't," said Vivian. "He's not here."

"Oh, give me strength."

"So Dad never said anything about California? Or the name Telos?"

"Vivian, you're confusing me. Why are you doing this? This isn't a joke, is it? *Please* get Jesse, would you."

The conversation was getting her nowhere. Vivian put the matter to rest and reassured her mother that she'd get Jesse to ring once she got back to his "summer camp". The call ended on a hopeful, delusional note that nearly brought Vivian herself to tears. She hung up, ruminating on everything that had remained unsaid – not just since she'd got to Mount Hookey, but for years and years before that.

Jerome glanced at her from the driver's seat.

"No luck?"

Vivian shook her head.

"Well. Like you say. Maybe this Blucas man can help. Right?"

She shrugged.

When they got to Dos Amigos they turned down the gravel road and the Buick struggled with the troughs and potholes. The dashboard sounded like it was going to come loose. Jerome drove with one hand on the wheel, the other pressing down the moulded plastic to stop it flying up. Vivian began to feel sick as they approached the crash site. She recognised the bits of farm machinery, the outhouse where she'd hidden from the sun. The prairie looked even more bleached than it had the day before, like she was viewing it through the fog of a migraine.

"My God," said Jerome. The Buick rolled gratefully to a stop. "What a mess."

The smashed truck was still there, pitched downwards into the foundations of the farmhouse. The carcass of the dead foal, too. The birds had already been at it.

Jerome got out of the car. Ex-policeman, of course – his first instinct when presented with something like this was to go and take a closer look. Vivian stayed in the passenger seat and didn't even undo her seat belt. It was all too real, this. Jerome looked back at her through the windscreen, made no expression, then went and did a tour of the truck.

He limped back, frowning. He rapped on Vivian's window. Again, something he must have done hundreds of times. *License and registration, please.* She was sick with worry. She wound down the window.

"Nobody here, Vivian," said Jerome.

For the moment, she didn't know if this was good or bad news.

"Nobody?"

"I can see where you had your tussle," he said. "And there's a hell of a lot of blood on the seats and the dash. But there's no one here."

Vivian stared out of the windscreen. When she didn't say anything, Jerome slapped the roof of the car with his palm and hobbled around looking at the ground. He squinted and bent over, one hand on his back. He did this in several places, then returned to Vivian's open window.

"Yup," he said, "there've been other cars here. Recently."

"Police cars?" she said.

He shook his head. "If it was the cops this whole place would be cordoned off by now. No one finishes up a crime scene this quick."

"So... what does that mean?"

"Means your guy probably woke up. Maybe both of them did."

"So I'm in trouble, then."

"Not as much trouble as if you'd killed him, but yes. Trouble." Jerome gave her a look that was something like pity. He surveyed the carnage again and said, "Listen. As a policeman I shouldn't be saying this, but: maybe you should skip town while you can."

"But Jesse. And Nathan."

He sighed.

"If this guy is alive and well, he'll come back for you. You know that, right? I guess I can talk to the police, but I can guarantee they won't want to get involved. Hell, your guy might have already gone to the police with a hole in his head and a description of you."

"He's got more than that," said Vivian.

"What do you mean?"

171

Glenn had all her details from when she'd signed up for the Sanctuary. Even her address back in London. Even if she flew home, they'd find her. She didn't reply to Jerome. She leaned over, reached around the steering column, and started the car. Jerome took the hint.

19

THEY WENT back and picked up Minnie before heading to the mountain. Vivian offered her the front seat but she deferred and sat in the back, eating refried beans from a Tupperware she'd brought with her. She offered them round but Vivian said she wasn't hungry.

The drive to Mount Hookey was a couple of hours. No matter what direction they were pointing in, the mountain seemed to fill the whole windscreen. Half an hour in they passed a police car in a layby, a speed gun pointing threateningly out of the driver-side window, and Vivian ducked out of sight as if looking for something in the footwell.

When they came up the 55, Vivian had the same feelings she'd had when she first arrived. When you didn't care to look at the detail, Mount Hookey was like any other worn-out frontier township. Then she began to see the crystal shops and the yoga retreats and the men and women in robes. Doubly unsettling, now she knew her father had started the whole thing. The place was her inheritance.

Had everyone known? Was that why everyone was so complimentary about her and Jesse's energies? Glenn had always talked about her being family. Then again, perhaps they hadn't known to begin with, but had subconsciously noted the likeness between John of Telos's serene, smiling face and her own.

There was no going back to the Sanctuary now, obviously. It was probably wise to avoid town altogether. The person she really wanted to see was Mr Blucas, the one who lived in the cabin. He was probably the only person who knew all about Telos but was no longer faithful to the cause. Perhaps he knew more about Jesse than he'd let on when she'd first met him. He certainly knew more about her father, and right now that seemed almost as important as finding her brother.

She planned to park at the motel and hike up the mountain from there, but at the intersection in the middle of town she suddenly said, "Go right here."

Jerome looked at her.

"Here? Why?"

"Just want to check something."

He turned right, and then right again, at Vivian's instruction, and they drove slowly down Vista until they reached Shelley and Troy's house. Vivian could see before the car had come to a stop that things had not gone well. The large living room window was shattered and the door to the house was wide open, and someone had sprayed an upside-down triangle in black paint on the front of the house and on the garage door. The front yard was churned with tyre tracks, and Vivian could see some of Chason's toys pressed into the mud.

"Too late," said Vivian. In all the confusion at Wing's, she'd forgotten to tell Shelley what Forrest had been planning.

"Jesus Christ," said Jerome.

Vivian heard Minnie sucking her teeth behind her.

"These *people*! What in the hell is wrong with them?"

"She made some enemies at the Telos Sanctuary."

She opened the door and the smell hit her straight away. The plan had obviously come off beautifully. Jerome got out after her and retched and spat.

"All this talk of goddamn world peace," he said from behind his hand. "And they're happy to do this to each other. I just can't even... God *damn*."

"Please, Jerome!" said Minnie from inside the car.

Vivian pulled up her T-shirt so it covered her nose and mouth, but the stench of the sewage was already in her. She held her breath and approached the front door, which was also defaced with the inverted black triangle, which she guessed had some kind of negative runic power. She saw an oil drum lying on its side in the living room, spilling its contents. It did not contain oil. There were two jerry cans on the table in the kitchen. The carpet in the hallway was glistening.

Vivian called out.

"Shelley?"

She inhaled carefully through the narrow slit of her lips.

"Troy?"

When she got no answer she went around the side of the house to the back yard. The kitchen windows were broken too, and the stuff was sprayed all up the patio and the back wall. Forrest and the others must have used a hose or something. God knows how they did it.

Vivian came back and got in the car.

"Oh my," said Minnie. "I'm sorry, dear, I don't mean to be impolite, but did you tread in something?"

"This is insane," said Jerome. "It's the goddamn *end of days* in this town! That's it. Enough. I'm going to get some good po-lice up in here. I don't care if I have to call them in from another county."

"What about me?" said Vivian.

"What about you?"

"I thought we weren't going to get the police involved."

"I didn't know it had got so crazy. Look at this place. Kidnapping and vandalism. Not to mention the number of drugs arrests they could make up here."

"But what if the thing with Glenn comes up?"

"Better we let them know first. And like Minnie said, you can claim self-defence. You've got an ex-sheriff here to back you up.

That's got to count for something. And *this*—" he gestured to the house "—they can't ignore this."

"You're a nice young woman," said Minnie. "I'll tell them that."

Vivian wasn't sure that was true, and wasn't sure she wanted the police involved anyway.

"Take me to the motel," she said. "We can decide what to do there."

"Oh, I've decided," said Jerome.

Jerome pulled a violent U-turn and they made their way to Cedar Lodge. Minnie kept sniffing and coughing politely, but there wasn't much Vivian could do. Back on the main road they passed half a dozen more men and women in robes, a couple with rods, too.

"You see these people?" Jerome shook his head. "Can you imagine Nathan in a get-up like that?"

"It's not a crime to dress funny," said his wife.

He turned to Vivian suddenly, and the tone of his voice had changed. "And your dad never talked about any of this?"

"No. He didn't even tell Mum, I don't think."

"He must have been a piece of work."

"That's enough, Jerome!" said Minnie.

He must have been, thought Vivian. They drove on in silence.

The Cedar Lodge parking lot was empty as usual, although when they pulled in Vivian could see that one of the rooms on the first floor, two doors down from her room, was occupied. The light was on and the door was open. It was strange to think there were other guests. Vivian had got used to thinking of the place as her own.

She checked reception. No Troy, no Judy. She came back to the car and led Jerome and Minnie up the stairs of the fire escape to her and Jesse's rooms. Perhaps, she thought, it was time she broke a window and had proper look in room 29.

Before they got there Vivian recognised the voices of the new guests. She looked into room 32. Shelley was perched on the edge of the bed, knees together, looking very small. Chason was asleep in a carry cot balanced on the bedside table. Troy, stooping, was making sure everything in the room was in order.

"You got your tea and coffee things here, Mom. Wait. No, just tea. The kettle's a bit temperamental. What I usually do is use one of these plastic spoons to kind of flip the switch. Like this, see? Just to be safe. What else." He went into the bathroom. "You need a hairdryer? Mom?"

Shelley didn't answer. He came back out, ducking under the doorframe, and saw Vivian and her surrogate parents waiting outside the room.

"Oh," he said. "It's you."

"It's me," said Vivian.

"No robes?" he said. "What is it, dress-down Friday at the Sanctuary?"

"I saw what they did to your house," said Vivian. "Sorry."

"Right," said Troy. He turned back to his mother. "I should get back to the desk," he said. "You want that hairdryer or not?"

She shook her head.

"When did it happen?" asked Vivian.

"Night before last," said Troy. "You want something?"

"I tried to stop them," said Vivian. "I know who did it, if that helps at all."

"I know who did it," said Troy. "Fucking Glenn and everyone. You took the night off that night, did you? Didn't want to get your hands dirty?"

"I wasn't there," said Vivian. "Glenn drugged me and drove me out into the desert."

Troy scratched the back of one massive hand and frowned.

"Sure, whatever," he said. There was a long pause. Chason burbled something and Shelley winced, but he went back to sleep. Troy raised his voice and spoke over Vivian's shoulder to Jerome and

Minnie. "I know it looks like there's a party in here, but you need to head down to reception."

Vivian started to speak but Jerome took a laboured step past her into the room.

"Sheriff Jerome Carter," he said, and extended his hand. "Retired," he added, before Minnie could say anything. "This is my wife."

"Was it your house?" Minnie said to Shelley. "That is all so, so sad. I am so sorry."

Shelley looked up but didn't say anything.

"They're helping me find Jesse," said Vivian. "And they're looking for their son. Nathan. They got him, too. Telos got him."

"Has he ascended?" said Shelley. Everyone seemed to give her the same look of weary pity, except Minnie, who went and sat on the bed next to her and patted her knee and said, "It's okay, dear."

"So," said Troy. "Glenn kidnapped you." There was an uncertain amount of sarcasm in his tone.

Vivian nodded.

"But you're here now."

"I got away," said Vivian.

"You do something to his face?"

Jerome and Vivian exchanged a look.

"I knocked him out," said Vivian. "With the rod."

Troy laughed out loud.

"No shit. That's why he looks like he walked into a wall. And with his own rod. That's perfect."

"It wasn't his rod."

"Ha ha!"

"How do you know? About what he looks like?"

"He was up here looking for you. Earlier."

Vivian scrunched her toes in the ends of her hiking boots.

"Was there someone else with him?"

"No."

"What did you tell him?"

"I told him to get the fuck out, or I'd do the other side of his face for him. Dipshit acted like he knew nothing about the house."

Minnie was steeling herself against Troy's coarse language. She had her eyes closed and seemed to be muttering silent prayers.

"I don't think he did know," said Vivian. "He was in the truck with me two nights ago. And then he was out in the desert."

"Bullshit. He runs that whole operation, and they do whatever he tells them to."

"It was a girl called Forrest."

"It was more than one girl, I know that much. You see the size of those oil cans? Jesus, fucking *barrels* of the stuff. Anyway, I'm not talking about who actually did the thing, I'm talking about who *inspired* them to do it. 'Course Glenn was never going to actually do the business."

"Listen, Mr…" Jerome said, and waited for Troy to tell him his name, but Troy just looked at him. "We'll get some police up here to settle this, don't you worry."

"Don't you worry about it, sir," said Troy. "I'm going to settle it myself." He began rolling a cigarette. "So you're going up the mountain are you, Viv?"

"Can't hang around down here anymore," she said.

"You going with her?" Troy asked Jerome.

"Well, I don't know…"

"With your hip, Jerome?" said Minnie. "Please."

"I'll come with you," Troy said to Vivian. Then he said to Jerome, "Would you mind watching the desk for me?"

"The desk?"

"Reception desk. There's nothing to it. It's not like anyone's going to check in."

"I—"

"Thanks, Pops. Don't worry, we'll find your boy. You ready to go now, Viv?"

Vivian didn't know. She supposed she was. She hadn't planned on having an accomplice. Shelley was looking at her son with her mouth open. She looked like she was going to say something. She put her hand over her heart, but as soon as she'd taken a breath Chason stirred in his carry cot and her words were lost in his wailing.

20

TROY HAD an old canvas rucksack that he filled with bread and Twinkies and boxes of cereal from the kitchen, and he took a litre of the motel's warm, eggy water in Minnie's thermos. Then he zipped up his enormous, padded jacket, put in one earphone, and was, apparently, ready. Vivian didn't know if she was ready or not. She could quite easily make it as far as the Blucas brother's cabin in the woods, but if they were really going looking for the fountainhead, for Telos itself, they could be out in the wilderness for days. The peak of the mountain had snow on it. Troy was wearing tennis shoes, for crying out loud.

The boy seemed upbeat, though.

"Thanks for this, Pops," he said to Jerome again. Jerome and Minnie were standing at reception, arms around each other's waists, as if waiting to wave their children off to boarding school. "If anyone turns up looking for a room – I mean, they won't – but if they do, just put them anywhere and I'll sort it out when I get back."

"You still got the pager I gave you?" Jerome said to Vivian.

She nodded. She had visions of trying to type on the stiff, rubber buttons while caught in a blizzard.

"I got this," said Troy, and waved his phone.

"Careful with that," said Jerome. "You don't know who's listening."

"Weren't you going to call the police?" said Vivian.

"Not on the phone. I've still got my police radio."

"Which he's not supposed to use," said Minnie. "They've *told* you, Jerome."

"No one's going to need to call anyone, yet," said Troy. "We're just going to go and take a look around. Right, Viv?"

"I suppose."

"Alright. Then mount up."

Troy went back to the room to say goodbye to his mother, and Vivian waited in the parking lot. He came back smelling of some sort of herbal skin cream that Shelley had rubbed all over him. His bag looked bulkier than before, and something made of glass or metal was clinking inside.

"What is that?" Vivian asked.

"What's what?"

"That noise."

"Just supplies."

He loped past her and struck out for the 55, into the trees, away from town.

Yet another bright and flawless day. The forest was in deep silence, the air dry and resinous and sweet-smelling. They walked until they met the creek that flowed through a concrete tube under the road, and Vivian hiked up into the trees. Birdsong and the crunch of pine needles. Troy's music was hissing from one dangling earphone, and it made Vivian flush hot and cold with irritation. She would much rather have gone alone.

"Why did you want to come with me?" she said.

Troy looked up from his phone. "Huh?"

"Why did you want to come up the mountain?"

"I said. I want to know what's up here too."

"You said you were going to settle something."

"Yuh-huh." He didn't elaborate on that. "Look, someone's just filled my house with a couple hundred gallons of human shit. Wouldn't you want to know what it is that would push someone to do that?"

They walked on in silence for a bit.

"What do you think it is?" Vivian asked.

"Don't know."

"I mean, it's not a Crystal City. Is it?"

She hadn't meant the last two words to come out as a question.

"Maybe it's a revolving restaurant. Gift shop. Must be something. Otherwise where's everyone going? Where's Jesse gone?"

Vivian couldn't and didn't answer. She came back again and again to the vision of her brother dead from exposure, his bones and his baseball cap bleaching in a gully somewhere. Troy didn't seem overly concerned. He'd put his other earphone in and was marching ahead and punching the air. He seemed fired up for something.

After an hour's walking they hit the treeline and were faced with a barren, Martian landscape of reddish rock and scree.

"We've come too far," said Vivian. "We've got to go back."

"What do you mean, too far? We're on the mountain aren't we?"

"There's someone we need to find."

"I know. Jesse."

"Mr Blucas."

"*Blucas?* What? Why?"

"Different Blucas. His brother."

She told him about the last time she'd met him, and about the photo she'd found, though she omitted the part about her dad. Troy clicked his tongue and sighed.

"Two Blucases. Unreal. This place, man." He scanned the mountainside. "I need a smoke."

He lit one of his special cigarettes and drank some water from the thermos. When he was done smoking he put it out carefully with his fingers, unzipped his giant coat, and tucked what was left into the breast pocket of his plaid shirt.

"I don't get it," he said, still surveying the upper portion of the mountain. "You can't hide anything up here."

He was right. There was nothing besides bare rock and dirty snow and sporadic clumps of grass and lichen and wild flowers. If Telos was anything like the Sanctuary down in the town, it would be impossible to conceal.

They tramped down again. Vivian kept thinking she saw paths through the forest, but they always lasted for a few paces and then met some impassable terrain. They came to a ravine that may or may not have been the same one she'd fallen into when she'd followed Judy. There was no way of knowing. It had been too dark, and she'd been unconscious when Mr Blucas had carried her back to his cabin.

The light among the trees dimmed and Vivian began to feel hollow and hopeless. Just as she was about to suggest heading back to the highway, she heard rustling in the undergrowth. There was a squealing sound, so high-pitched as to be almost inaudible, followed by a grunt, then silence. A low muttering. Troy heard none of it because he still had his earphones in, and he looked confused when Vivian suddenly stopped.

"Oh brother," somebody growled.

She turned around to see Mr Blucas – the second Mr Blucas – dressed identically to when she'd first met him, holding a limp rabbit by its neck. He squinted in the half light, sighed.

"What is it?" he said. "Got lost on the way down, did you?"

Then he was gone. Vivian watched the bushes springing back into place where the man had been, and it seemed for a moment that he had been another figment of her imagination.

"Jesus," said Troy. "It looked just like him!"

"They *are* twins," said Vivian.

"I know, but I mean… it's kind of amazing. It's like someone gave Mr Blucas a bath and a gym membership."

She set off in Mr Blucas's lumbering wake, with Troy some way behind her.

"Mr Blucas," she shouted through the trees. "I need to talk to you."

She found him again in a clearing, spinning around like he was lost. They faced each other.

"Please, Mr Blucas," said Vivian.

He sighed again, so fiercely it sounded like a bark, and went over to the trunk of a cedar. He bent down, fished around in the dry needles, and uncovered a clump of mushrooms which he cut with a penknife and put in his knapsack. Then he went on to the next tree and inspected a snare he'd set. He adjusted the size of the loop. Troy was wise-cracking somewhere in the bushes but she wasn't listening to him.

"I need you to tell me about Telos, sir," she said, while he rummaged in his knapsack. "I need you to tell me what's up the mountain."

Mr Blucas stood up very suddenly.

"I told you, missy, to get gone. There is nothing here. The mountain does not have the answers. I don't have the answers. You're wasting my time and you're wasting your time. It is not real. None of it is *real*. This here—" he took the body of the rabbit out of his bag and waggled it in front of her face "—this is real. That's all you're going to find up here. Now. I told you to git. And if you don't, Lord help me, I will be angry with you, and when I am angry I am liable to do you some unconscionable physical discourtesy."

Troy started laughing.

"Well, I can see who got all the family's brain cells."

"Who the hell is this?"

"Friend of your brother's."

"Get a haircut."

"That's what your brother says!"

"Please, Mr Blucas," said Vivian. "It's not what you think. I'm not just another hippy."

"You look like one." He turned to Troy. "He sure does."

"I'm nothing to do with Telos," said Vivian.

"You had a rod."

"I know."

"So?"

"I just pretended to join," said Vivian. "To find my brother. That's all. I'm not here looking for enlightenment or whatever."

"You sure about that?"

She paused.

"I'm just looking for my brother."

"And how the hell should I know where your brother is?"

"He went to Telos. I thought you'd know what that was."

The man looked at her, then looked up at the sky. His face looked very old in the slanted, burned-out light of the evening.

"I don't know anything about that."

"You were there right at the beginning though, weren't you? I saw it. In the paper. You and your brother and the other guy—" she didn't want to say her father "—Mr Owens."

He frowned.

"Graham? How do you know about him?"

"Mr Owens?" said Troy.

There was silence, then all three of them started at a sound that came from further up the mountain. A strange gurgling roar, not particularly loud. It sounded like someone doing a bad impression of a lion.

"Damn it," said Mr Blucas, and looked in the direction of the noise.

"What is that?" said Vivian.

"Cougar." He turned back to them. "This was your plan all along, right? Filibuster till it gets dark and I feel sorry for you and I take you in for another night? Get another free meal out of me? You know what you are, your generation? You're selfish." He pointed a thick, calloused finger at her. "That's why you all love Telos so much. Pretend you're meditating on the great cosmic spirit, but all you're doing is thinking about yourself all goddamn day."

The cougar growled again, closer.

"You can come back to the house," said Blucas. "But I'm not feeding you again." He looked Troy up and down his full height. "You? I don't even know if you're gonna fit."

And he set off down the mountain without a torch, seeming to know his way by smell, and apparently not caring if Vivian and Troy kept up with him.

"Mr Owens," Troy said in Vivian's ear. "Family? Right?"

She said nothing.

"Your dad?"

Again she didn't reply.

They walked a little further and she finally said, "Don't say anything to him," nodding to the dark shape of Blucas.

"No way," said Troy. "No fucking *way*."

It was almost completely dark by the time they reached the cabin. They came at it from the back, and the window was four dull squares of orange. The wood burner was lit inside, and the smell of smoke was rich and peaty. Mr Blucas didn't so much as show them inside as forget to close the door. He had taken up a seat by the fire and had stuck his knife into the rabbit before Vivian and Troy had crossed the threshold.

"Like what you've done with the place," said Troy.

"You can go and sleep with the cougars if you don't like it," said Mr Blucas. He stripped the animal of its skin as easy as peeling a banana.

"Gross," said Troy. The boy was nearly bent double under the cabin's roof. He went and sat on the bed and folded up his legs and looked like some kind of optical illusion. Out came his phone.

"That goes away," said Mr Blucas.

"Why?"

"It goes away, or it goes in the fire."

He dug the blade of his knife into the rabbit's belly and the guts slopped into a metal bowl he had waiting. Troy did as he was told, and for once didn't have some smart-alecky reply.

Vivian watched Mr Blucas lever himself off his stool and spit the rabbit's carcass and remove the top of the wood burner with thick gloves. He balanced the spit on top and turned it a couple of times. It was as though he was completely alone in the cabin. When the fat started hissing he turned it again, then poured himself something brown from a brown bottle and took his seat and spat on the floor.

"So, you saw me in the paper," he said. "And what paper was that?"

"I don't know. An old one. From the eighties."

"Right. Well. Good sleuthing, you found me."

He spun the rabbit on the spit and it seemed he had nothing else to say.

"Please, Mr Blucas."

"Stop that. You're not in middle school. My name's Piotr."

"I need you to tell me what Telos is. *Where* Telos is. I'm just going to get my brother and leave. I'm not going to tell anyone about this. Or you."

"Damn right you're not." He wielded the spit like a cutlass and pointed it in Vivian's face. "How do you know Graham?"

"Doesn't matter."

"It sure does matter. *No one* knows Graham. He made sure of that, the old bastard."

"What do you mean?"

"I mean, if he *knows* you know, then you need to watch your back. Jesus."

Vivian found she was clenching her jaw so tightly her whole neck and shoulders were starting to cramp up.

"I don't," she said. "He's dead."

"Dead? Then who's in charge now?"

"I don't know." Shiv, perhaps, Vivian thought.

"How do you know he's dead?"

"I just do."

"Oh for crying out loud," Troy interjected. "Just tell him."

"Tell me what?"

"I will, if you won't," said Troy. "Piotr, you're looking at the heir apparent."

"What's that?"

Vivian wished, not for the first time, that Troy hadn't come with her. She looked at him and shook her head, and he just splayed his enormous hands in a helpless gesture.

"He's playing hard to get," he said. "We need to give him something."

"Baloney," said Piotr. "You've got some mouth on you, boy."

Vivian turned back. "No. He's telling the truth."

Piotr looked from Vivian to Troy and back again.

"You're his daughter?"

She nodded.

"And your brother, he's signed up to the course?"

"I haven't heard from him in weeks."

"Your dad put him up to it?"

"No. None of us knew anything about what Dad did."

Piotr Blucas looked at her steadily.

"Figures," he said. "Good God. That man."

He didn't speak again for some time. He had two more slugs of his brown homebrew, then slid the rabbit from the skewer and, true to his word, devoured the whole thing by himself without offering anything to Vivian or Troy.

When Piotr was finished he wiped his mouth with the sleeve of his plaid shirt and threw the bones out of the door. He came back inside and patted his pockets and sighed a heavy sigh.

"One of these?" Troy said. He fished under the long black curtain of his hair and produced a cigarette he'd tucked above his ear. He held it out as a peace offering. His arm reached halfway across the cabin from where he was lying.

Piotr regarded it, and Troy, with suspicion. He took it and grunted, and then spent a moment lighting the cigarette from the embers of the wood burner. He sat back in his chair and exhaled a cloud of smoke. It had the pungent, spicy aroma that followed Troy everywhere.

Vivian was about to try coaxing him into saying something when he began of his own accord.

"We were in at the ground floor, so to speak," he said. "Me and Janek. That's my brother. The money I made from that whole thing. Jesus, it does not bear thinking about."

Another very long pause.

"We didn't actually make up the Telos stuff. Well, the name maybe. That was Graham – your dad's – idea, I think. I don't even remember. But the mountain thing, that's not new. Native Americans always used to think this place was spiritually significant. Then the Spanish claimed it as a holy site. Like a Mount Sinai of the New World. Then it was the Dutch and English and so forth. Then the hippies wanted it. In the sixties everyone started coming back here. I don't even know why your dad wanted to start it in the first place. It might have been a joke. He might have even believed all this mountain spirit nonsense at the beginning. I don't know. He was difficult to read."

"I know," said Vivian.

"Sure you do," said Piotr. "At any rate, it was clear pretty quickly that he couldn't keep the whole show on the road by himself. That was when he got me and Janek involved. Add a few more cast members."

He sniffed. "He thought three was a good number. You've seen all the triangles, right? And twins added a nice bit of mysticism."

"How did you meet him?"

He took a long drag on the cigarette.

"Grateful Dead concert," he said.

Troy sniggered from the corner.

"Seriously?" said Vivian.

"From way back." He stared at Troy until he stopped laughing. "At first he just hired us for decoration, but then we all had jobs to do once the thing started making serious money. Graham was the visionary, I guess. He fine-tuned the mythology. He had all the ideas about how to monetise it. I'm a certified accountant, if you can believe that. Janek... I don't know, he did the heavy lifting. Odds and ends. Manual labour. Debt collection sometimes."

"Debt collection?"

"It happened."

"If you all made so much money then why are you here? And why is your brother... like he is?"

Another couple of puffs on the cigarette. He looked at the lit end and frowned, as if unsure of what it was he was smoking.

"Your dad was the real businessman out of all of us. If he was a hippy at the start, he sure as hell wasn't after a few years of profit. He was the one who took Telos public. That was the beginning of the end."

"Public?"

"I mean he turned it into a franchise. International Church of Telos became Telos Incorporated. That must have been, what, '87, '88? Your dad appointed himself CEO. Can you imagine that? Head of the board during the week, and come Friday night he puts on his goddamn dressing gown and comes down here to be John of Telos, Ascended Master." He shook his head and gave a laugh that sounded a lot like the cougar. He looked at Vivian seriously. "I'm not going to mince words, young lady, your father was a selfish son of a bitch. He cut Janek loose because he didn't think he was pulling his weight. Then when Janek broke his NDA, your dad ruined him. Financially and otherwise. And I don't just mean in court. Those initiates will do anything for the good of Telos."

Vivian remembered the local paper that Janek Blucas had shown her – the burned-out house, the triumphant headline. Blucas had got what was coming to him, just like the members of the Telurian Mission, and however many others.

"Didn't you want to help him?" she asked.

"Me? Back then I was making too much money to give a shit. Janek said he'd never talk to me again, and he was right to. Then, in a couple of years, your dad jettisoned me too. Heaved me over the side of the good ship Telos, right about when he went back to the UK. I had the good sense not to lose my money and my mind on a lot of legal nonsense." He held up the cigarette, now not much more than a damp stub, and sniffed. "Say, boy, what is *in* this?"

"You're still here, though," said Vivian, before Troy could answer.

"Yes, ma'am, I am still here. Your powers of deduction are astonishing."

He sniffed again. She just waited for him to carry on, rather than risk embarrassing herself with any more questions. Eventually he cleared his throat and spat something that looked like a whole oyster onto the floor.

"I left Telos and spent all my earnings and had a good old time. Twenty years of partying doesn't do a lot of good for the soul, though. After all that, found myself back here, wandering California looking for something more spiritually fulfilling. The mountain called to me!"

He made an epiphanic gesture with his hands.

"Are you serious?" said Vivian.

"No, I'm not serious. I wanted to be anywhere else in the world but someone needed to keep an eye on my brother. You know what that's like, am I right?"

"He thinks you're dead," said Vivian.

"I'm dead *to him*, that's for sure. Still doesn't talk to me. I just go to his place sometimes and bring him food and blankets and such. Poor son of a bitch."

"But why are you up here?"

"I ain't living in town, no thank you. Don't want anything to do with any of that. I see what the Telos thing has turned into and I tell you, with God as my witness, I am ashamed. It was different when we started. In the seventies there was a kind of optimism about it. It was *fun* being a hippy. I don't know when it got so serious. Nowadays, these kids..." He flicked the butt into the fire and it made a small tongue of flame. "Like the goddamn Hitler Youth," he said.

They sat in silence for a few moments.

"So there's nothing up here? Apart from you?"

"I told you," said Piotr. "Just me and the rabbits."

"There must be something. Why do they keep sending people up the mountain?"

"No one gets *sent* up the mountain. They just come up here of their own accord, because they think they're going to find the answer."

"And what happens to them?"

"What do you think?" he said. "What happened to you?"

The bruise on Vivian's head felt like it was swelling afresh in the heat of the cabin. What about the violet man she'd seen? She still refused to believe he'd been a mere figment of her imagination. She'd nearly killed herself trying to catch him.

"But everyone talks about Telos like it's a real place," said Vivian. "Even the people who are in on it."

"Oh, Telos is real," said Piotr matter-of-factly. "But it's nowhere near here."

"It's not?"

Piotr leant forward and put his elbows on his knees.

"What did they say about your brother, exactly?" he said, cocking one ear in her direction. "He went up the mountain? Or he went to Telos?"

"Both."

"Nope," said Piotr. "Not the same thing."

"What do you mean?"

"What did they say, word-for-word?"

Vivian tried to remember. Glenn and the initiates had said a lot of words, and not many of them had made sense.

"He had some special energy. And they'd kind of fast-tracked him through the course. Through the – what are they called? – stones."

"And now he's ascended. Am I right? Thirteenth Stone?"

"That's right."

Piotr looked at his feet and seemed to be smiling, though Vivian couldn't see his face properly. He scuffed the floorboards with the toe of his boot.

"Now, miss, I don't know if you'll consider this good news or bad news." He raised his head and looked past her to Troy. "Give me that," he said.

"What?" said Troy.

"The phone."

"Why?"

"Thirteenth Stone was your dad's idea. It's been nearly thirty years. But... well, I'll show you."

Troy handed over the phone. Piotr spent a few minutes scowling at the screen, like Vivian remembered her mum doing, poking slowly and precisely with the tip of one finger.

"You know what you're doing with that, grandpa?" said Troy.
Piotr ignored him.

"Also," Vivian said, remembering something suddenly. "Your brother. He mentioned something about a big house."

Piotr laughed through his nose. "Uh-huh," he said. He kept prodding at the phone. "We used to recruit the smart ones. Send them to head office."

"Head office?"

"I mean, we didn't call it that, obviously. Was your brother smart?"

"I guess so."

"We got them to research Telos's competitors – self-help stuff, spiritual stuff, any new bit of hokum that someone had decided was the new thing – and then we'd fold it into the franchise. I suppose the point was to make sure we could offer anything you could get elsewhere. We never missed a trick. The initiates didn't mind. They thought it was all for the good of Telos. All part of the one truth. We got them doing pretty much everything. Research and development. Sales and marketing. Hell, they probably got your brother designing the goddamn website."

Piotr handed over the phone. It was street-level view of an office building, maybe ten storeys high. It had greyish cladding and the windows were small and there was a half-empty parking lot outside the front doors. It was flanked by a laminate flooring wholesaler on one side, and the Contractors State License Board on the other. The address read: 9815, Lot A1, Business Park Drive, Sacramento CA.

"That," said Piotr, "is Telos."

21

SHE STARED at the photograph until Troy snatched his phone back, and after that stared at the palm of her hand where the phone had been. Troy started laughing through a mouthful of Twinkie.

"I knew it," he said. "I said it. Didn't I say it? I mean, I said Upper East Side, but this is way better."

Piotr got up unsteadily and poured himself another drink. He went and drank it by the window, then scowled as if he'd seen something. He began scratching his tongue with his dirty fingernails.

"That's it?" said Vivian. "That's all Telos is?"

"You sound disappointed," said Piotr.

"In *Sacramento*!" cried Troy. "It's just too *good*!"

Vivian looked into the fire until the surface of her eyes seemed to dry and crisp. She felt unutterably bleak. The truth was this: she *was* disappointed. It had been nice to entertain the idea, however briefly, however ironically, that there really were answers somewhere up the mountain. That there really was a path she could follow that would bring her to something more meaningful than the life she was currently fumbling her way through. Even after the business at the Sanctuary, and the kidnapping, and Shelley, and the Carters, it was still a shame.

"Better than being dead," said Piotr, with his back to them.

"I don't know about that," said Troy. "You ever been to Sacramento?"

"What is your *problem*, boy?"

"I mean, it's no Crystal City, and that's being very generous."

"If your brother's there, he'll be okay. Physically, anyway."

As much as she wanted to believe that, it didn't tally with what Glenn had said, and it didn't tally with an unnameable feeling she had about Jesse and his whereabouts. A certainty that other, more naïve people might have put down to some empathic bond between twins, but which Vivian couldn't explain so easily.

"He's here, though. I'm sure." She stopped short of saying she could *feel* it. "Glenn definitely said he went up the mountain. He said he had, what was it... *truly ascended*."

"That's what they always say."

"Maybe he never made it to Sacramento. Maybe he stayed here."

"You think they give them a bus ticket and let them make their own way there? No, miss, someone will have made sure he got there."

"But they said they didn't know where he was. What if he got away from them, and came up here on his own?"

"Yikes," said Troy. "No offence, Viv, but I saw your brother and he was no mountaineer."

Piotr went back to staring out of the window. He buffed the dirty glass with the cuff of his shirt. Vivian came over. She couldn't see anything besides the reflection of the man's face, ghoulish in the firelight.

"Are you sure you haven't seen him?"

Piotr was scowling again.

"He's my age. My height. Looks... well, he looks like me."

"What the hell have I been smoking?" he said, loudly.

"Mr Blucas?"

He whirled around to look at Troy.

"You put some kind of special ingredient in that cigarette?"

Troy held up his hands in a gesture that could have been either a protest of innocence or an admission of guilt.

"Mr Blucas..."

"You seeing this? Am I going crazy?"

He pointed out of the window. Vivian came to his shoulder and peered up the mountain. From over the next ridge came a faint glow that looked like sunrise, though the day had only ended a couple of hours ago.

"I see it," said Vivian.

And then, the violet man. Just as Vivian remembered him, and just as Forrest had described him. He drifted like an *ignis fatuus* along the top of the ridge, and the trees showed up purple and black either side of him. He stopped and seemed to admire the view and then disappeared, leaving his glow behind him.

"Well," said Piotr, "this is a *fine* new piece of theatre."

"I've seen him before," said Vivian. She was already moving towards the door of the cabin.

"Your dad used to do this shit, you know. Wander the mountain in his purple robes just when the initiates happened to be having one of their meditation sessions. Then, ta-dah! Throwing more money at it these days, looks like."

"What is that?" said Troy. "Some kind of laser show?" Extricating himself from the bed seemed to take a lot of effort so he was just craning his neck.

Even if it was, Vivian wasn't going to let him go again. She left the window and started to fiddle with the latch on the door.

"What are you doing?" said Troy. "Cougar's still out there, Viv."

"It's him," she said.

"Who?"

She didn't answer that. She flung the door open and ran out into the chill darkness of the mountainside.

"You're going to get eaten," yelled Troy.

Vivian had no torch but the lingering haze from the violet man was enough for her to see her way. The going was steep. She hauled herself up between the trunks and the roots, dislodging small avalanches of earth and stones behind her. She was vaguely aware of Troy, or Mr Blucas, cursing in her wake – maybe the cougar, too – but she didn't stop and she didn't look back. When she reached the top of the ridge the violet figure came back into view, his head a little pink moon floating up and out of the trees. There was a kind of grace to the way he moved, as if he passed through the physical features of the mountain rather than around them. A fine piece of theatre, indeed.

She emerged from the treeline. It was freezing. The upper slopes of Mount Hookey looked scoured and blasted in the moonlight. The violet man was way, way ahead of her, almost at the point where the snow began.

She went down into a gully and began climbing the scree. She slipped every two or three steps but by now she was so cold she didn't even feel the sharp edges of the rocks when they met her palms. She only knew she was bleeding when she tried to sweep a strand of hair out of her eyes and ended up leaving a warm, sticky smear across her forehead.

In a minute or two the violet man was out of sight. Vivian straightened, looked up the mountain. She felt a sudden, dizzying surge of blood to her head, then toppled over onto her side and started sliding down the way she'd come.

The descent somehow lasted longer than the climb. She slipped and rolled past the point where she'd emerged from the trees, down into some lower portion of the gully. The landslide roared around her, throwing clouds of freezing white dust into her nose and mouth. Then her coat snagged on something and she stopped falling, and the avalanche diminished to a trickle of stones and then to silence. She lay on her back and looked up at the stars, and then up the mountain. The violet man was gone. She'd lost him, again.

She lay very still for some time. She saw the dark shapes of Piotr and Troy at the top of the gully. The echo of their voices seemed to reach her before the voices themselves, from the opposite side of the mountain. They began to slither down after her.

Vivian sat up and turned around to see what had broken her fall in the first place. Something was tangled in the drawstring of her hood. At first she thought it was a tree root, until she began to untangle the cord and felt the shape of the fingers, curved and hard as talons. She scrambled to her feet and fought to swallow whatever was coming up out of her.

She stared at the hand. At some point Troy appeared by her side.

"Jesus," he said. "Who is it?"

"I don't know."

She scanned about and saw more of the outline of the hand's owner among the fragments of rock. A shoulder, a knee, the toe of a shoe. A stiletto, looked like.

Piotr caught up last. He was less out of breath than Troy. He saw the body and grunted.

"There you go," he said quietly. "That's your dad's legacy." He sniffed. "My legacy. Poor stupid kid. I'm going back. I hope this is enough to convince you to do the same."

He made to leave but Vivian didn't move. She crouched down where the forearm projected up into the sky and began carefully clearing the rocks away from the rest of the body. Troy shone the torch of his phone. It picked out a string of brightly coloured beads, set against the dull, blue sheen of dead flesh. Vivian brushed gravel away from the face.

"Oh God," she said. "It's her."

"Who?"

"That woman. Eenoo, or whatever."

"From the trailer park!" There was a degree of excitement in

Troy's voice that made Vivian uncomfortable. "Well, fuck me."

"She's been up here before," said Piotr. "I've seen her."

Eenoo was no bigger than a child, curled up in masses of crystals and beaded jewellery and a huge fur coat. She had lost her hat somewhere in the fall. She looked mummified.

"I'm not staying up here," said Piotr. "You can do what you want. I've told you what I know."

Vivian stood up. She looked to the summit of the mountain again.

"What about the man?" she said.

"The *man?*"

"We all saw him."

"Have you lost your mind?" Piotr said. "Are you not seeing *this?*" He pointed at Eenoo's body.

"He might know about Jesse."

"He's a goddamn actor! It's a stupid magic show! Man's got LEDs in his pants or something!"

"I want to keep going."

"Then you do that, miss. But be prepared to end up like this one here."

He stared at her for a moment, waiting for her to change her mind. Troy was circling the body, taking pictures on his phone. He took a couple of himself, too, next to the body. Vivian could see him selecting filters and effects with great care.

She didn't say anything else. Piotr huffed and set off up the side of the gully.

"What do we do about her?" Troy shouted after him.

"Nothing," said Piotr over his shoulder. "Meat wagon will pick her up."

"Meat wagon?" said Vivian.

"It's been up here almost every night this week." He'd reached the top of the ridge and was nearly out of earshot when he stopped and called back to them. "You think that's the only body on the mountain right now?"

Vivian and Troy stood in silence on either side of Eenoo's shrivelled form. The wind scoured the mountainside and sent eddies of dust swirling around their feet. Troy was still snapping away, stopping occasionally to flex his fingers.

"This is *wild*," he said.

Vivian looked up the mountain. Back to the body. Back up the mountain. Why that urge to keep going? What was she hoping to find? Her father, up to his old tricks, in his purple dressing gown? No – they must have hired a new John of Telos to replace the dead one. But why do that at all? It seemed a ridiculously convoluted illusion to no discernible purpose. Unless they were deliberately *luring* initiates up to the summit? That seemed too sinister a motive, even for Telos – and besides, Glenn had tried to dissuade their students from going up the mountain on their own.

She thought about it for a minute or two, though there had never really been any doubt in her mind.

"I'm going to follow him," she said.

"You're what?"

"I'm going to keep going."

"Why? Didn't you hear what the old man said?"

She didn't reply.

"C'mon, Viv. We're on the same team, aren't we? You know this is all nonsense."

"I just have a feeling, you know—"

"Jesus, Viv, this is not the time for a Road to Damascus moment."

"It's difficult to explain."

Troy looked at her. He shone his torch directly in her face, and then back at his.

"I'm freezing," he said. "And I've got like seven per cent battery."

"You don't need to come with me."

She didn't *want* him to come with her, that was the truth. He seemed relieved.

"Well. If you must. I mean, I've got what I need." She wasn't sure what he meant by that. "And I'm not exactly equipped to strike for the summit." He pointed the torch beam at his huge sneakers. The rubber toe opened like the mouth of a puppet.

"Can I take your phone?" Vivian asked.

"Er." He stood awkwardly for a second and blew into his hands.

"For the torch."

"I think I might need that. To get down."

"Can I have the bag, then? With the food?"

He paused again.

"I guess so."

He slid his rucksack off his shoulders and handed it to Vivian. She hefted it and the bottles clinked inside.

"Oh wait," said Troy. "I should probably take those out." A slight pause. "Reduce the weight."

She undid the top of the bag and took one of the bottles out and handed it to him.

"What's in these?" she said.

He didn't answer, and went about slotting them carefully into the huge pockets of his jacket. He also took out a cigarette lighter that he'd left in the bag.

"Troy?"

He patted himself, then he looked up, satisfied.

"Good luck then, Viv. Don't know why you're doing this, but... well, I hope you find what you're looking for." She would have found him callous if she'd not been so desperate to be alone. "And if you don't," he added, "totally up for a road trip to Sacramento."

He gave her a strange one-armed hug, and she felt the bottles press against her ribs. He looked at Eenoo's body one last time and shook his head.

"Careful how you go, alright?" he said. "Page that old man in the motel if you're in trouble."

He turned and loped back to the edge of the forest, the same way Mr Blucas had gone, the beam of his torch a few feet in front of him. He clinked all the way along the top of the ridge. Once he was out of sight, Vivian rubbed her hands together and found a weirdly slick residue on her fingertips. She sniffed at them and wasn't totally surprised to find that the bottles had been filled with petrol, and that Troy was looking for a kind of closure all his own.

22

VIVIAN LEFT Eenoo where she was. It didn't feel right to be shovelling rocks back on top of her, now she'd been discovered. She was in enough trouble as it was after the incident with Glenn, and the last thing she wanted to be doing was dragging bodies around the mountainside and getting prints and fibres all over the deceased. Best to leave the scene untouched, she thought. Or at least, best not touch the scene any more than she already had.

The gully was obviously not the safest way up the mountain, so she looked for another route. She didn't need Troy's phone after all. There were stars and most of a full moon, and above her the peak looked like some vast and intricately sculpted dessert. The ribs and roots of the mountain were thrown into sharp relief, and it was to these that she was drawn. She managed to claw her way out of the gully onto a bright saddle of rock where the going was narrow but at least firm underfoot.

Vivian was a few hundred feet above Eenoo's body when she heard the gurgle of a diesel engine. The wind was stronger up here and she strained to listen. It was distant, but not so far away to be coming from town. The noise was followed by a spot of bright artificial light that suggested, at first, that Troy had come back with his torch.

The light moved with some ease over the fractured terrain of the mountain, in time with the spurts of engine noise. It swept the landscape like a searching eye. A spotlight, fixed to the back of some kind of vehicle.

Vivian huddled behind an outcrop and thrust her hands deep into her pockets. Not even two coats could keep out the wind's savagery up here. The spotlight cast its gaze once or twice in her direction, and she sat motionless in the pool of shadow it cast. The truck came close enough for her to smell its exhaust and hear the irregularities in the cadence of its engine, and then it rolled into view in the gully below her. The spotlight rested on Eenoo's tiny body.

Two men hopped out of the cab – she recognised neither – and wordlessly hauled the corpse out of the rockslide and threw it in the back of the truck. Its elbows clanged against the sides of the flatbed. Then they got back in their seats and went on their way.

Vivian watched the meat wagon until it was out of sight over the next ridge. It made no more stops, which she supposed was a good thing. How many more had there been, over the years? And where had they been taken? Were Jesse, and Nathan Carter, and everyone else waiting to be discovered in some abandoned quarry somewhere?

The violet man would know. The violet man could answer everything. She was sure of that, sure in a way that she hadn't been about anything for a very long time. It was a childlike certainty; the kind of certainty she used to feel about her parents, that whatever trouble she was in they would be there for her, no question, and could make it all better.

Strong winds made for a treacherous ascent. Vivian went very slowly, sometimes on all fours, testing every foot placement three or four times before trusting her weight to it. After maybe an hour's climbing the terrain levelled out into a boulder field covered with patches of snow that had melted and refrozen, iron-hard. There was no sign of him. In the time she'd taken to get up here he could have passed right over the summit and started down the other side. Perhaps the meat wagon had picked him up, too.

She saw it when she was facing in the opposite direction. A faint rose-glow only detectable on the fringes of her vision. It came from a cleft in the rock where the boulder field met an icebound, unassailably steep face that went all the way to the summit of the mountain. She went on, over the broken ground. The refrozen snow patches were nearly fatal, polished to a high sheen by the wind, some deceptively thin and disguising deep crevices that could instantly break a leg or an arm.

The light from inside the cave grew more distinct. Vivian was drawn onwards and found herself under the cliff face and out of the wind. She reached the opening in the rock and saw outside a handful of initiate rods arranged upright in the snow like punji sticks. Things hung from them, the spoils of some primitive cannibal. She recognised those things. A fleece, a pair of unfashionable trainers, a baseball cap emblazoned with the words "Surf's Up!" and a picture of a dog in sunglasses riding a surfboard. She saw the design clearly under the snow crust, and her heart made one huge beat and then seemed to stop completely.

She went inside. It was quiet and suddenly, impossibly warm. She heard voices ahead – no, a single voice, a woman's, and one that by now she knew very well.

"I brought you some books from your room," Judy was saying. "I didn't know which ones you wanted so I just got a selection. You like the chair? Better than being on the ground, all dirty and freezing."

Silence.

"I don't know how long I can do this for. Everyone's talking about you. More and more people coming up here every day. Some people, they don't know the mountain so well, and you know, well, they're getting into trouble."

There was still no reply, but Vivian felt, with that same unshakeable certainty, another presence in the recesses of the cave.

"So maybe, I was thinking – and I know it's not my place, Telos forgive me, what with you being the Ascended Master and all –

maybe you could, you know, *show me the way*, and I can pass on your teachings, and then, well, you wouldn't need to be here, would you?"

Vivian saw Judy's shadow waver in the violet light. She seemed nervous.

"Shiv's just going to keep looking. And your sister. Oh my stars, I don't even know what they did with your sister."

Vivian's heart started painfully and she pushed through to where the cave widened, catching and tearing the sleeve of her coat on the rock. Judy turned and gasped. She was wearing several layers of robes, her sacred drum, and a woollen hat with earflaps that somehow contained all her hair.

Jesse was sitting on a foldable chair in the middle of the cave. Pulsing. Irradiated. Angelic. He was wearing shorts and a T-shirt, but the violet light seemed to pass through them almost unhindered, just leaving the silhouette of the sports logo on his chest. Vivian looked at him and her first thought was: his posture is better.

"No, miss," said Judy, holding up her hands as if to shield him. "No, no, no, you can't be here. You can't have him. I am so sorry, for what they did, but you *cannot* have him."

Vivian looked past her.

"It's me, Jesse," she said. "It's Vivian."

He angled his head slightly to look at her, and his face seemed a bright, expressionless vacuum.

"What are you doing?" she said, and her voice sounded very loud, and the words somehow clumsy when put next to his serenity. She waved a hand vaguely in his direction. "How are you doing this?"

Judy made a squawking laugh.

"You think he's just going to come right out and *tell* you? You think he'll just give up the secrets of Telos like *that?*" She tried to snap her fingers under her mittens. "Miss, I know he's your brother, and I am sorry for misleading you, but there's just no way you can understand what's going on here."

Jesse still made no reply. He seemed not to recognise his sister at all. Vivian's eyes prickled.

"What's wrong with him?" she said.

"Miss, there is nothing wrong with your brother. Really, *nothing*. I mean that very literally, with Telos as my witness. There is nothing wrong, and everything right. Are you hearing what I'm saying?"

"I hear it. I don't understand it."

"Jesse has *ascended*. Jesse has seen Telos. I mean, he has really *been* there. He has visited the Crystal City and has spoken with the Telurian Elders and he *knows*."

"Knows what?"

"Everything! More than knows! He has gone *beyond* knowing into pure *being*."

Vivian blinked a couple of times but had nothing to say to that. She looked at her brother again, sitting perfectly still, perfectly upright, his features showing – if anything at all – a very vague curiosity. Just the spectacle of him was incredible. So, what was it? LEDs woven into his clothes, like Piotr had said? Some kind of phosphorescent face paint? Maybe they were things you could buy from the Sanctuary gift shop, another little tributary of the Telos Inc. revenue stream.

"Does he speak?"

"Well now, miss, he's not on our plane anymore so—"

"He doesn't need to, right, right. Communicates through violet waves or something."

"How'd you know that?"

Vivian took another step towards Jesse. She wanted, more than ever in her life, to throw her arms around him, to cuddle him like a baby. But there was also something unsettling – more than that, frightening, unknown, unknowable – about the way he looked now.

The receptionist made a half-hearted attempt to block her.

"Now, I've told you, you can't have him. Shiv can't have him. No one can have him."

Vivian ignored her again.

"Jesse, stop this," she said to her brother. "I mean it."

She was doing her mothering voice, the one she sometimes used at home, as if that might reaffirm their old relationship. She was always the one who looked after him – *properly* looked after him, as opposed to her parents, who simply paid for his therapists and sometimes bought him a mindfulness colouring book or a model sailing boat to dismantle.

"Jesse, this is stupid."

"You do *not* speak to an Ascended Master like that!" snapped Judy.

It's okay, said Jesse, and Judy put her hand over her chest and backed up against the cave wall and looked like she was having a heart attack.

The voice was recognisably her brother's, but also not recognisably human, and though he'd only said a couple of syllables they seemed not to match the movements of his bright, violet mouth. Judy continued a long, violent gasp that sounded like a sink draining, her drum clattering against the rocks behind her. Vivian waited for Jesse to say something else; waited for his light to go out, for his spine to bow into its customary curve, for his voice to reclaim its slightly infuriating nasal whine. A long time passed, but none of these things happened.

She's right, said Jesse.

"Who's right? About what?"

She took steps left, right, forward, trying different angles to gauge whether it was, in fact, her brother. Of course it was. His Surf's Up! cap was on a punji stick outside, the same one she'd bought him on their holiday to Santa Cruz, nearly fifteen years ago. Santa Cruz! It was only a day's drive away. Had their father come to Mount Hookey then, too? Had that been a business trip? She couldn't remember him spending much time with them at the beach…

I figured it out, said Jesse.

"Figured what out?"

All of it, he said.

Another long silence.

"I don't know what you mean by that," said Vivian. Why was she speaking so quietly? Her mothering voice had evaporated entirely. She had the feeling she was in church, addressing some higher power.

"Tell us!" said the receptionist, suddenly, breathlessly. "Show us the way!"

It's not what you think, said Jesse.

Still Vivian tried to read the expression on his face but found nothing. He seemed neither happy nor sad. Seemed beyond those things, in some way. Seemed to be sitting at a great distance from her, even though he was physically only a few feet away.

"How are you doing this?" she said. "With the light?"

I figured it out, he said again.

"Figured what out?"

The thing.

Vivian remembered the scraps of paper she'd found in his jacket. "What thing?"

The thing I was looking for. The thing everyone is looking for.

"He means the Crystal City," said Judy.

It's difficult to explain.

"Well, I need you to explain," said Vivian. "What will I tell Mum? Did you think of her? I've come a long way for you, Jesse. And this is all…" She looked around the cave and then back at the blank, radiant orb of her brother's head. "I'm frightened. You are frightening me."

Don't be.

"Then tell me what the hell's going on."

I can show you, he said.

"Yes!" said Judy, now almost prostrate on the floor of the cave. "Show us! *Show us!*"

Jesse considered this for a moment. He looked at his sister.

"Alright, then," she said. "But if this is some kind of prank…"

It isn't, he said.

She believed him. It didn't seem at all likely. Jesse had been a perennially serious child, and not the pranking sort at all.

He nodded and then got up and made to leave the cave. His steps were deliberate, poised. Vivian watched and didn't recognise him. She missed his clumsy flat-footedness. He both was and was not who he seemed to be – the kind of impostor she sometimes met in her sleep.

"Oh my stars!" said Judy, also getting to her feet. She was still barely able to catch her breath. "Oh my goodness gracious! Miss, he is showing us the way! The way to Telos! Oh my heart!" She ran after Jesse, then stopped, came back, folded up his chair. "Shall I bring this? What about the books?"

Jesse kept going, out onto the frozen mountain. He was still in his shorts and T-shirt – barefoot, too – but seemed not to notice. He picked his way gracefully over the boulder field, with Vivian slipping and tripping and grazing her knees some way behind him. When she was close enough, she scrutinised his skinny body for wires, battery packs, paint smears. She saw nothing of the sort, and the longer she spent in his light, the more she considered the possibility that Piotr had been wrong, and Troy had been wrong, and this was no piece of theatre, and while that made no sense whatsoever she had no choice but to keep following her brother and lean into the dream.

23

WHEN THEY reached the edge of the gully where she'd found Eenoo,
Jesse stopped and looked down. Vivian stood beside him, a little apart.

"I've got your coat, by the way," she said. "If you want it."

He didn't. He wasn't even shivering.

"Where's this thing, then? Somewhere up here?"

He just stared down the mountain.

"Can you give me a clue?"

It's difficult to explain, Jesse said again, and didn't move. Vivian
waited a minute or two.

"What are you thinking?" she asked.

I'm not, he said. *I don't.*

Judy finally caught up. She'd had trouble keeping her balance
with the drum strapped to her back.

Jesse had obviously heard it before Vivian – or, perhaps, had had
some sort of extrasensory premonition – because at the bottom of
the scree slope appeared the meat wagon again, shuddering over the
uneven ground with its spotlight.

"Oh dear," said Judy. "Oh no. That'll be Shiv's boys. They see you,
they'll take you away in the back of that thing."

"You know about this?"

"Do I! Poor Shiv can't catch a break."

"Poor Shiv?" said Vivian. "There's a dead woman down there."

"I know. Such a shame."

"It's a bit more than a shame."

"It's their own choice to come up the mountain, miss. He tries to

213

stop them. That's the rule. You're not allowed up here until you're ready. But they try anyways." She looked at Jesse and her eyes reflected him, teary from the cold or perhaps a deep spiritual love. "Who wouldn't, if they knew he was here?"

"I don't think this is Jesse's fault."

"If I may be frank with you, there's no other reason they're coming up here. That's why Shiv wants him. He's causing a lot of headaches back in Sacramento..."

"You know about Sacramento, too?"

"I know about the *earthly* Telos, yes."

"Shiv told you that?"

"Shiv doesn't tell me anything. Not intentionally, at least."

At first, Vivian had trouble understanding the weird doublethink this required the receptionist to perform – to see behind the curtain, and to know the essential falseness of Telos, and yet to buy into it anyway. But then, she thought, Judy seemed exactly who Telos was aimed at. Wealthy and dissatisfied and, if the glimpses of her marriage were anything to go by, lonely as hell. And watching her now, basking in Jesse's reflected light, she obviously thought her faith had paid off.

Jesse himself turned and went along the ridge, and his words drifted, bell-like, behind him.

There's another way, he said. Vivian didn't know whether this was meant to be a straightforward comment about their route down the mountain, or something more cryptic.

The drone of the truck came and went. It sounded busy. Jesse led them around the edge of the boulder field and appeared to be heading back up the mountain. They reached a plateau which was split by what Vivian could only describe as a chasm, a dreadful seam of black even in the moonlight.

Jesse descended into it without a word.

"Jesse?" Vivian called after him. "Are you sure?"

He wandered away from her. She had memories of them trying to navigate Oxford Street during the height of Christmas shopping, she constantly steering him away from the bright lights and dark alleyways and still somehow losing him every five minutes. What a long time ago that was, now. Had it even happened?

This is the way, said Jesse, from inside the abyss.

The caves wormed their way blindly into the mountain but Jesse knew every fissure and tunnel, and always moved with an assurance that Vivian thought so foreign to him. She herself was no spelunker, and found the experience wildly disorientating.

The only person who spoke was Judy. She continued muttering under her breath, and occasionally got excited and said things out loud, like, "We're close! Oh boy, are we close! I can feel it. Can you feel it?"

Vivian ignored her and fished around in Troy's bag for something to eat. So strong, that smell of petrol! How had she not noticed it before? She found a box of cereal and ate it awkwardly with one hand as she clambered around the rocks, since Jesse wasn't slowing or stopping. She offered some to Judy, hoping it might stop her speaking.

"No thank you, miss," she said. "Shiv and me, we only eat organic. Well, I do. I'm trying to encourage Shiv but he's got a lot to think about. Anyways. I don't want to enter Telos weighed down with a lot of toxins. Maybe you should think about that, too."

Vivian finished the packet in the darkness.

"Shiv's your husband, then."

"Twenty-five years, now."

"And he's in charge. Right?"

"Only since last year. He got a promotion." Then she whispered, "His boss *passed on*."

"Yeah," said Vivian. "I know."

"You know?"

"Your husband had me kidnapped. Did he tell you that?"

"Oh, kidnapped, what a lot of phooey!"

"I think they were planning on killing me. Glenn and the other one."

"Well, if that's true, that's on Glenn's conscience, not Shiv's."

"But everyone works for Shiv, right? He must call the shots."

Judy stopped briefly. Jesse continued into the labyrinth and the place got darker still.

"My husband may not be perfect, but I'll have you know he has deep Eastern wisdom. His parents were from Rishikesh. Do you know Rishikesh?"

Vivian shook her head.

"It's in India. Do you know India?"

"Yes."

"Rishikesh is energetically *very* significant. Shiv, he's got that energy, in spades. He'd be an Ascended Master by now, if he wanted to be. But someone's got to look after the earthly side of the business, don't they? Who do you think orders all the crystals? Gets the books printed? Who deals with the indemnity forms and the NDAs and the insurance and taxes? The IRS tried to shut us down last year! The whole programme! And if anyone gets a whiff of this business with the initiates, coming up the mountain when they're nowhere *near* ready, then we'll be in a whole lot more trouble. So yes, sometimes he has to get his hands dirty, for the good of the family. I'm not saying I always agree. But it is what it is."

"Was that it? He was worried I'd find Jesse's body?"

"What's that? No, miss, you're misunderstanding me. He knew Jesse wasn't dead. He wanted you to tell him where Jesse was. He thought you knew."

"Oh," said Vivian. "And you didn't want to tell him?"

Judy looked longingly at Jesse, who was some way ahead of them now.

"No I did not," said Judy. "It's bad enough I let slip I'd seen him at all. See, Shiv doesn't believe that Jesse has *truly* ascended. At first he was worried that your brother had just wandered off and was going to give a whole load of Telurian secrets to the papers... Then I told him I'd seen him up the mountain. Looking like he does. All that gorgeous light! Now he's worried that this is some kind of game your brother is playing. If Shiv gets his hands on Jesse, well, I don't know what he'll do. Take him away from here, that's for sure. He's got some temper, you see. He's not at all happy with the trouble Jesse's been causing. But *look* at him, Vivian! If that isn't an Ascended Master, I don't know what is!"

"Why didn't you tell me where he was? When I first got here?"

Judy shrugged her drum.

"Same reason. I didn't want you taking him away from me. And all your posters... The world and his wife would've been up here looking for him! He belongs here, miss. He belongs on the mountain. And if I may be so bold, he belongs to me. I found him." She paused. "Wait, you're not still hoping to take him home with you, are you?"

Vivian watched her brother. He was climbing a ledge and slithering around on the flowstone like some luminous axolotl. She had no idea what she was planning on doing with him.

Judy kept pestering her about her intentions but she just murmured something about getting left behind and went on. The air became colder and fresher and she began to see patches of indigo, like trails of spilled ink, in the cave ceiling. The odd star. They heard the sound of rushing water. Jesse climbed down, momentarily out of sight, and they followed him into an icy underground stream, nearly waist-deep, that sapped what little feeling remained in Vivian's hands and feet. Judy thrashed and gasped in the darkness. Her drum finally detached itself from her back and bobbed through the water where Jesse stood glowing.

"Oh my," said Judy, still unable to catch her breath. "Oh dear. Won't I need that in the Crystal City? Jesse?"

Jesse waded on ahead. The river got shallower and the cave opened up and he emerged onto a stony shoal. They were back below the trees. His body illuminated the thick, wrinkled trunks of the cedars. Vivian smelled mulch and earth.

"I don't understand," said Judy. "We're not in the mountain. Are you sure this is the way? I'm sorry, I know it's not my place to question, but..."

This is the way, said Jesse.

He was waiting on the river bank, unperturbed by the fact that he was wet through and the air temperature wasn't much above zero. Vivian didn't know what time it was, but it must have been nearly dawn.

She came and stood beside him while Judy caught up, and still couldn't think of anything to say, settling on a completely unsatisfactory, "Are you okay?"

I'm okay, said Jesse.

The words echoed strangely, even though they were no longer in the cave. Vivian listened carefully to him. There seemed a layer of deep silence around him. She couldn't even hear him breathing.

"This thing—" she said.

I wrote it down.

"But you can't just tell me."

No.

"But it's words?"

Not really.

"A picture?"

Not really.

"Then what is it?"

A shape.

"What kind of shape?"

It's difficult to describe. It describes itself, if you know what I mean.

"You're frightening me again, Jesse."

You'll understand when you see it. It's simple. I figured it out.

She looked at him, bewildered. Another memory came back to her. Jesse, at the dinner table again, staring a hole in his mashed potato and occasionally scribbling something in a notepad, or if there was no paper, just scratching it into the varnish of the tabletop. A frown so deep it made him look not quite human. The answer always the same when she or her parents or the help asked him what was wrong: "Just trying to figure something out." How old had he been then? Seven or eight? His whole life had been one long figuring out.

"Are you going to come home?" said Vivian. "After you've shown me the thing, obviously."

Why? he said.

"Because I miss you. Mum misses you."

Okay, he said, but it seemed he cared neither one way nor the other.

"Don't you want to come home?"

I don't want anything anymore, he said.

Vivian didn't know what to say to that. As soon as Judy arrived he started wandering away from her again.

"We're outside again," said Judy. "Why are we outside? Do you not think I'm ready? I was so sure I was ready! Is it because I lost the drum? Jesse?"

Nobody replied.

The sun came up not long afterwards. It lit the forest gold and green and the mountain seemed to Vivian more beautiful than any tacky pink Crystal City that Judy might have been looking for. The river tumbled over a series of waterfalls and at the bottom of one they found Judy's drum lying on its side in an eddy. She tried to retrieve it with a stick but only succeeded in poking it further under the water.

They followed the river through its various cascades and meanderings. Vivian didn't know what side of the mountain they were on, but Jesse still seemed quite sure of where they were going. Judy kept looking wistfully at the rapids, hoping, no doubt, that her sacred instrument might bob to the surface somewhere she could retrieve it. She'd gone very quiet.

The river eventually emptied into a black pool about the size of a tennis court, ringed around with trees. It was still and deep and oily and there was a smell about it that seemed more offensive than just stagnant water or rotting vegetation. Jesse stopped on the edge. Vivian wondered whether he had meant to bring them to this specific spot. They waited. Then they heard it again: the deep-throated rumble of an engine with a lot of horsepower.

Jesse withdrew slightly into the forest. Vivian, too. He seemed less incandescent in the daylight, but there was still no answer to how he was doing it at all. Apart from the answer he had given. The Answer, with a capital "A".

"Do you think they saw us?" said Vivian. "I mean, up on the mountain? They can't have followed us. Right? Judy?"

Judy was some way behind them, looking despondent. She shrugged.

The noise of the truck got louder and Vivian saw it emerge on the far side of the pool, nose-first, like an animal at a watering hole. She and Judy ducked down. It performed a series of awkward three-point turns between the trees until it was able to reverse down to the edge of the water. There was a hiss of pneumatics and the bed of the truck was raised to a forty-five-degree angle and its cargo slid and tumbled out the back. Vivian watched the bodies of Eenoo and three others she didn't recognise hit the surface of the water and disappear almost instantly.

She turned to Judy.

"Sure," she said, "deep Eastern wisdom."

24

THEY TOOK the same overgrown logging road the truck had arrived on and followed it till it met a highway that might have been the 55, though Vivian wasn't sure. Jesse went on silently. He had nothing to say about what they'd all seen. His feet made no noise on the weed-cracked asphalt. Vivian and Judy followed, a pair of ragged disciples. The receptionist was sobbing quietly at the back, ashamed of the scene at the lake, or disappointed by the absence of the Crystal City, or missing her drum, or perhaps just bone-tired like Vivian was.

Three bends in the road and things became familiar. They crossed the creek that led to Piotr Blucas's cabin and came up through the forest and then Vivian saw it, the unhappy bear with his neon sign, and the western corner of the Cedar Lodge Motel. He was taking them back to room 29. Vivian was absolutely certain of that.

It couldn't have been eight a.m. yet and the streets were quiet, at least at this end of town. No one saw them as they crossed the parking lot and entered the lobby. Inside, Jerome and Minnie were asleep on the sofa. Jesse's radiance lit their faces and the furniture and they both seemed to give easy, childlike smiles and stirred slightly. Seeing Jesse in this setting, surrounded by normal things, forced another recalibration in Vivian's brain. No writing it off as her imagination when it was combined with the stink of cigarettes, and cheap furnishings, and the lines and grey hairs that belonged to the Carters. Yes. The light was real, or none of it was real.

She thought, briefly, that she might speak to Jerome and get him to report what they'd seen up the mountain to his police contacts. But her brother wasn't stopping, and the thing, the answer, was waiting for her. Besides, she'd have to tell Jerome and Minnie that there was a chance their son was decomposing at the bottom of a stagnant lake, and she wasn't sure she was ready to have that conversation yet.

Troy wasn't there.

"Who's been watching reception?" said Judy, and nobody replied, and this started her crying again.

Vivian followed her brother through the double doors and up the steps, the same way she'd come on the morning she'd checked in.

"It's in your room, isn't it?" she said. "The thing."

Yes, he said.

"I have the key!" said Judy, hurrying up the stairs behind them. Jesse answered by producing his own from his pocket. That was two of them, then. And the third, who had that? Mr Blucas?

"I don't understand," said Judy. She sounded more despondent than ever. "Why didn't you tell me you wanted something from your room? I could have brought it up for you. You didn't need to come back here."

Jesse turned the key to room 29 and opened the door and stepped inside. He didn't need to turn on the light. The glow from his flesh showed up the walls and furniture, as far as could be seen. For the most part, the room was filled – to the ceiling in some areas – with towering piles of books and papers. Vivian went in after him. She inspected the spines of the books and recognised titles from her conversation with her mother. Perhaps one in four of them were part of the Telos imprint. The rest were a mixture of self-help, spirituality, theology and quantum mechanics. Marcus Aurelius' *Meditations*, next to Feynman's lectures, next to J. B. Purelight's *The Healing Power of Dogs*. Hundreds of them, all well-thumbed and annotated and divided up with bookmarks and coloured Post-It notes.

"These all yours, Jesse?" said Vivian.

He didn't answer.

"What were you doing in here?"

"What do you *think* he was doing?" said Judy. She was starting to sound ratty.

"You knew about all this? And you put me in the room next door?"

Why hadn't she made more of an effort to get in? She needn't have bothered looking for the key. The walls in the motel were so thin she could have just put a fist through from her room into his.

Jesse manoeuvred through the maze he'd built for himself until he reached the desk in the far corner. He stopped and looked around as if he'd lost something, and he cast kaleidoscopic shapes and blotches onto the walls, and, just to add to the general trippiness of the space, his room also had some complexly patterned wallpaper, its design fibrous and spider-webby and more conducive to madness than mindfulness, Vivian thought.

Jesse opened the drawer in the desk and shut it again. The desktop itself was curiously empty. The kettle had gone. The TV was also missing, and the bracket that had once attached it to the wall.

"What is it?" asked Vivian. "Jesse?"

"*Shush!*" said Judy. "Why must you keep *bothering* him?"

He still didn't reply.

The room was close and stuffy and the light was odd. It reminded Vivian of when she'd had the flu, as a child. She'd been confined to her bedroom for five days, waking and sleeping in a persistent, feverish twilight. Figures who may or may not have been her parents materialising at the foot of her bed with water and boiled sweets, their voices coming to her from some other dimension. That same feeling she had now – that she'd had pretty much since she'd arrived – of being unable to distinguish what was a dream from what wasn't.

She put down the book she was idly thumbing – *Mein Leiben,*

Meine Weltansicht, all in German, its margins crammed with more text than the body of each page – and took a couple of paces towards him. From this distance she saw that the pattern on the walls did not repeat. In fact, it wasn't a pattern at all. It was all tiny numbers and letters from the Greek alphabet, interspersed with brackets and mathematical functions and symbols she didn't recognise. Thousands of equations, or perhaps just one enormous equation, or perhaps not an equation at all, perhaps the scrawlings of a madman. Vivian had only studied mathematics as far as GCSE and as far as she was concerned she could have been looking at the runes Judy had used to embellish her posters, or the "sacred geometry" Forrest had talked about non-stop back at the Sanctuary. As well as the symbols and numbers, Jesse had written notes to himself in the same minuscule handwriting. They were like the notes she'd found in his coat. Some were very simple. *Try cutting out sugar,* said one. Another said: *renormalisation group running of the three gauge couplings in the Standard Model does not meet at EXACTLY same point if hypercharge is normalised so that it is consistent with SU(5) or SO(10) GUTs i.e. GUT groups which lead to a simple fermion unification.*

She was aware, from a curious warmth in the back of her head, of her brother standing behind her.

It's not here, he said.

Vivian turned and had to squint in the glare that came from his forehead.

"What's not here?"

The thing, he said. *I wrote it down, and now it's not here.*

She looked again at all of his wild annotations and calculations.

"And you say it's, what, a shape?"

Yes. It's the *shape.*

"And this shape is, like, a spiritual thing? Or a scientific, quantum-physics-type thing?"

Both.

"Both."

There's no difference. They're the same. It's all the same. It's all one thing. You'll understand when you see it. He paused. *Only it's not here.*

"Where did you write it? Or draw it? Or whatever."

He put his thumbs and forefingers together. *On a circle.*

"Of paper?"

Yes.

"The thing they put the glasses on?"

"Oh, *please*," said Judy.

Yes, said Jesse.

Vivian felt herself trying to smile. It had been a long time since that had happened. It manifested as a dull ache at the corners of her mouth.

"All this, Jesse," she said, gesturing at the walls and the books and the sheaves of paper, "and you wrote the answer on the back of a coaster?"

"Why are you smiling?" said Judy, and her voice was shrill with desperation. "*Where's the coaster?*"

Vivian looked at them both. She had a pretty good idea where it was. She heard a door opening down at the other end of the motel. Someone roused by Judy's screeching. Soon afterwards, a clanging of feet on the steps that led up from the lobby. Urgent muttering, something about someone never bothering to use a comb.

Judy and Vivian turned to look at the door and saw Shelley on one side, with Chason strapped to her chest, Jerome on the other. Minnie hobbled in between them to complete the triptych. A few moments of mute incomprehension passed, then a gasp, then a lot of talking.

"It's him! It's really him!"

"Vivian? That you?"

"Decided to wake up, did you? *Great job* watching reception."

"What is this? Some kind of shenanigan?"

"Should we call a doctor? Sir, are you sick?"

"No, he's not *sick*, for goodness sake."

"Where's Nathan?"

"I can't believe it's really him. *Is* it him?"

"Oh yes, dear, did you find Nathan?"

"I don't understand what I'm seeing here."

"Did you take a coaster from this room?"

"We haven't taken anything, please just calm down, ma'am."

"Did you see Nathan at *all*?"

Vivian didn't contribute to any of this. The questions and accusations and counteraccusations reached a chaotic pitch before she stepped in.

"Can you drive us to the end of Vista?" Vivian asked.

"Who?" said Jerome. "Me?"

"Anyone," she said.

"Now, just hold on a second—"

"I haven't seen Nathan," said Vivian. "I don't know where he is. He might be in Sacramento. He might be..." In her mind's eye she saw the bodies flopping heavily into the lake, their descent marked by a quiet gurgling. "I don't know. I did find Jesse, though. This – this is Jesse. I don't know why he looks like this. He found something out, and the thing did this to him, and the thing is somewhere down that turning at the end of Vista. In Mr Blucas's place. On a coaster. I think."

More silence followed.

"I don't understand," said Jerome.

"I don't understand either," said Vivian, "but I'd appreciate the ride. I can tell you about the mountain and about Nathan on the way."

"Well, alright," said Jerome. "But—"

"Now, hold on," said Judy. "We can't *all* go to Telos, can we? This isn't fair. This isn't *fair*! I found him! I should be the one to go. I've had enough of all this, Jesus, I've had enough, I want *out*. I'm so *tired*, I can't *take* it anymore…"

She descended into gibbering and Minnie came forward and put a consoling arm around her. Vivian pushed ahead and left the room, and this time Jesse followed her. Shelley and Jerome parted in silence, awe on one side, confusion on the other.

"No Troy?" Vivian asked.

Shelley stared and stared.

"Shelley? Did Troy come back?"

She blinked and came to.

"Oh. Yes. Bless you. He came back late last night. But he went off again."

"Where?"

"I don't know. Said he had some things to do."

They all trooped down to the Carters' Buick. Jerome got behind the wheel and started the engine but had nowhere to go. Nobody knew what to do with Jesse. The four women stood around the car in a loose semicircle, until Minnie opened the passenger-side door and gestured inside.

"You take it, dear," she said.

Vivian climbed in the back. Minnie helped Shelley into the middle, then Judy, and then got in herself. Vivian looked around the interior of the Buick. Seven of them, including Chason, still strapped to his mother's chest. It was very tight.

"Wait, we don't all need to go."

"That's what I was saying!" said Judy.

"I'll follow wherever your brother leads us," said Shelley.

"I've got to drive," said Jerome.

"I've got to keep an eye on Jerome," said Minnie.

The car was moving before she'd even shut the door. They pulled out of the motel and headed into town. Jerome had his window open so he could lean on one elbow, away from Jesse. One eye was half-closed in the violet light, and he kept glancing to the right and making the Buick swerve.

"You might want to buckle up, boy," Jerome said, and Jesse just stared straight ahead. "You sure he's okay?" he said to Vivian, over his shoulder.

I'm okay, said Jesse.

"They dress you up like this? The cult, I mean?"

"Please watch the road, Jerome!" said Minnie.

"What is it, some kind of make-up?"

Nothing from Jesse this time.

"I don't think it is," said Vivian.

"I saw something like that once," Jerome continued. "At a carnival in Carson City. I was just a kid. They said they had a real, honest-to-God angel in one of the tents, who'd crash-landed in the desert or something." Vivian saw him frown and shake his head, as if the memory still brought him disappointment. "Turned out it was just some special paint and a couple of spotlights. I saw him behind one of the trucks when the carnival was packing up. Just a regular guy. He was trying to get a feel of one of the lady acrobats."

"Oh, Jerome, please," said his wife.

"Still had some of that paint on his ear."

"It's not *paint*," said Minnie.

"Then what is it?"

"I don't know. Maybe they're into all of that – what's it called? – *genetics* stuff. Maybe they've been experimenting on him." She stuck her head between the two front seats. "Jesse, dear, did they do a, you know, science experiment on you? Honey?"

No, said Jesse.

"How do you feel?"

I don't feel anything.

Didn't think, didn't want, didn't feel. Just what were they going to find on the back of that coaster, Vivian thought. And did she want to find it at all?

"Oh," said Minnie. "Well. At least you're not sick. Don't you want a jacket?"

No, said Jesse.

She turned to Vivian, tried to look at her over the three other heads that were between them. "You found him up the mountain? Like this?"

Vivian nodded.

"Just walking around?"

"More or less."

"But no one else?"

"No." She saw the vision of the bodies again. "I mean… no."

"But Nathan might be… where? San Francisco, did you say?"

"Sacramento."

Shelley, who'd been watching Jesse in a trancelike state since they'd got in the car, suddenly straightened up and blinked. Chason opened his eyes, too.

"Sacramento," she said. "That's where Troy said he was going."

She went back to gazing at Jesse. Chason looked around as if unsure of where he was, and his huge, brown eyes were drawn back to the purple glow from the front seat. He was the calmest Vivian had ever seen him.

25

VISTA STREET was still virtually deserted. One of Mount Hookey's regular citizens – though, of course, you could never *tell* they were regular until you started talking to them – was checking his mailbox. Someone opened the door of the video rental store and stood on the step with a cigarette. No inkling of what was in the car, or what was up the mountain, or what was written on a coaster somewhere in Mr Blucas's archives.

They were coming up on Shelley and Troy's house when Vivian heard sirens and saw three police cars appear in the rear-view mirror. Jerome glanced up.

"Jesus, would you look at that. Years without even visiting the place, and now they're behaving like it's goddamn *Miami Vice*."

"Did you call them?" said Vivian.

"I told them about the vandalism, is all. Look at it!" They happened to be just passing the graffitied front of what had been the House of Telos. "Don't know why they need their sirens on, anyhow."

They kept on to the end of the road. Vivian looked over her shoulder. The police cars didn't stop outside Shelley's house. They caught up with the Buick and one of them curved around in front with a squeal of tyres. Jerome slammed on the brakes.

"God*damn* it! What is this?"

The other two squad cars pulled up behind their rear bumper. The doors of the car in front opened and a pair of police officers stepped out and adjusted their belts.

"Jerome?" said Minnie. "What did you tell them?"

Vivian had a premonition.

The first officer was a young man with a young face, but he had a kind of middle-aged fatness around his waist. He had a healthy crop of pimples, too, and it seemed he couldn't yet grow a beard thick enough to conceal them, though he was trying. He approached Jerome's window, studied Jesse for a long time, then peered past his shoulder to see Vivian squeezed into the back seat.

"Glad you boys came," said Jerome. "Was beginning to think this place wasn't on any of your maps."

Vivian relaxed slightly to hear him speak like that. An ex-sheriff was a good card to have in the deck.

The officer wasn't convinced. He leaned forwards to get a better look at Jesse. The top button of his shirt was undone, and Vivian saw, hanging from his neck, a purple crystal shard.

"I need you all to step out of the car," he said.

"I think there's been a mix-up here, Officer…" Jerome looked at his badge. "…Gallardo? Say, I used to work with an Esteban Gallardo, you're not—"

"Step out of the car."

"Listen, I'm po-lice. I'm the one that's been radioing you."

Officer Gallardo's hand went to his gun.

"Now hold on, there's no need for that, we're getting out, my God…"

Jerome opened his door and raised his hands. The four women on the back seat shuffled out after him. Jesse didn't move.

The second officer came over. This one looked wiry and mean. Humming with steroids or amphetamines or both. The sinews in his forearms stood out like he was under some invisible torture. He tapped on the passenger-side window with the butt of his nightstick.

"What's with him?"

Nobody answered.

"Hey. You trying to be funny? Turn off the lights and get out."

Jesse was off in his own universe.

"Hey. Out, motherfucker."

"That'll do, officer," said a voice behind all of them. "Need that one in one piece."

They turned. The doors of the other two police cars were open. Half a dozen men had got out. Four of them were police. Glenn and Shiv were there, too.

"What is all this, then?" said Shiv. "You all going for a hike? Family picnic? Dangerous up the mountain. Judy, you of all people should know that."

Judy was shamefaced and silent.

"Who are you?" said Jerome. "You're not po-lice."

"Nope," said Shiv.

"Well, listen up, son, because I *am* po-lice."

"Nope," said Shiv again. "You're retired. These fellas filled me in. Lewiston's finest. They're sick to death of you nosing around, by the way. They say you come in and use their coffee machine. Finish it up half the time."

Jerome breathed heavily through his nose.

"You going to arrest me for stealing coffee?"

"I can add that to the list of charges, if you'd like."

"The list?"

"Are you kidding?" said Shiv. "I don't even know where to start with all of you. How about attempted murder? Glenn? Do you want to fill them in?"

Vivian looked at Glenn. His head was heavily bandaged, and she could see the yellowing edge of a bruise underneath. He had a slight speech impediment, from swelling or a lost tooth.

"She beat me," he said. "Left me to die."

"It was self-defence."

"Beat me with a sacred rod of Telos."

Officer Gallardo seemed to take particular offence to this, and his jaw began to work hard on something.

"I had to," said Vivian. "He was going to—"

"Going to what, dear heart?"

"I don't know. You were going to do something."

"I was going to ask you about your brother, Vivian. That was all. We all just want your brother to be safe. We want everyone in our family to be safe."

"There's bodies up on the mountain," said Vivian to the other officers. "They're dumping them in the lake."

Minnie and Jerome looked at each other. The police didn't seem to hear her, or they heard her and didn't care.

"You want me to cuff her?" said Gallardo.

Shiv nodded at the Carters. "And these two. They helped."

"Says who?" said Jerome.

"Says the owner of the restaurant you picked her up from. He got the licence plate, everything."

Officer Gallardo clopped forwards in his leather boots and spun Vivian around so she was facing the car and wrestled her hands behind her back.

"Now just hold on a minute!" Jerome cried.

The handcuffs bit into her wrists and she looked down into the Carters' car and there it was, the same rod she'd used to beat Glenn, just lying there in the footwell. Gallardo's mean partner saw it at the same time. He went around her and reached into the car and held it triumphantly over his head. Its tip was still speckled with dirty, brown blood.

"I had to," she said. "Listen to me, I *had* to. They threw me in a truck and took me out into the desert and they were going to *do* things."

"Threw you in a truck!" said Shiv. "Against your will! Unthinkable!

You want to talk kidnapping, let's talk about kidnapping. Where are you planning on taking that radiant young man in the front seat there?"

He nodded at the Carters' car. No one answered.

"You thought you could just walk into town with him and no one would *notice*?"

"He's an Ascended Master, asshole," hissed the officer holding the rod. Vivian looked into his eyes. He was deadly serious. They were all in on it. No need to even pay them off.

"Take them in, officers," said Shiv. They all began unhitching cuffs from their belts.

"This is *absurd*," said Jerome. "We haven't done anything."

The wiry officer waggled the bloodstained rod in his face, then spun him round.

"Look here, junior, I am a county *sheriff*! Get your damn hands off me!"

They began to frogmarch the Carters back to one of the cars. One of them tried to get Shelley into bracelets, too, and Chason started screaming.

"No, forget her," said Shiv. "She's done."

They left her alone but Chason kept going. Some of the residents of Vista Street had come out of their front doors to watch what was going on, standing in their robes with cups of coffee.

"Get these people back in their houses!" Shiv hissed at two of the officers. "They'll see who we've got in the car. Judy, you're going home. I don't know what I'm going to do with you. Jesus Christ. You got someone watching the motel?"

"Shiv, I—"

"My God, Judy. I give you *one job*."

The officers herded the onlookers away from the scene. Gallardo began to manoeuvre Vivian towards the patrol car behind the others, but Shiv grabbed him by the arm to stop him. Vivian smelled his aftershave, the leather of his jacket. His silver hair was heavily gelled. A salesman, just as Troy had thought.

"Let me talk to her a second, officer," he said abruptly. "Alone."

Gallardo let her go and went to the other car. Shiv took her to one side.

"Has he told you?" he said.

"Told me?"

"Jesse. Has he told you. What the thing is."

"I don't know what you're talking about."

"I guess you don't. Otherwise you'd look like him, right? You'd be giving us the full Cirque du Soleil performance."

Vivian looked back at the Buick. Jesse was still sitting in the passenger seat. He was exploring the intricacies of the air conditioning.

"You know about the thing?" she said.

"Of course I know. Why do you think I'm looking for him? I mean – I know *of* it. Obviously I don't know what it is. Jesse is the only one that knows that. Could be anything. Some kind of equation. A theory. A diagram. I don't know. Maybe it's just words. A sentence, that explains everything. Maybe it just says, 'drink eight glasses of water a day'. Maybe that's the secret. Right?" He smiled again and it made him look ugly. He looked around to check that he was out of earshot of the police and then lowered his voice. "Whatever it is, Vivian, if it gets out it's going to make a lot of people very *unhappy*. You understand? If he's found something, then that poses a significant challenge to Telos as a, uh—"

"As a business?"

"As an ideology," he said. "There's also the fact that whatever solution it is he figured out came to him as a result of the Violet Path. So… you know. Technically, it's our IP. So we should be the ones to say if other people get to see it. You understand? Problem is, it's in his brain. So we're going to need access to that brain." He paused. "At the *very* least we need assurances from him that he won't tell anyone else about it."

"Your wife said you thought he was just putting on a good show."

"A show? Have you *seen* the guy, Vivian?"

"Yeah, I've seen him."

"You think he's making all this up?"

She shrugged. "I guess not."

"Okay then. So, Telos needs to know what he knows. It's in his interests. And yours. And your mom's. And if you can't see that," he said, suddenly abandoning all pretence of diplomacy, "you're fucking stupid."

"What?"

"She wants her retirement fund, doesn't she? You want a nice inheritance? If your brother wants to compete with Telos, you can say goodbye to all that."

"What do you mean?" she said.

"Your dad's cut," said Shiv.

"You know about Dad?"

"Yeah, I know about your dad. I know he kicked my ass for twenty years as senior partner. Do *you* know about your dad?"

"Yes. I mean, no, I didn't. Not until I got here."

"So you know that your family still gets an annuity from any profits Telos makes?"

"I didn't know that."

"Telos goes under, you and your family go under. So while we're on the subject, best not to mention the bodies either. Tends to be a brand-killer." He winked. "Of course, the opposite is true, too. If your brother can give us the edge against our competitors – and, let me be quite honest, I want to see Rhonda Byrne dead and buried – figuratively – aha – then your family will do very well out of the whole thing."

Vivian hadn't considered that.

"Who's Rhonda Byrne?" she asked.

"Seriously?"

"You could have told me all this in the Chinese restaurant."

"Could I?" he said. "Right there, in front of everyone? No, no, Glenn was the man for that job. He's better at getting answers, too. Usually. The paternal touch. But, well, you know what happened there. So here I am. Telling you. Asking you to save my family, and yours. Though I guess they're kind of the same thing, aren't they? One big happy family."

Vivian tasted a slight saltiness in the back of her mouth, something that usually heralded a sustained period of vomiting.

"I can't tell you anything," she said, "and neither can Jesse."

Shiv sighed and looked like he might hit her. He was wearing the kind of rings that could do a lot of damage.

"We were going looking for it," she added quickly. "When you stopped us. I think I know where it is. The thing. It's written down on a coaster."

"Are you shitting me?"

"No. That's what Jesse said."

"And where is it?"

"I'll show you. Someone took it."

"Then someone *else* knows what the thing is?"

"I'm not sure. I don't think so, otherwise we would have seen him."

"I hope you're right. I really do." He gestured to the Carters' car with his chin. "Lead on, Ms Owens, lead on."

26

THEY TOOK the Buick up to the end of Vista and turned onto the dirt road that led to Janek Blucas's place. Officer Gallardo drove, while Vivian sat in the back with Glenn and Shiv either side of her. Jesse hadn't budged from the passenger seat.

Glenn kept looking at her meaningfully. The only time she caught his bruised eye he shook his head and turned away again. She kept thinking of him with his hands around her neck, out on the barren prairie, spitting and swearing like a man possessed.

"Such a shame," he said. "You were such a sweetheart, Vivian."

"Should have known better, Glenn," said Shiv. "She's got her old man in her."

The car rattled and protested all the way up the mountain until they reached the fork just above Blucas's barn.

"Here," said Vivian.

They stopped. The right-hand path was too steep to drive down. Everyone apart from Jesse got out of the car and looked down the ridge. There was the junkyard and the warehouse and Janek Blucas's tricycle parked outside. Shiv was unconvinced. He rapped on Jesse's window and Jesse wound it down.

"You fucking with me?" Shiv said.

No, said Jesse.

"I think you're fucking with me."

"We're not," said Vivian. "The guy that has it lives there."

"I've seen that bike before. That's the hobo's bike. The one who's always at the motel."

"Mr Blucas. He's the one that steals things from all the rooms. If anyone's got the thing, he does."

"The hobo?"

She nodded.

"Jesus Christ. I've got to go in there?"

"Do you want it or not?"

Shiv stared at her a moment and then turned to the officer.

"You stay up here and watch him," he said, and nodded at Jesse.

Officer Gallardo fiddled with the crystal around his neck.

"I don't know, Shiv. Just me? If he's an Ascended Master, I can't exactly—"

"Jesus Christ, just stay with him. Make sure he doesn't wander off again. An Ascended Master will still take a bullet."

"Excuse me?" said Vivian.

"Figure of speech."

She looked at the police officer, who was still massaging his crystal between thumb and forefinger.

"Don't hurt my brother," she said.

He blinked. She didn't think he would. She turned back to the car.

"Jesse?" she said. "Are you okay?"

I'm okay, he said. His voice cast a momentary silence over everyone.

"Jesus," said Shiv. "For someone who's found enlightenment, he's not exactly selling it, is he?"

Shiv, Glenn and Vivian stumbled down into the gully. Shiv was in brogues made of snakeskin or armadillo hide and he slipped and slid all the way to the bottom. Vivian's hiking boots served her well, although she was still cuffed and Glenn had to keep hauling her upright. He seemed to take a certain pleasure in this.

They made their way through the rusted shells of cars and trucks to the door of the barn. It was closed this time. Shiv tugged it open without knocking and went inside.

It seemed Janek Blucas was out. The place was quiet as a tomb, and had the same smell of putrefaction. Shiv spun on the spot and looked at the shelves of trash bags, the piles of books and videos and old electronics and parts of cars, a rich and varied garbage-scape that seemed divided into dozens of distinct biomes of ephemera.

"It's here somewhere," said Vivian. "Probably in one of these bags."

Shiv spun and grabbed Vivian by the front of her coat. She heard and felt a seam rip somewhere behind her armpit.

"I've been quite clear on the whole not-fucking-with-me thing, Vivian."

"I'm not fucking with you," she said. "Everything Mr Blucas finds at the motel, he brings here. He's the only person that could have it. Your wife doesn't have it. That's obvious. Jesse doesn't have it. Mr Blucas is the only one who can get in and out of the rooms."

Shiv turned to Glenn.

"Go get Jesse. Bring him down here. I don't know what I'm meant to be looking for."

"It's on a coaster," said Vivian.

"A coaster, sure, sure. Go get him."

Glenn obeyed and went back out the way they'd come, leaving Vivian alone with Shiv, handcuffed. Shiv opened one of the bags and pulled out a fistful of brown and curling newspapers. He threw them to the floor and went to the next one. Papers, magazines, takeaway menus.

"You've got to be kidding me."

He hurled the whole bag from the shelf, then did the same with two more, tore up a bundle of envelopes that had been tied together with garden twine. Pieces of Mr Blucas's archive flew into the air and skittered through the dirt and under his feet.

He turned and glared at Vivian with his hands on his hips, as if expecting answers from her.

Vivian heard a click. A voice, thick with mucus.

"You pieces of garbage."

Neither of them saw Mr Blucas before he unloaded both barrels of his shotgun. The sound of the explosion was immense. It echoed around the barn like artillery. Vivian threw herself to the ground and paper fragments showered her like confetti.

"Can't you see I'm trying to do *good work* here?" said Mr Blucas. "How am I s'posed to figure all this out with you sons of bitches *meddling*?"

She still couldn't see him, but she heard his sluggish footsteps. He reloaded, fired again. She felt the roar of the shotgun's barrels, followed by the whine of shrapnel and a patter of paper flakes. She went down on her belly and began squirming her way towards the door.

"Been working on this for years! Getting everything *just so*! Getting everything in order so I can understand it and let you know what the point is and now you're coming here mussin' everything up!"

He came across the bundle of letters Shiv had disordered and let out a desperate moan. The gun cracked twice more. A piece of the shelves missed her by an inch and landed in the dust in front of her face. She crawled into a different aisle, past piles of *The Violet Path*, past Shiv, who was cowering behind them.

"Sir..." he was saying, "sir, we didn't mean to intrude..."

She heard Officer Gallardo yelling something from outside. He appeared in the open door with his own gun. His radio was crackling. He let off two rounds into the barn. Mr Blucas replied in kind, blowing two holes clean through the timber of the warehouse. The next time she saw the police officer's silhouette she managed to get to her knees, then her feet, and ran for the exit under his covering fire. She tripped on the threshold and fell onto her chin, her hands still cuffed behind her back. Another *crack* from Blucas's shotgun blew apart the doorframe and covered her with splinters.

She took cover behind one of the old car wrecks, her back to the fender. She closed her eyes and heaved the air in and out of her. The firefight went on behind her. Gallardo was still frantically calling for backup, more cars, a helicopter, an ambulance, everything.

Some stray shot pinged off the bonnet and she ducked further down.

Who was the ambulance for? Was Shiv injured? She opened her eyes and looked up the slope to where the Carters' car was parked. All four doors were open, and the front seats were both empty.

Two more police cars arrived in a storm of dust, sirens blaring. The same two that had stopped them back on Vista. She could see Jerome and Minnie sitting in the back. Their officers scrambled down into the gully and took up positions behind the pieces of junk metal. Vivian was back in her Western movie. A good old-fashioned shootout.

It felt as if it went on for hours, though it was probably only a matter of minutes before Blucas's shotgun fell silent. Vivian's ears rang. She was sick in the grass beside her but couldn't hear her own retching. Then, after another few minutes, the hiss and bleep of Gallardo's radio again.

"You alright?" said an officer who had taken cover behind the car with her. He glanced at her bracelets and seemed unsure as to how much sympathy she deserved. She nodded and tried to wipe her mouth with her shoulder. The officer went ahead.

Vivian turned and peered over the bonnet. Officer Gallardo had gone inside, but his partner was crouched in the weeds by the door of the warehouse. Just above his head were two ragged holes from Janek Blucas's last stand. At his feet were two bodies, and when he looked down and checked their pulses his face reflected a rapidly dimming violet light.

* * *

The ambulance still hadn't turned up after quarter of an hour, but Officer Gallardo was willing to take matters into his own hands for the sake of an Ascended Master. Vivian convinced him to undo her handcuffs, and he drove her and Jesse to the hospital in Lewiston, sirens on, the speedometer not dipping below 90mph once. Out past Wing's, past the burned-out husk of the Telurian Mission, past the Telos Sanctuary, whose triangular window still hadn't been replaced. The whole thing was nearly over before it started when they came across Forrest on the ramp to the freeway. She was performing some kind of ritual dance, right in the middle of the road, and she flapped her arms and shook her tambourine at the car as if trying to get them to stop. She knew. Somehow, she knew it was them. Gallardo had to hurl them halfway into the scrub, and for a few fearful moments it felt like they might lose a tyre on the passenger side. He hauled them back onto the asphalt, and Forrest diminished in the rear-view mirror, howling in despair like a wolf at the moon.

Vivian sat in the back of the car with Jesse's head in her lap. He was breathing, but not moving, a piece of the police officer's shirt bandaging his head. Above his left eyebrow it was completely red, with a satiny sheen that suggested the thing was already saturated. There was blood filling the channel between his cheek and his nose. Even with his head bound up, she couldn't unsee the injury that was beneath the dressing – a hole in his skull not half an inch in diameter, but black at its centre, and so deep it seemed she could stick her pinky through it and touch whatever goo was inside.

"How is he?" said Gallardo over his shoulder.

"He's getting cold," said Vivian. "His eye is doing this thing. Twitching, sort of."

"How's his aura?"

"I can't see his aura," she said shortly.

The glow of Jesse's skin had almost completely gone. It was

strange for Vivian to watch him – on the one hand slipping away, on the other coming back to the world, the old Jesse, unilluminated, with his moles and frown-lines and the sparse, furry moustache their mother had always disliked.

Officer Gallardo squeezed on the accelerator and the car bucked and wriggled its way through Lewiston's rush-hour traffic, which seemed in no mood to get out of the way of another car, even a police car with its sirens on.

They pulled up outside the hospital at a wild angle and Officer Gallardo braked so violently that Jesse nearly rolled into the footwell. He and Vivian leapt out and were joined by two paramedics who had been lazing in the back of their ambulance. A stretcher was prepared and Jesse was wheeled along to the emergency room, joined by doctors of increasing stature and expertise as they went. The air in the hospital had a stringent antiseptic smell, but with something troubling underneath, as if the odours of death and disease had only been concealed rather than eradicated. It seemed altogether too noisy in here, too, Vivian thought. Then she remembered: this was just what the world was like outside Mount Hookey. Noise and smell and busy people.

At some point Jesse and his stretcher crashed through a pair of double doors and Vivian and Officer Gallardo weren't allowed to go any further. They sat on rubbery chairs in the corridor. Gallardo played with his policeman's cap. A nurse came out and asked them both questions. Gallardo told her, straight off the bat, that Jesse was an Ascended Master and required special kinds of treatment and specific all-natural foods. After that the nurse spoke mostly to Vivian.

Did he have health insurance, she asked? No, he was from the UK. Did he have travel insurance, then? Vivian didn't know, but it wasn't at all likely that Jesse had considered those kinds of minutiae. Was he covered by Vivian's insurance? No, Vivian didn't have any insurance herself. Could she see their passports? No, she couldn't, Vivian said.

The nurse looked down and scribbled something on her a clipboard and got up and went back through the double doors.

"He'll be okay," said Gallardo. He retained a slight Mexican accent that Vivian hadn't detected until now. "As long as they don't pump him with all their chemicals. Half the time you come out of these places sicker than when you went in." He paused. "Or they put a microchip in you, so the government knows what you're thinking." He paused again. "We should really have taken him to a shaman."

Vivian turned to face him, squeaking on the vinyl upholstery. Who would have thought, to look at him, that these were the things he carried round with him in his head? Who would have imagined that this was the way he viewed the world? A police officer! To protect and to serve! And he wanted to take a man with head trauma to a witch doctor. It terrified her, in moments like this, how little she knew – how little anyone knew – of the skull-sized universe that lay behind someone else's eyes. When had anyone glimpsed even the tiniest fraction of Jesse's interior life? When had anyone glimpsed hers?

"He'll be fine here," she said.

"I don't know about that. Maybe we could at least get a shaman to visit him here?"

"No shamans."

"I know a cheap one who helped my cousin's baby. She had an indigo child. You know indigo children?"

"Are you all into this?" said Vivian, interrupting.

"What?"

"The whole police department. Are you all initiates?"

"Most of us," he said. Then he corrected himself. "Enough of us."

"So Shiv isn't paying you to do all this. To keep out of town."

"Shiv paying *us*? That's crazy!"

"You know it's all a setup, don't you? You know none of it is real."

He gave a condescending smile.

"Please. I'm Seventh Stone. People have been trying this on me for years."

"Trying what on you?"

"What you're doing."

"But it's true. I went up the mountain, there's nothing there. No Telos. Nothing at the end of the rainbow."

"You found your brother, didn't you? You saw him. We all saw him. Are you going to deny that he ascended? Energy like that? Come on."

"That's different," said Vivian. "What Jesse found is totally different."

"Different how?"

She couldn't answer that. Would she ever be able to answer that? She changed tack.

"I wasn't lying before, about the bodies."

He gave that smile again.

"I know. They went up before they were ready. It's their own fault, *The Violet Path* is quite clear on what happens if you try to get into Telos without the proper training."

"But they're *dead*. Shiv's dumping them in the lake."

"They get to be a part of the mountain. I think that's kind of beautiful."

"But you're a police officer!"

There was a moment of conflict in Gallardo's face. He frowned and his eyes seemed to point in different directions. His radio sounded. He answered. Someone was calling him back to Mount Hookey.

"I have to go," he said. "The scene needs securing. But I'll come back as soon as I can."

"You don't have to," said Vivian.

"I will. And I'll bring the initiates."

"I'd rather you didn't."

"I don't really have a choice…"

"What are you going to do with the others?"

"What others?"

"The sheriff and his wife."

"That depends on what's happened to Shiv. He'll decide what to do with them. If he's… you know. Still with us."

"Did you see what happened to him?"

He shook his head.

"Glenn?"

"I don't know."

"They've not done anything wrong. Jerome, I mean."

"It's out of my hands, I'm afraid."

"Jesse would appreciate it," she said. "Me and him, we're the same. You must know that. Same energy. He wants what I want. You're not going to take Shiv's word over the word of an Ascended Master, are you?"

He thought about this.

"You are his twin, aren't you?"

"That's right."

"I don't know… I've got my Eighth Stone certificate coming up."

"So. Help us out, and I'll make sure you get a personal audience with Jesse when he wakes up. Deal?"

"You think he'd do that?"

"Sure he would."

"I don't know. I'll see what I can do. Maybe I can set bail for them…"

His radio went off again.

"I've got to go."

Another stretcher came rattling between the two of them, accompanied by another cluster of nurses, one of whom was holding a saline drip over his head. By the time it had passed, the police officer had turned on his heel and was plodding down the corridor to the exit.

Vivian watched him go and slumped into her chair. No one came out of the double doors for some time. She drank several tiny paper cones full of water, until the cone began to disintegrate and she crushed it and put it in her pocket. She saw a payphone down the corridor where there was a queue four or five people deep. She wanted to call home. Needed to, in fact. She wanted to hear her mother's voice – that was an entirely new feeling. She would happily have listened to her talk about her bladder infection or the state of the guttering or the decline of terrestrial TV for days. She decided to wait, at least until there was some definitive news about Jesse.

Eventually, a doctor came and found her. His face had the colour and sheen of liver, as if both heavily sunburned and Botoxed. Sweat was beading between the very black, very sparse hair on his brow – a transplant that hadn't quite taken root yet, she assumed.

"Vivian?" he said.

She looked up.

"Jesse's sister? Yes. Obviously. The passportless pair. Aha. Well. We've had a good look at your brother. Come through and I can tell you what's what."

She followed him through the double doors, past half a dozen empty beds and another one that contained a man who was screaming and whose odour of high proof alcohol made Vivian's eyes water from several feet away, and into an office.

The doctor parked himself in a chair and looked at some documents on his desk. He wheezed as if trying to pass something uncomfortably from his digestive system. He picked up two pieces of paper and looked from one to the other. Vivian surveyed the office. There were photographs of him at various body-building meets hung on the wall behind his chair.

"How is he?" said Vivian, when the doctor wasn't forthcoming.

"Now, this is the thing." He kept looking at the papers, as though he couldn't tell them apart. "Doctor Heben, by the way." He squeezed the life out of her right hand and then was quiet again and frowned as best he could with his taut and swollen brow.

"Doctor?"

"Here's the thing. Your brother. He's been taken to surgery to get the foreign body removed."

"Foreign body?"

"Metal fragment. You say he was shot? He wasn't shot."

"There was a shooter."

"Sure, I heard. But he wasn't shot. It was shrapnel."

"Is he going to be okay?"

"Who?"

"My brother."

"Well, here's the thing," he said again. "The guys are pretty sure they can get the critter out of there."

The guys. The *critter*.

"But?"

"We put your brother through an MRI and CT scan. To see just what the damage was. Magnetic resonance imaging. Computerised tomography. Real good kit. Expensive, too. We weren't sure whether the injury had touched the brain."

He looked at the two bits of paper again. He seemed to be relishing the suspense. Outside, the screaming man was wheeled somewhere out of earshot.

"And had it?" said Vivian.

He turned one of the sheets of paper around. She'd seen these kinds of pictures before. A scan of the brain, divided into layers like so many slices of ham. She only had time to look at it briefly but saw nothing alarming.

"See now, this," said Doctor Heben, "this is a normal brain. I know what you're going to say – no such thing! Right? But seriously. This is a brain functioning what we'd *call* normally." He pointed at a few of the thumbnail images. "This bit lights up, this bit lights up, depending on what job it's doing. This is a brain just going about its business."

He now turned to the second piece of paper. Vivian found she was shuddering in anticipation. Something was wrong. She knew it. How would she tell her mum?

"This is your brother's brain," said Doctor Heben.

She looked at the scans. At first it seemed there had simply been something wrong with the machine, or wrong with the printer. There was no detail there. It was just a series of slightly misshapen ovals, white on black, like the phases of the moon.

"What is it?" she said.

"Well, *look* at it. The whole thing's lit up like Broadway! We've not got different parts talking to each other in there. Every single neuron is on full blast. Constantly. It's like he's thinking everything at the same time. Or nothing. Depending on how you look at it. I have never seen anything like this. And I've seen a lot of brains!"

Vivian didn't say anything.

"We're pretty confident we can get that object out of there," he said. "But looking at this…"

"What?"

"Well, I'm sorry, Vivian, but the damage might already have been done."

He mopped his brow. Vivian looked again at the blazing circles on the page. No, she thought, that brain wasn't damaged. Far from it. He'd just figured it out, that was all.

"Now, here's the thing," Doctor Heben started up again. "A little bird tells me you haven't got any insurance?"

27

VIVIAN SPENT the night in the emergency room, horizontal on three plastic chairs, but not actually sleeping. Even if she had managed to drop off, Doctor Heben was in and out of theatre every half hour to keep her abreast of developments. He didn't actually seem to be performing the operation himself. Vivian never worked out whether he was a surgeon or a consultant or a radiographer or what. She considered the possibility that he was just a secretary with ideas above his station. He went back and forth like an errand boy, occasionally looming over her, his clipboard trapped under one massive bicep, and reassuring her that Jesse was stable, and that "the guys" were doing a fantastic job.

Once, in the early hours of the morning, he came out and said, "Settle something for us, would you: does the Queen actually *live* in Buckingham Palace, or is it just for show?"

Vivian said she didn't know. He made a clicking noise with the side of his mouth and went back into theatre.

The sun came up and any hope of getting to sleep evaporated. Vivian knuckled the grit from her eyes and went to the bathroom to throw some cold water in her face. She hardly felt it. The kind of fatigue that rendered the whole world grey and lukewarm. She'd approached at least ten different people in various waiting rooms before someone relented and changed one of the Carters' fifty-dollar bills so she could get a coffee. She drank it black and unsweetened and thought about calling home again.

The gears of the hospital began to grind. More seats got filled, phones began ringing. Vivian sat with her coffee and watched the waiting room's tiny television.

She was about to hunt for sugar when the woman who had given her change suddenly piped up, "Well would you look at that. Seems somebody finally had enough." And she laughed a short, vindictive laugh.

The TV was showing a local news channel. The reporter was standing in front of a barn shot full of holes. There had been an incident in Mount Hookey. Two men were dead, including the shooter. There was Gallardo, palm to the camera, trying to usher the reporters away.

Poor Mr Blucas. She thought of him and his estranged brother, and suddenly the idea of losing Jesse became more real, and more unbearable.

Two dead. Who was the other one? Shiv? Glenn? A police officer? Or were they referring to Jesse? Perhaps Gallardo had reported him dead so no one would come looking for him. But then, the fact that the shooting was getting reported at all suggested that Telos Inc. did not have control of the situation, so maybe Shiv had been killed after all.

"Should've let the shooter keep going," said the woman who was sitting next to her. "That whole place needs cleaning out. Send in the pest control." She did her unpleasant laugh again.

"What's that supposed to mean?"

"No-good beatniks. Thought we'd seen the last of them in the seventies. This generation's worse than the last one!"

She blew on her own coffee and slurped it loudly. Vivian resisted the urge to slap it from her hands and turned back to the TV, feeling suddenly protective of Jesse. Of the others, too: Shelley, Forrest, Eenoo. Maybe even Glenn? No, not Glenn.

"They're just lost," she said.

"They're just *lazy*, is what they are. Too much money and too little sense. They need to go out and get themselves proper jobs."

Vivian was suddenly aware that Doctor Heben was standing behind her shoulder, also watching the TV. It had been a couple of hours since his last visit.

"Have they mentioned your brother?" he said.

"Not by name."

"Someone should let them know. Get a reporter down here."

"I'd rather keep things quiet."

"The guys would love to do an interview."

"I don't think Jesse would want that."

The coffee woman was scowling at her, now. Vivian got the impression that if she wasn't going to tell the reporters about Jesse, then this woman would. She got up and took Doctor Heben to one side.

"How is he?" she asked.

"Oh, right," he said, and he gave two thumbs up. "Mission accomplished."

"Why didn't you tell me?"

"I'm telling you now, aren't I?"

"Where is he? Is he awake?"

"Oh, no, no. They're moving him to another wing. He's good and sedated. Won't be awake for a day or so. And he'll be kept in here for at least a week. You want to see what they did?"

"I want to see Jesse."

"That's what I mean."

She followed him for what seemed like miles through the corridors of the hospital. It was like changing terminals at an airport. They needed a monorail or something. The going was slower still because Doctor Heben had a poised and unnatural way of walking that seemed designed to show off the muscles of his torso. It was clear that he had also chosen a doctor's coat that was slightly too small for him, for this same purpose.

Every part of the hospital seemed to be in a state of low-level panic, and she was glad when they reached Jesse's cubicle and Doctor Heben pulled the curtain around them.

Almost the entire top half of her brother's head was bound in clean bandages. Only his right eye was visible, and this was closed. Its lid looked yellowish and swollen. Something about his eyelashes, matted with some kind of gunk and trembling almost imperceptibly, brought her to the brink of violent tears. His glow was gone. His face was the familiar mixture of grease and sweat and dead skin cells, just like everybody else's. She didn't know whether this was a good or bad thing.

She felt a sob coming, ambushed it, swallowed it deep down into the pit of her stomach.

"What happened with the brain damage?" she asked.

"Won't know for sure for a couple of days," said Doctor Heben. "We'll do a scan when he's awake and the swelling's down."

"You say he'll be in for a week?" She was only half thinking of the cost.

"At least. We'll look after him. He'll be comfortable here, don't worry. This is a good hospital. The Lewiston Hilton – that's what the guys call it. Ha ha!"

She looked at Jesse again. He was swaddled like a baby. Tubes in his nose, tubes coming from under his blanket.

"Do you have somewhere to stay?" asked Doctor Heben.

"I'll figure something out," she said.

"You know your way around the town?"

"I think so."

"You want a good gym? I can recommend somewhere."

He kept talking until he realised she wasn't going to reply. She perched on the edge of Jesse's bed and squeezed his foot. There was no response. At some point Doctor Heben slunk away from the cubicle, and Vivian was finally alone with her brother, listening to the machine that was doing his breathing for him, and she stayed there until it was completely dark outside.

She booked herself into a hotel across from the hospital where the sheets were clean and everything worked and the staff were charmless and forgettable. The other guests were a mixture of travelling executives and relatives of patients who were being treated across the road. She didn't speak to any of them. She sat in her room on the edge of her bed, alone again, and watched the reports of the shooting in Mr Blucas's barn. Initiates fretted around the police cordon. Officers left the scene of the crime carrying little see-through bags of evidence.

What if the thing was in one of those bags? What if, right now, it was in the process of being filed away in the Lewiston police force's evidence room, barely even glanced at by some weary desk clerk, cigarette in hand, on the tenth hour of his shift? Just any old paper coaster, curling at the edges, showing – well, what exactly? Would Jesse be able to remember it, when he came around? Or figure it out all over again? Would he even want to?

She went back to see him early the next morning, but his eyes weren't open, and the tubes were all still in him, and the machine was still beeping interminably. She sat with him for most of the day. Doctor Heben came by a few times, making notes, and seeming happy enough with Jesse's progress. He affectionately thumped Jesse's shoulder and said things like, "Attaboy!" and, "Come on, champ!" and then smiled at Vivian and went on his rounds.

In the afternoon Vivian thought of something.

"Jesse," she said, and squeezed his hand under the bedclothes. "I've got to go out for a while."

There was no response.

"I'll be back soon," she said. She got up and left. She went to the main entrance of the hospital and asked for directions to the courthouse and the police station.

Lewiston was not a big town and crossing from one side to the other only took twenty minutes. She passed the bus station and the xeroxing place where she'd copied the posters of Jesse. That seemed a long, long time ago. There wasn't the slightest whiff of Telos about the town and this unsettled her. It just made the ruse feel more elaborate, as if all the streets were a sophisticated film set designed to conceal the Telurian reality of the place. She looked for crystals around the necks of passers-by, for robes poking out of sleeves and collars. A woman came towards her in a lavender-coloured blouse and Vivian crossed the road to avoid her.

The courthouse was a large colonial-type building that seemed on the flimsy side. Another piece of set, looked like. Vivian went in and spoke to the clerk and found that Jerome and Minnie – full name Minerva, it turned out – had been granted bail. It wasn't an extortionate amount, either. Whether it was Officer Gallardo's doing or not, they'd only been charged with DUI and bail was set at a thousand dollars each. Vivian still had twice that amount in the wad of cash that the Carters had given her in the first place.

She paid the clerk and three hours later she was standing with them on the steps of the police station. They'd aged ten years overnight. Minnie still held onto her Tupperware of leftovers, which she had somehow been able to keep with her in her cell.

"You're a dear, sweet thing to think of us," she said, and clutched Vivian's arm with both her hands. "What on earth happened? Where is your brother? Is he still at Mount Hookey?"

Vivian was watching the police officers coming and going, singly and in pairs, carrying cups of coffee, twirling their nightsticks. None of them gave her or the Carters a second look. How many of them were initiates, she wondered? All of them? *Enough* of them, as Gallardo had said.

"We shouldn't hang around here," she said.

"Right," said Jerome.

They found a litter-strewn park somewhere back towards the hospital and sat together on a bench. Vivian took the middle, Minnie and Jerome like her parents on either side. She told them what had happened in the barn, where Jesse was now. Minnie shook her head and tears leaked from the corners of her tiny eyes.

"But is he better?" she asked.

"He's not awake yet."

"Did they get all that paint scrubbed off him?" asked Jerome.

"It wasn't paint."

"Wasn't, huh? Then what was it?"

"That was just how he looked," said Vivian.

Jerome frowned and opened his mouth, but his wife said, "More things in heaven and earth, Jerome." She dabbed at her eyes.

The three of them sat in silence and watched a mother spinning her child on the roundabout.

"I'm sorry I had to bail you with your own money," said Vivian.

"Nonsense," said Minnie. "Who else's money were you going to use?"

"And I'm sorry I didn't find Nathan."

Jerome and Minnie looked at each other.

"What were you saying before, in the street," said Jerome. "You said something about... Jesus, I don't even want to say it. Bodies? On the mountain."

"Some of the initiates, when they go up the mountain..." Vivian kept watching the toddler spinning around and around. "Well, you know. It's a mountain. And they're in robes and sandals. It's freezing up there."

"But you said Nathan was in Sacramento?" said Minnie, and seized Vivian's bicep again, tight enough to leave a bruise.

"He could be. I mean, he should be."

"Then we should go and get him."

"I don't think it'll be that simple."

"Well, we're not just going to go back to Gazelle, are we? Jerome?"

Jerome shook his head.

"We should still look into it. If there's a chance…"

"But you're on bail," said Vivian. "Aren't you meant to stay around here?"

"We'll come back," said Jerome. "We'd like to know, Vivian."

Vivian looked either side of her. Minnie's fingertips were still digging into her arm. She thought of Jesse, wondered if he was awake yet.

"Alright," she said.

She took out the Carters' envelope and counted how much of their cash was left and began to plan her final pilgrimage to Telos.

28

BACK IN the hospital Jesse was still comatose. Vivian found the doctor at his bedside, explaining to a nurse why most people's bench-pressing technique was all wrong. Vivian gave them the number of her new phone, a cheap "burner" she'd picked up from a liquor store for thirty dollars, told them to get in touch if there were any developments. She gave her brother a kiss on his bandaged head and tried not to cry again and went back to join Jerome and Minnie at the main reception.

There were a few tense minutes while Jerome attempted to hire them a car. The man in the hire place checked his licence over and over, looking up, looking down, but the false DUI claim from the Lewiston police departments hadn't yet caught up with whatever database the car hire company was using. In an hour they were on the freeway in a little Japanese automatic that smelled of strawberry bootlaces and caustic cleaning products, and the sun was hovering just above the barren hills to the right of the road.

They hardly spoke on the journey. Minnie alternated between weeping silently in the back seat and exclaiming with surprise when the satnav said something out loud. Vivian couldn't remember the exact address but had entered "Sacramento business park" and hoped that she'd recognise the place when she saw it. Jerome concentrated on his driving. Getting pulled over now would be the end of them.

When they got to Sacramento it was dark. It turned out there were four business parks in and around the city, and they visited all of them before Vivian recognised the laminate flooring wholesaler and got Jerome to pull into the parking lot. The Telos building itself was as she remembered, without any defining features. It could have been the headquarters of the IRS, as far as anyone on the outside knew.

Jerome turned off the engine and made to get out.

"Wait," said Vivian. "If we try and go inside they'll just turn us away."

"Or worse," said Minnie.

Jerome sat back in his seat and closed his door and stared ahead at the building.

"Are you sure this is it?" he said.

"Pretty sure," said Vivian. "That's the big house."

"The what?"

"Nothing. It's just what somebody called it once."

She thought of Janek Blucas again, and the ruin that Telos had brought him – that her own father had brought him. Why couldn't she have had a family like the Carters? Why couldn't she have had a dad like Jerome?

They sat and watched and Jerome put on the air conditioning with the heat turned right up. It was nearly seven o'clock, but most of the lights in the office were still on. The windows in the building were small but occasionally Vivian saw people moving inside. Was that a robe she saw? It was difficult to tell. It could have just been someone in a blouse, or an ill-fitting shirt.

Vivian checked her cheap phone. No word from the hospital.

After half an hour a few people emerged from the entrance. It was difficult to see them properly in the street lights, but they seemed as unremarkable as the building they'd left. Two men in shirts and ties and sensible slacks. A woman in jeans and a woollen jumper. Vivian's heart got uncomfortably tight. What if it was just an office after all? She'd only had the information from Piotr Blucas. How long had it been since he'd left the Telos operation behind him?

"I don't know about this," said Jerome, quietly.

"Let's just be patient," said Minnie.

Jerome sniffed. "Never thought I'd be staking out my own son."

The woman in jeans came towards them and Vivian and Jerome sank in their seats. The woman got into her own car and reversed out of the space and drove slowly past them.

"There," said Vivian, sitting up and pointing.

"Where?"

"Bumper sticker."

There was a purple triangle stuck to the inside of the rear windscreen, and next to it a white oblong that said: "Telos Welcomes You!" It was the same one Vivian had seen in Shelley's living room.

"Well, I'll be…" said Jerome.

They kept watching. More people left and went to their cars and bikes and scooters. Some made prayer-hands to each other before saying goodnight. One wore a rucksack that Vivian was fairly sure had a sacred rod poking out of the top.

And then she saw him. He looked no different from the portrait photo the Carters had on their mantelpiece. He was in a well-tailored suit and his shirt was undone at the top and the only strange thing about him was that he wore no socks under his shoes.

Jerome and Minnie were out of the car before anyone had said anything. They went running across the parking lot while Vivian struggled releasing herself from the seat belt.

"Oh Nathan!" Minnie cried. "Oh son!"

"Nathan, it's us!" said Jerome.

Vivian ran after them, her heart somewhere up around her ears. This was not how it was meant to go. There were still initiates leaving the office behind him – Ascended Masters, no less, according to Glenn's definition. Jerome was slow with his cowpoke's hobble and they hadn't yet reached Nathan, but they'd got his attention. He was staring at his parents with total bewilderment. He didn't even seem to recognise them.

Minnie was brought up short by the look on his face.

"Nathan, baby! You're okay!"

Nathan had been talking to another man in a suit, middle-aged, who looked like an accountant from his wireframed glasses and breast pocket of biros. He looked at this man and raised his eyebrows, made to leave.

"Nathan?" said Jerome. "It's us. It's your mom and dad."

The pair of them stopped and turned.

"I'm sorry," said Nathan. "I think there's been a mistake."

"This is private property," said the accountant, more unkindly.

"Nathan, come on now," said Jerome.

"What did I tell you," said Minnie. She was shaking. "They've done something to his brain. Just like they did to your brother."

Nathan glanced briefly at Vivian, and then back at his mother.

"Bless you," he said. "But I've never seen you in my life."

"We've got cameras all along here," said the accountant with satisfaction.

"Please, Nathan…"

Minnie went to embrace him, and as if drawing a concealed weapon, the man in the glasses made an inverted triangle with his fingers and started a high-pitched humming. Nathan did the same.

"Lord have mercy…" said Jerome.

"Nathan, you're coming home. You've got to come *home* with us."

Visions of Jesse, and home, interposed themselves between Vivian and the scene that was unfolding.

The accountant was now blowing through the triangle he had made with his fingers. Nathan held his own triangle at arm's length from his body. He had a look on his face that was difficult to read

in the haze of the street lights but which didn't seem a million miles
from pity.

"I'm sorry," he said. "I think there's been a mistake."

"You get going, Nathan," said the accountant. "I'll keep them
here and get security."

"No need for that," said Nathan.

"No *need*? After everything that's happened? Shiv and Glenn?
You think we should let these two crazies loose, poisoning the
energy round here?"

"They're not crazy, it's just a mistake. Bless you."

"A mistake," said the accountant. "Get gone, Nathan. I'll deal
with them."

"We don't want any trouble," said Jerome.

Nathan backed up.

"Oh son," said Minnie, barely audibly.

He looked at the other man and then turned and disappeared into
the shadows of the business park's topiary. The accountant increased
the frequency of his blowing.

"Easy there," said Jerome. "We're going."

"No…" said Minnie.

"We're going," Jerome said again. "You don't need to call anyone,
son. It's a mistake, an honest mistake. We'll be on our way. You watch."

Vivian scanned the parking lot. Nathan was already nowhere to
be seen.

Jerome had to drag his wife by the elbow back to the car.
Minnie was in ruins, stumbling and looking over her shoulder and
occasionally collapsing completely. "I don't understand," she kept
saying, and, "What did we do?" Over and over and over.

The other man was still making his triangle symbol at them, right
up until they were all back in the hire car. Jerome started the engine
but didn't go anywhere.

"I don't want to leave him," said Minnie from the back seat.

"We're not leaving him," said Jerome. "I just didn't want that lummox calling security and getting us locked up for second time in twenty-four hours. Jesus, Mary and Joseph. What in hell have they done to him."

"What did we do?" said Minnie yet again.

"It's not our fault, Minnie."

"We brought him up good..." Minnie said. "Why's he doing this?"

"We'll find him," said Jerome. "We'll ask him."

The accountant wouldn't stop watching them until they left. Jerome drove them out and made several slow laps of other lots of the business park. Most of them were completely empty, seeing as it was after seven. No cars or people. No Nathan. He could have caught a bus by now and be miles away. Jerome still had the car's heater on full and the satnav kept trying to firmly direct them back to the same spot they'd just left, and Vivian became sweaty and irritable and desperate. She worried that she shouldn't have left Jesse at all. She checked her phone again. There was still no word from the hospital. What if Gallardo had returned in her absence, and wheeled Jesse away to see his cousin's shaman?

Jerome stopped the car in lot B4 outside Telfer Express Refrigeration and a big billboard of a snowman winking. They had all been silent for the last few minutes, and Jerome's usual stoic pragmatism seemed to have evaporated. He rested his head on the steering wheel and stayed like that for a moment.

"We can come back tomorrow," he said, into the instrument panel. Nobody answered.

Vivian looked in the wing-mirror and thought she saw someone moving on the verge between the lot and the main road. The figure seemed abnormally tall and thin, well over six feet, and drifting among the palms and the yuccas like it was one of them, uprooted and carried by the wind. She turned from the mirror to the verge itself, but there was nothing there.

While she peered into the wickerwork of shadows, she heard the door on the opposite side of the car opening. At first she thought that Minnie had taken matters into her own hands and gone off charging into the night to look for her son on foot, but Minnie was sitting directly behind her, and there was the sound of someone getting into the car, not out of it, and the car wobbled with a new weight.

"Sorry about that, everyone."

Vivian turned away from the verge and looked in the back. It was Nathan. He was out of breath. He leaned over and pulled his mother into a hug and she just gaped silently and the tears started again. He sat up and looked around the interior of the car and then at Vivian.

"Who are you?" he said. "Dad? What happened to the Buick?"

They drove out of the city until they found a McDonald's, halfway to the airport, where Nathan thought it would be safe to pull in. Jerome gave him an incomplete and slightly confused appraisal of the situation. It was forgivable in the circumstances. He kept trying to hug his son with one arm while he drove, snaking his arm at painful-looking angles between the two front seats, and the hire car wove all over the freeway to a riot of horns. Nathan just laughed and told him to keep driving and he'd explain everything once they'd gotten somewhere. He apologised again and again for pretending not to recognise them – they really *did* have cameras everywhere, as the accountant had said, and the forecourt of Telos's head office was no place for a family reunion.

"I shouldn't really be doing this at all," he said as they took the off-ramp and passed under the restaurant's golden arches. He suddenly checked out of the rear windscreen, as if worried they might have been followed. "But just seeing you again. It's been so long. I hadn't even realised how long it had been. You looked so sad. I am so *sorry*, Mom. I can't believe you came all this way. I can't believe you found me in the first place."

"You've got Vivian to thank for that," said Jerome.

Minnie had still barely spoken. She just beamed and squeezed her son's thigh, and sometimes leaned over and squeezed the rest of him.

They parked up and went inside. Nathan still seemed nervous and kept checking over his shoulder despite all the hugging and backslapping. Jerome went to the counter and ordered while Vivian and the others found a booth. When the food came Nathan looked around again and then bit into his cheeseburger ravenously. He half closed his eyes while he chewed and groaned with pleasure.

"Oh my God," he said with his mouth full. "I can't remember the last time I ate junk like this…"

Minnie and Jerome laughed, bright-eyed, delighted just to be watching their son eat; proud, too, of him and his youth and his appetite. Vivian felt suddenly like a third wheel. An intruder in their wholesome family unit. She was envious, too, and not for the first time. When was the last time she'd sat like this with her parents in a McDonald's? It had definitely happened. Different chain, perhaps. She couldn't pinpoint the year, but there was a scene very like this somewhere in her memory. She and Jesse had been maybe eight or nine years old. Jesse had dismantled all the free plastic toys that came with the meal, as was his wont, and Vivian had got upset, and their dad had gone and bought them all the same meals again, just to get the toys, and the table had been piled high with burgers and fries that no one wanted to eat.

Vivian chewed anxiously on the straw of her milkshake and checked her phone under the table. Still nothing.

Nathan groaned with satisfaction again and wiped his mouth with the back of his hand.

"Well," he said, "I suppose I owe you an explanation. And an apology. I'm just so sorry. I mean, I know I've said it, but... I really am, Mom, Dad. I'm sorry. You must have been worried sick."

"Oh Nathan," said Minnie. "We're sorry. What did we do wrong?"

"Wrong?"

"You running off like that!"

"What? Oh, Mom, nothing. *Nothing*. It wasn't you. Oh, man. Listen. I didn't join Telos for real." He realised how loudly he was speaking, stopped, looked round the restaurant. Someone came past with a tray of drinks and he waited until they'd gone before he continued. "I was worried about Joy."

"Joy?" said Vivian.

"His girlfriend," said Minnie.

"She signed up before me," said Nathan. "Went crazy for it. Moved to Mount Hookey, stopped answering her phone. So I went after her. Dad, I remember you saying how weird it was up there. Joy, she was... just gone. I don't know. So hard to keep things in perspective when everyone's telling you what you thought was the real world isn't the real world. I very nearly got sucked in myself. I mean, I *did* get sucked in. But the thing that kept me sane was I started looking at the whole thing from a legal point of view." He turned to Vivian. "I'm a lawyer, by the way."

"I know," said Vivian. "You went to Brown."

He nodded. "This Telos thing. God*damn*. The whole thing is crooked. Fraud, coercion. Unlawful imprisonment. No one gets to leave – not that anyone wants to. You know they get their initiates to give them power of attorney? Can you believe that? They take your phone. Then they give it back to you when you get here, but they're listening and reading everything that goes through it. You were right about the cops, too, Dad. They're part of it."

"Then why are you still here?" said Minnie.

"I'm gathering evidence, Mom."

Minnie looked unspeakably proud again.

"I'm sticking around here long enough to get a case together and bring them down. Everything we'd need to get them to court is in that office." He laughed. "Shit, I really thought I was going up the mountain when they said I was ascending. Couldn't believe it when they put me in a minivan and brought me here."

"Where are you living?" asked Jerome.

"They put us all up in hotels. And Telos own the hotels, so that means they control the phones and the TV and the internet. Which is why I shouldn't really be here. People will talk if I'm not back in my room soon. They're probably already talking."

He worked at some stuck bit of food with his tongue, slowly, thoughtfully, as if just now realising the extent of his mistake.

"What happened to Joy?"

"I don't know. She's back in Mount Hookey, I think. Never made it past the Sixth Stone. I mean, come on, she worked in bakery. There's no way she's paying to get further than that."

"A case?" said Vivian. She'd been worrying at the word. She hadn't forgotten what Shiv had said to her on Vista Street. That the Telos family was her family, figuratively and literally. That a challenge to the Telos brand would compromise all of them financially.

The three Carters looked at her as if they'd forgotten she was there. Nathan nodded.

"The guy I'd really like to get in a courtroom is the one who started it. Classic narcissist guru type. Called himself John of Telos. He's the one who put the whole system in place. The guy must be in the Fortune 500, but I can't find his real name on any of the paperwork. I bet he's got the private jets, the yachts, all of it. Like that Osho guy. Remember him? Up in Oregon? Must be some piece of work." Jerome smiled at this. "Anyway, he's not been on the board since last year, looks like. Maybe he's already dead."

Vivian chewed all the way through her straw, accidentally inhaled it, and then spat it out onto the vinyl tabletop. Jerome and Minnie glanced at each other. Their son sensed something was amiss.

"What?" he said.

"It's just—" said Minnie.

"I think I want to go," said Vivian.

To hell with it. To hell with all of them – Glenn, Shiv, her dad. To hell with the Carters, too, and their all-American, white-picket-fence, swing-chair-on-the-veranda, meat-loaf-making happy family. Nathan could do what he liked. She didn't care whether Telos made front page news or it carried on duping sad, lost Gen Z-ers for the next hundred years. She just wanted out. She wanted to get back to Jesse, and to get home, and to never have to think about any of it ever again.

"We've only been here twenty minutes, Vivian," said Jerome.

"It's been an hour, with the drive."

"No, it's okay," said Nathan. "I need to get back. It feels kind of edgy being here, anyway."

"But you can't just go back! When will we see you again?"

"Give me another few weeks? A month? I need to pick my moment."

"Vivian, you still got that pager I gave you?" said Jerome.

She dug into her coat pocket and handed it over. It felt good to be rid of it. Nathan laughed.

"You been hanging onto this, Dad? Surprised they still work." He inspected the screen and pressed the buttons experimentally, and then looked up at his father. "You reckon you can hook me up with the Feds? Would be good to know they had my back. Before I make a run for it."

"FBI?" said Jerome. "Yes, I suppose I can."

Vivian got up out of the booth.

"What is it, dear?" said Minnie.

"Are we going or not?" said Vivian.

She couldn't stop thinking of Jesse, now. Visions of him came to her in waves, like a migraine. Perhaps he was awake, and that psychic bond she'd always thought was such horseshit was pulling her back to him. The Carters reluctantly started to move.

"We're going, we're going," said Jerome.

"Dad said you were at the Sanctuary, right?" Nathan said. "Looking for your brother? We should talk when I get out. It would be great to have you as a witness. And tell me if I've missed anything. I wasn't at the Sanctuary – I went through the Telurian Mission. Same kind of thing, of course. All roads lead to Telos."

There was a whole lot he'd missed, about her dad, and bodies up on the mountain, but she didn't want to get into it now.

"I'll let you know," she said. Then she turned to Jerome and said, "I need to get back to the hospital."

"Okay, Vivian, we hear you." He seemed a little annoyed at her insistence.

"Maybe I can drive," she said.

"You're not on the insurance."

"I'd prefer it if I drove."

She held out her hand for the keys.

They had to drop Nathan off somewhere near the business park so he could get back to his accommodation. It was a detour Vivian could have done without. She kept seeing Jesse's hotel room, from the perspective of his bed. The migraine was getting worse. She could barely see the road in front of her.

She drove fast, ignoring Jerome and Minnie's protests. They'd been on the road ten minutes when the sirens and flashing lights appeared in the rear-view mirror.

"Well that's great, girl," said Jerome. "Just great! Now we're all for it! Why you got to drive like a goddamn maniac?"

Vivian slowed slightly, one eye on the speedometer's needle. The police car came up hard on the driver's side, and then sped past her. It was followed by another three emergency vehicles. They blared through the traffic and were soon out of sight.

"Okay," said Jerome, shaking his head, "you got lucky. Now, pull over and let me drive. You even got a licence?"

She ignored him and pressed on the accelerator and moved ahead through the wake of the police cars.

Before reaching the labyrinth of the business park, they all noticed the orange glow on the horizon. The smoke found its way into the currents of the air con. Minnie was holding her nose, and Nathan leaned forward between his father and Vivian to see what was happening.

"That happened quickly," he said. "Didn't notice it on the way out here. Anyone?"

Nobody said anything, and Vivian suspected they were all, at that moment, having exactly the same premonition. Another couple of fire engines came screaming up the freeway and took the same exit that the satnav was suggesting. The fire and the business park got closer. Nathan had wanted Vivian to drop him somewhere far from the office building, but he didn't protest when she drove them all through lots A4, A3, A2 and back to the spot where they'd first seen him. Just as she'd thought. Telos was going up in flames.

They pulled up behind the police cordon and got out. The heat was incredible. Firefighters yelled at the onlookers to keep back, but there were so many, too many, like a festival crowd, like Woodstock, the initiates clearly distinguishable by their humming, and by the triangles they were making with their fingers, and by the looks of utter desolation on their faces. There were half a dozen hoses directed at the fire but it was nowhere near under control. Now and then a window exploded and the initiates began a new round of wailing.

"Shit," said Nathan. He folded his arms on the open car door and rested his chin there, like he was watching the sunset. A good few minutes passed.

"What happened?" said Minnie at last. "Jerome?"

"How should I know?" he said. "But like Nathan said – it's gone up pretty fast. Doesn't look like an accident to me."

They all watched a bit longer, transfixed. No, it wasn't an accident, Vivian thought, and she thought of the palm trees, and the shadow among the palm trees.

"Does that mean you can come home now?" said Minnie, hopefully.

Nathan didn't reply.

"Son?" Minnie came up behind him and rubbed his shoulder. "What do you say?"

He turned around.

"Huh?"

"You going to come home?"

He looked back at the blaze, and then back at his mother.

"I don't know," he said. "I suppose so. Case is done."

"What do you mean?"

"The amount of evidence in there? Come on."

"Oh," said Minnie. "Well, never mind. You'll get more cases."

Nathan looked at her and blinked away the ash.

"You could always help us," Minnie suggested.

"What do you mean?"

"With our case."

"What case?"

"Your father and I…" Minnie said. "We're here on bail."

"On *bail?*"

A heated discussion ensued. Vivian tuned them out. She wanted to get back in the car and on the road back to Lewiston. She watched Telos going up like the *Hindenburg* and wondered whether this in itself would be enough to unravel the whole operation. Possibly. She was strangely apathetic about it. It was just Jesse she worried about, now.

She felt another throb in her temples, and the vision of the hospital room materialised again. A projection on the cinema screen behind her eyes. She turned away from the burning building and blinked hard and tried to look beyond the illusory image. With her back to the fire the darkness of the parking lot congealed and another illusion seemed to appear in the background of the first. A giant and two dwarves, it looked like. She squinted. Two regular-sized police officers were leading an inhumanly tall man to their car. The man clinked as he walked. He saw Vivian.

"Hey Viv," he said, and he grinned and raised his cuffed hands and flicked her a "peace" sign.

It took several moments of configuring his limbs and head before he'd fit in the back of the police officers' car.

29

VIVIAN DROVE back to Lewiston without the Carters. Nathan didn't think it was a good idea to just walk away from Telos, even after the fire. Perhaps something could be salvaged from the office once the whole thing had burned out, he thought. Perhaps he would wait for another six months for the franchise to get back on its feet, and start the process of gathering his evidence all over again. Minnie and Jerome wanted him to go back with them to Gazelle in the meantime. Vivian had gotten in the car and driven away before they'd reached any kind of agreement.

She drove on through that vast American darkness, nothing on the radio, the film reel of Jesse's hospital room playing on and off across the windscreen. She thought she saw faces crowding around him, faces she didn't recognise as the taut and characterless oval of Doctor Heben. She felt Jesse's total disorientation, and silently apologised to him, over and over again, knuckles white on the steering wheel. She felt it, and she felt him.

It was after midnight by the time she arrived at the hospital, and she was worried about visiting hours. She knew he was awake, and knew she needed to see him, but it was surely too late for her to be allowed onto the wards. She tried calling the hospital from her mobile as she entered the outskirts of Lewiston but predictably only got Doctor Heben's answerphone.

The drop-off point outside the hospital was empty and she left the hire car there, half on the kerb, and headed for the main entrance. The automatic glass doors were open, but only enough to admit one or two people at a time, giving the impression they had been forced or short-circuited in some way. Vivian slotted herself through the gap and found the reception empty. There was an unattended mop and bucket in one corner. Two of the phones were ringing and not getting answered.

She broke into a run and headed down the corridor. She passed a solitary nurse walking in the opposite direction, who skidded to a halt and opened her mouth and raised a hand as if to try and stop her. Vivian kept on. She took the stairs instead of the elevator up to the third floor. When she came through the double doors at the top she heard a good deal more commotion. Doctors and nurses and clerical staff rushing in all directions, shouting over Vivian's head as she made her way towards Jesse.

"What the hell's going on? Are we evacuating or what?"

"Don't go down there. Do *not* go down there."

"Is it a shooter? Someone said it was a shooter."

"Religious nuts."

"Should we be helping?"

"Has anyone called the cops?"

"How'd they get in?"

"Some of them *are* cops!"

The doors ahead of Vivian were flung open dramatically. She stopped. They all stopped, the doctors and nurses and janitors. There was a procession up ahead, moving with a weird solemnity through the mayhem of the corridor. Twenty people, or thereabouts, most of them in robes. A few in police uniform. One of them was ringing a handbell, the tone of it so familiar to Vivian, even after all this time, that it felt like someone hammering a masonry nail into her forehead. The twenty-ish people were carrying Jesse aloft like a funeral bier. His eyes were open, but his body was limp, and he was dragging a saline drip along the floor behind him. Some of the nurses were pleading with the initiates to put him down but were quickly hustled away with much humming and finger-triangle-making. The procession halted when Vivian wouldn't move out of its way.

Forrest was at the head of the group. There were others Vivian recognised: Peace, Officer Gallardo, the man from Mount Hookey Crystal Visions. Was that the woman who had been asleep in the back of her car when she'd gone to visit Telos Now?

"Put him down, Forrest," Vivian said.

Forrest shook her head. "I won't let you take him from us. Not again."

"Who told you he was here?"

Forrest didn't answer.

"Who told you?" Vivian repeated.

"*He* told us. We felt it."

"Did you tell them, officer?" said Vivian, turning to Gallardo. He looked embarrassed.

"He needs to go back to the mountain," said Forrest. "Look at him! Look what's happened to him!"

"He's sick, Forrest. You need to put him down and let the doctors look after him."

"The *doctors*? Lord have mercy, have you seen the job the *doctors* have done on him already?" She picked up the saline drip, which was still attached to Jesse's arm, and flapped it about.

"You're confused, Forrest," said Vivian. Then she spoke over the top of her. "You're all confused. My brother doesn't have any answers for you. I'm sorry. I'm really, really sorry. Honestly."

"She's a liar!" She recognised the voice. It was Judy. "I was there, Vivian! On the mountain! You know he knows! You know he has the answers, and you *took* him from us and hid him here because you want the secrets of Telos all to yourself!"

Vivian felt the heat flaring in her face.

"Look, fine, he found something, but—"

"She admits it!"

"—it's not what you think. There's no Telos. There's no Crystal City."

"You *saw* him Vivian!" crowed Judy. "You saw his light!"

"We *all* saw his light!" said Forrest.

"But it's not like that. He *thought* his way to the answer. He just thought, and thought, and *thought*, for his whole life, until he was miserable, just fucking wretched, and that's how the answers came to him. You saw his room, Judy. You know what he went through to get to wherever the fuck it was he got to. And you can bet it was an answer that only he understood. It wasn't even an answer! A shape, he said! He found a *shape*, that could only be described by itself! Do you think that's going to help you?"

"She's talking a whole lot of nonsense," said Judy. "His room is covered in Telurian runes, and it's the most beautiful thing I ever saw."

"They're not runes!"

"Then what are they?"

"I don't know. Calculations or formulae or something. If you really want the answer, you don't need him. He wrote it down. Or drew it, or whatever. It's out *there*, somewhere in all that garbage. You go to Mr Blucas's barn, and take your time, and you'll find it. You don't need Jesse. Leave him here. He needs to get better. Please. He's ill, he's so, so ill."

"Out of the way, Vivian."

"Please put him down," said Vivian. She was sobbing, now.

"We're taking him back to Telos!" said Forrest. "We're taking him home!"

The procession started moving again.

"Please," she said, "put my brother down."

"The Master is returning!" said Forrest, and she clanged her bell, and the initiates started humming again. Jesse's head lolled to one side, but Vivian couldn't tell if he had moved it himself or if it was from the jostling beneath him.

"Jesse? Can you hear me?"

"He is coming home!" shouted Forrest.

"Jesse..."

"He is returning to Telos! Praise be!"

Vivian shoved her way through the bodies and tried to get an arm around her brother.

"That's enough, girl," said Officer Gallardo. "You don't know what's best for him."

She tried again, pulling at Jesse's arm. He ragdolled to one side again, and then blinked, very slowly, and there was something in his eyes that was closer to boredom than to fear.

"I said that's *enough*," said Gallardo.

He pushed her backwards. Vivian heard the tone of the bell behind her, Forrest's bell, and she whirled around, and in a near perfect déjà vu the brass rim came down between her eyes and she crumpled and tasted the antiseptic linoleum of the hospital floor as the procession moved on around her.

She opened her eyes in a bed, flattened there by a shaft of hot and hazy yellow sunlight, NorCal sunlight, the kind that suggested a dust storm had only recently passed outside. She blinked three or four times but nothing got clearer. It felt like someone had rubbed petroleum jelly in her eyes. She tried wriggling her fingers and toes and succeeded. She licked her lips and they were dry and papery and seemed they would slough off completely if she kept working at them with her tongue. She thought about turning her head but knew instinctively that this was far beyond her means, something she would have to work up to in the coming days and weeks.

She was still in the hospital, that was clear. In a bed. Tube up her nose. Her room was completely silent, though she could hear the distant clopping of feet in the corridor beyond. It took her a minute or two to remember why she was there, and then she thought of Jesse, and it felt like some red-hot geological fault had opened up in the front of her skull.

She closed her eyes again and drifted in and out of something darker and more foreign than sleep. Hours or days might have passed. The next time she opened them properly she felt a little more lucid. Doctor Heben was standing at the foot of her bed. Behind him there was a painting hung on the wall – one of many hundreds or thousands of reproductions, she was sure – of a lone cowboy atop his horse, looking down from a mesa over the great, wide promise of the open plains. She stared at this for a long time before Doctor Heben said something.

"Together at last!" he said with a grin. "The head trauma twins! Ha ha ha!"

Vivian frowned, felt again that horrid splitting sensation in the front of her head. Three times she'd been knocked unconscious since she'd arrived at Mount Hookey. Three was an energetically significant number. Three points to the Telurian triangle. Forrest had taught her that.

The doctor came forward and obscured the cowboy painting.

"Come on, Vivian, up and at 'em! Your brother will be gone before you've had your breakfast!"

He jerked his head to the side, and Vivian looked over.

Jesse was sitting up in bed. He was awake, and looked thin and sad. He did a kind of smile where one corner of his mouth twitched horizontally, not really a smile at all. Vivian studied him. He still had bandages around his head. She raised a hand and felt the fabric around hers. They must have looked completely indistinguishable.

"Pulled a lot of strings to get you two in the same room," said Doctor Heben. "Technically, Jesse should have been discharged by now. While we're at it, there is the matter of your insurance…"

Vivian very slowly squirmed herself until she was also propped up in her bed.

"Easy there," said Doctor Heben, arranging her pillows and her blanket and her tube.

She looked at Jesse, and he looked back with a thousand-mile stare.

"What…"

She dislodged the word like a stone caught in her throat. The doctor gave her a sip of water that dribbled into the cracks of her lips and stung.

"What happened?" she said. "Where are the others?"

"What others? Oh, you mean the nuts?"

She nodded.

"Me and the guys sorted them out, don't you worry." He flexed his chest under his doctor's coat. "I didn't get the call until after you'd gone down. They were halfway to the parking lot with poor old Jesse!"

"Sorted them?"

"Uh-huh. Should have seen it, Vivian. All that sitting still, vegan diet, all the rest of it – they didn't put up much of a fight. Those guys need to eat some red meat!"

Her forehead sent two or three waves of pain, like sonar, through her whole body.

"They just left?" she said.

"I wish! Ha ha ha!"

She shook her head. "Then what?"

"They've been camped outside for the last five days. Doing their rituals and their seances and what have you. Someone needs to teach them how to play the drums, that's for sure. Gee whiz. I couldn't think straight. Police didn't seem to want to do anything about it, either."

Five days she'd been out. She hadn't thought it had been so long.

"Are they still there?"

"Nope. Packed up and shipped out this morning."

"How come?"

"Must be something to do with what's happening up at Mount Hookey."

"What's happening up at Mount Hookey?"

"The mothership's calling them! Ha ha ha!"

"What do you mean?"

Dr Heben scanned around the room.

"Give me a minute. I'll go find you a TV or something. You two got plenty of catching up to do, anyway."

He slipped out of the room and left Vivian and Jesse looking at each other. For a long time neither of them spoke.

"Hi," Vivian said.

Jesse's mouth did its strange sideways twitch.

"You okay?" Vivian said.

He nodded.

"Do you remember what happened?"

He shook his head.

"I mean, Jesse, do you remember anything about, you know…" What exactly was she angling at here? Was she still hoping he would just tell her? Was she, in fact, just as lost as the initiates, just as desperate for answers? "The thing."

This time he didn't move at all. He looked at her, then through her. His eyes were light-years away. There was nothing to read there. She wondered whether it was better for him to remember or to forget what he'd found. Perhaps it was a relief to be free of it. Or perhaps it was hell. She suspected the latter. To have known, and understood, and to lose it all. To have been fished out of the deep, calm waters of cosmic understanding and dumped back on this squalid bit of earth to gasp and flounder.

"Do you know what I'm talking about?"

He nodded again.

"Do you want to go back for it?"

He shook his head again.

Doctor Heben came swaggering back into the room with a tablet in one hand and a protein shake in the other. He found them staring at each other in silence and laughed.

"Take it easy on the psychic twin telepathy thing," he said. "Your head still needs a good old rest. Both your heads."

"I didn't think that was a thing," said Vivian.

"Oh trust me, it's a thing! And I'm saying that as a brain surgeon." He came between the two beds and showed Vivian the screen of the tablet. "Here," he said, apparently seeing no need to elaborate on his most recent remarks. "This is the story."

The article was from ABC7, a local news website. *ET Visits Mount Hookey, Steals Burrito*, read the headline.

"Lot of reporters going up to Mount Hookey these days, after the shooting and the nuts coming down here. And the fire in Sacramento? You hear about that?"

Vivian was watching some grainy footage from a phone. A figure was drifting down the main street of the town, emitting a violet light that illuminated the shopfronts. She recognised the shuttered front of Wing's, and the thrift store, and the luridly decaled windows of Mount Hookey Crystal Visions.

"When's this from?"

"From today," said the doctor. "I said – must be why those nuts hot-footed it back to their mountain."

She checked the date on the article. It was from seven o'clock that morning. It wasn't Jesse, that was for sure, but whoever it was moved with the same grace that seemed at once deliberate and totally aimless. They shone. Someone had found the coaster. The shape. The thing. But who'd found it? Blucas? He was meant to be dead. Shiv? Glenn? One of the police officers? Or someone else entirely?

"Pretty clever, right?" said Doctor Heben. "Wonder how they did it. My brother works in CGI, in Hollywood – docs all the big movies – he says it's pretty easy to do that. Can just do it on a cell phone these days."

"Jesse," she said. "You want to see this?"

She held out the tablet, but Jesse had rolled over onto his side, and was pointedly showing his back to both of them.

30

THEY WERE both discharged after another five days, during which Jesse continued to communicate only through nods and shakes and peculiar facial tics. Doctor Heben said it was nothing to worry about.

"Scans are all fine," he said. "Cognition is fine. His brain's as good as it ever was. Chattering away in there!" He tapped him on the top of his bandages. "He'll talk when he's good and ready."

Jerome and Minnie came to visit, unannounced, on the afternoon of their departure. Minnie seemed buoyant. She was wearing a new T-shirt from Sacramento that just said: "I've been to Sacramento". She was glad to see Vivian, and Jesse, and it soon became apparent why she was in such a good mood.

"They dropped the charges!" she said, and touched Vivian's wrist with her warm, grandmotherly fingers. "Whole thing got thrown out. Poof! No evidence, no nothing. The only two witnesses were the officer, Gallo, what was his name?"

"Gallardo," Jerome corrected her. He had a dark look about him that worried Vivian.

"Gallardo and the Indian gentleman. Neither of them showed up. Judge didn't seem to know what we were doing there. Tell her, Jerome."

Jerome was still standing, leaning on the wall, while his wife took the seat between the two hospital beds. He hitched up his jeans with his thumbs, glanced at the painting of the cowboy and said, absently, "Whole thing's unravelling, seems like."

"How do you mean?" said Vivian.

"Did you see the news? With the shining man?" Minnie interjected again.

"I did."

"Just like you, dear!" Minnie said, turning to Jesse. "Same colour, same everything. Did the doctors find out what caused it?"

"No," Vivian said quickly.

"Oh," said Minnie. "Well. Looks like you're not the only one they've been messing with, Jesse. Maybe someone will have some answers. Something in the water? Who knows! I just thank God that Nathan didn't end up in the same position." She put a hand over her mouth. "I am *so* sorry! What a terrible, selfish thing to say. And I haven't even asked you how you're feeling. You better, Jesse?"

Jesse nodded.

"Good." Minnie paused, as if unconvinced. "Few good meals and you'll be right as rain, I'm sure. Your mom a good cook?"

"She's okay," said Vivian. In fact, she'd never seen any evidence of their mother cooking in twenty-five years.

"I'll bet she is," said Minnie. "You know what, you two could switch beds and no one would ever notice. Aren't they just the *spit* of each other, Jerome?"

She smiled broadly at the pair of them. There was an awkward silence. Jerome was studying the painting again.

"Where's Nathan?" Vivian asked.

"He's gone back to Mount Hookey. All this hoo-hah with the shooting and the shining man and such. Thinks he can do a lot of investigating while everything's so up in the air. Which reminds me, Vivian – he asked me to ask you, would you mind telling him what you saw up there? In detail? With the mountain, and the…" she crossed herself, and spelled out "…B-O-D-I-E-S."

Vivian didn't want to think about it. She wanted to be gone.

"Alright," she said. "I'll tell him what I can."

"You're a good girl," said Minnie, and tapped her wrist again. "He thinks it could really help with bringing these bad men to justice. You'll see. Didn't he say that, Jerome? Corporate manslaughter, or… what was it?"

Another pause. She sighed.

"You'll have to excuse him, dear, he's still got a bee in his bonnet, even after all this."

Vivian looked at him. He fingered the frame of the painting and then muttered, "You could have taken the car back."

"Could have what?" said Vivian.

"Oh, Jerome! She's had more important things to think about!"

"The hire car! Thing got towed, and it was in my name! You have any idea the charges for that? On *top* of the late return fee from the hire place?"

"Oh," said Vivian. "That."

"Yes, *that*."

"Don't be such a grouch, Jerome. Today's a good day."

"It's costing us a fortune!"

"I've still got the rest of your money," said Vivian. "It's in my coat. I can pay you back when they bring me my stuff."

"Well, then," said Jerome, wrong-footed. "That's a start."

"You won't accept a dime from her Jerome," said Minnie.

"It's fine," said Vivian. "But it would be good if I could borrow enough to get to the embassy."

"Don't need to even ask, dear," said Minnie. "All that money's yours, as far as I'm concerned. You were the one that found our Nathan in the end. You sure you don't want to come and stay, before you go home? Get back on your feet? You could see Nathan and chat about, you know, the situation."

"That's kind," said Vivian. "But we're going to try and get back today or tomorrow, I think."

"So soon! Well, ring him, anyway. And you must write. Both of you!"

She turned and smiled at Jesse again, but Jesse was still staring into some hidden corner of the universe.

When the nurses had brought their old clothes, Vivian handed over the envelope of cash, far slimmer that it had been when she'd received it. She kept two hundred dollars to get her and Jesse to the consulate in San Francisco. They all hugged and said their farewells and exchanged telephone numbers. Minnie reminded Vivian to call Nathan, and Vivian said she would, but the promise was half-hearted.

"One thing you could do," Vivian said, just as they were leaving.

"What's that, dear?" said Minnie.

"If you go back to Mount Hookey—"

"Oh, I doubt we will."

"Well, if you don't, maybe ask Nathan to check in on Shelley. Remember Shelley? From the motel?"

"Yes, poor love."

"I think someone should make sure she's okay. And her son. Remember her son?"

"The beanpole!"

"He could do with some help, too. Legal help, I mean."

No chance of *his* charges getting dropped, Vivian thought. Caught red-handed next to a burning office block with a coat full of petrol bombs.

"I'll mention it," said Minnie. "But you can just ask him when you call him, can't you?"

"Yeah," said Vivian. "I suppose I can."

That afternoon, Vivian and Jesse left the Lewiston Hilton in matching coats and matching bandages, with combined medical bills just shy of half a million dollars that Vivian had no means of paying. *Whole thing's unravelling*, Jerome had said, and that was truer than he'd known. Despite her promise to Minnie, it really wasn't in her interests to ring Nathan and help put the final nails in the coffin of her own inheritance. If Telos collapsed, and their father's annuity stopped paying up, they'd have to get jobs. They would have to *work*. She struggled to see Jesse as a barista, or delivering flyers, or entering data in an office somewhere. Although, perhaps this would be different, since his enlightenment. Perhaps it no longer mattered to him what he did. Perhaps, even after his surgery, he didn't feel or think or want anything.

The grass outside the hospital was still scrubby and littered from the initiates' encampment. Vivian saw the remains of incense sticks, prayer flags, one dirty, purple robe. She didn't dare think what might have happened if they had successfully smuggled Jesse back to the mountain. She looked back at her brother, a few paces behind her, scowling slightly to be out in the sun. He still hadn't said anything. She held out her hand, and he took it, and they hung on to each other like two small children until they reached the bus station.

They took a Greyhound bus to the British consulate in San Francisco. Someone gave them temporary passports and – grudgingly, Vivian thought – a loan to cover the cost of their flights home. Vivian's story went no further than the mugging in Lewiston. She didn't want to tell them everything that had happened in Mount Hookey. Not all over again.

They spent the night in a hotel, Jesse still not speaking.

After they'd turned out the lights, Vivian asked, into the darkness, "Jesse? Did you know it was Dad? All along?"

There was a rustling of Jesse's pillow, but she had no way of knowing whether he was nodding or shaking his head.

The next morning they were both sitting in the departure lounge of San Francisco International airport watching their plane getting delayed for the third time. Vivian was studying the board. Jesse was trying to open the packaging of a club sandwich Vivian had bought for him.

"We've got to wait for information," she said. "Will you be okay if I go look around?"

He nodded, barely distracted from the task at hand.

She went off to explore the duty-free, keeping Jesse in her eyeline. She spent the last of the Carters' cash on a silk scarf and a chocolate Mount Rushmore for their mother. Then she found a quiet corner near the terminal window and called home. Nobody picked up, which perhaps wasn't a surprise given the time difference. But then, Mrs Owens was a light sleeper and, historically, could be brought to full alertness by the sound of a light switch getting flicked in a different wing of the house. The phone rang off and went to answerphone. Vivian listened to her mother fumbling through the recorded message, and could have listened to it another ten times. She left a brief message of her own, which said only that she'd found Jesse and they were coming home and mentioned nothing about their respective head trauma or their medical bill or the suitcase of pharmaceuticals she was bringing back from the hospital.

She hung up and worried a little, then came back and sat next to Jesse. He was still hard at work on the sandwich. She watched him picking at the cellophane, putting the seams of the packaging under various kinds of stress from various angles. He turned it over in his fingers and lifted it to the light. Studied its form and nature as if he had unearthed some precious artefact, bringing all the power of his intellect to bear on the thing. There was nothing in the world that deserved less than that, as far as Jesse was concerned. He held it before him and he looked and frowned, as if he knew, with enough time and enough thought, it would give up answers to much more than just itself.

His brow cleared suddenly. It was beautiful to watch, as if the sky was clearing after a heavy storm. He looked, briefly, like someone else – like the man she'd found up the mountain, and the man painted on murals and postcards all around Mount Hookey, with his knowing and contented half-smile.

"The shape," he said.

Vivian leaned in to listen.

"What's that, Jesse?"

He looked up from his hands and surveyed the departure lounge as if seeing it for the first time. Opposite him a man and a woman were trying to quieten their screaming baby, while an older child hammered on his phone, wearing a pair of enormous headphones that seemed designed to counter this specific scenario. Someone pushed a sophisticated and many-levelled cleaning trolley between the aisles, and collided with an old man's feet, and said sorry but didn't mean it, and the old man zipped his coat up and went on cursing under his breath long after the cleaner had gone on her way. Outside the darkened windows the planes taking off and landing and taking off again. The smell of jet fuel and discounted perfumes and grilled cheese.

"It's a miracle," Jesse said.

"What is?" she asked.

"All of it," he said.

A moment passed before he started frowning again. Vivian put her arm around his shoulders and his skinny arm wound its way between the small of her back and the chair and they clung onto each other in the middle of the chaos. They sat perfectly still. Such an odd pair they must have looked: identical human beings, with identical baseball caps concealing identically damaged and bandaged heads.

There was a general groan from their fellow passengers. The

flight to Heathrow had been delayed for a fourth time. The family opposite them looked despairingly at each other and then at Vivian. She glanced up at the board and pulled Jesse in a little closer, glad – overjoyed, in fact – that she and her brother would be able to stay as they were for at least another hour.

ACKNOWLEDGEMENTS

THANKS TO my editor Sophie Robinson, and copyeditor Dan Coxon, for their work on the manuscript at every stage; to my agent Jane Willis for her advice and encouragement; to Chris Vernon for being interested and insightful from the very beginning; to Mary and Dave and Carrie and Titus for giving me somewhere to live and write; and, above all, to Laura "The Most" Lomas, for reading and listening and being there, glowing, in my darkroom.

Special thanks to the residents of the real Mount Hookey, whose location must of course remain a secret. I think of you often, and with nothing but with fondness and gratitude.

ABOUT THE AUTHOR

NICHOLAS BOWLING is an author, musician, stand-up comic and Latin teacher from London. He graduated from Oxford University in 2007 with a BA in Classics and English, and again in 2010 with a Masters in Greek and Latin Language and Literature, before moving into teaching. He has also performed at the Edinburgh Fringe Festival and has recorded two albums and two EPs with Me For Queen.

He is also a critically acclaimed children's author, with *Witchborn* published in 2017 by Chicken House, and was followed in 2019 with *In the Shadow of Heroes*, which was shortlisted for the Costa Children's Book Award.

ALPHA OMEGA

BY NICHOLAS BOWLING

Something is rotten in the state of the NutriStart Skills Academy.

With the discovery of a human skull on the playing fields, children displaying symptoms of an unfamiliar, grisly virus and a catastrophic malfunction in the site's security system, the NSA is about to experience a week that no amount of rebranding can conceal. As the school descends into chaos, teacher Tom Rosen goes looking for answers – but when the real, the unreal and the surreal are indistinguishable, the truth can be difficult to recognise.

One pupil, Gabriel Backer, may hold the key to saving the school from destroying itself and its students, except he has already been expelled. Not only that – he has disappeared down the rabbit-hole of "Alpha Omega" – the world's largest VR role-playing game, filled with violent delights and unbridled debauchery. But the game quickly sours. Gabriel will need to confront the real world he's been so desperate to escape if he ever wants to leave…

"Inventive, playful bonkers writing… that ties up all the story's threads with a beautiful, pitch-black bow." *SFX Magazine*

TITANBOOKS.COM

For more fantastic fiction, author events,
exclusive excerpts, competitions, limited editions and more

VISIT OUR WEBSITE
titanbooks.com

LIKE US ON FACEBOOK
facebook.com/titanbooks

FOLLOW US ON TWITTER AND INSTAGRAM
@TitanBooks

EMAIL US
readerfeedback@titanemail.com